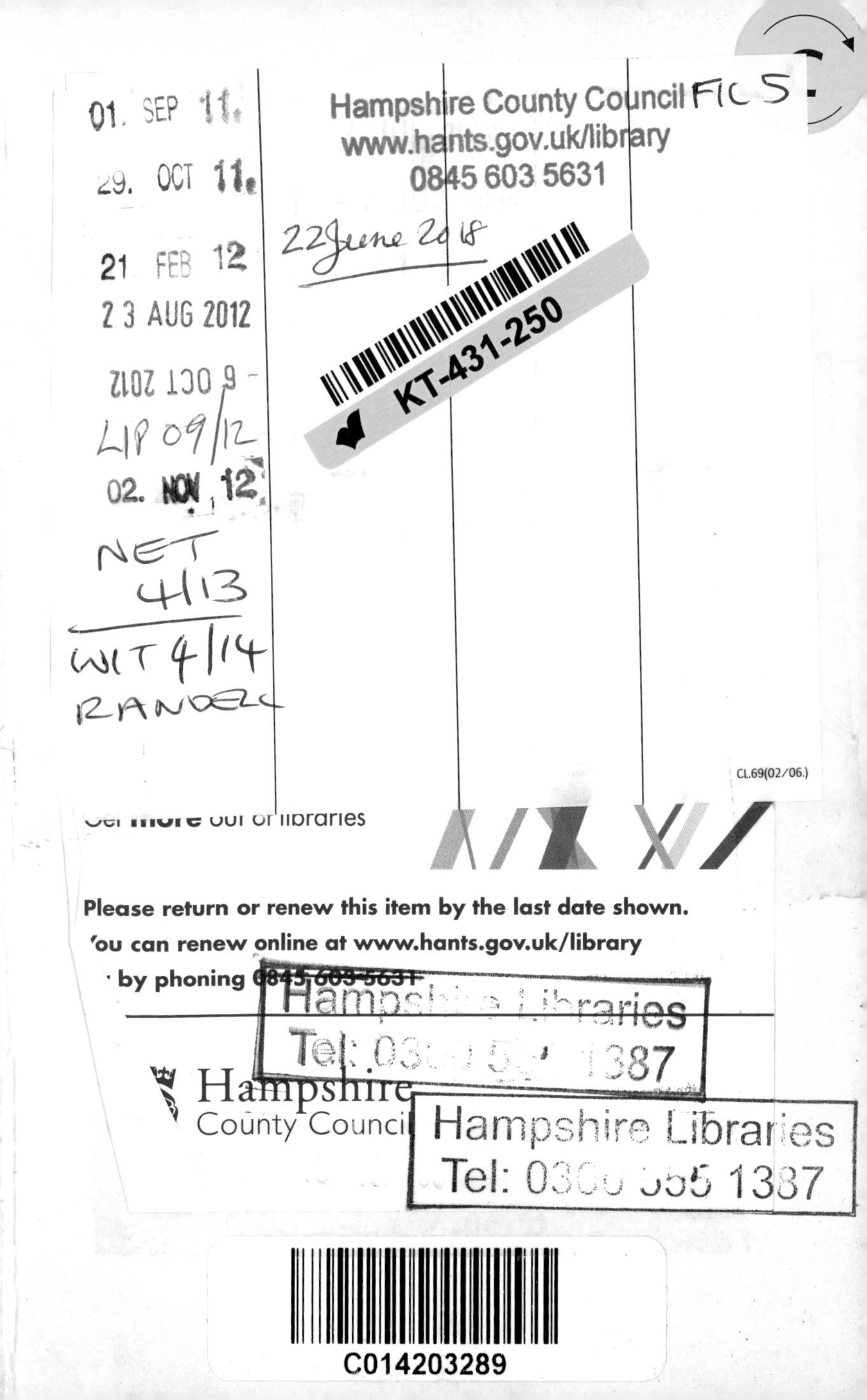

SPECIAL MESSAGE TO READERS

This book is published under the auspices of

THE ULVERSCROFT FOUNDATION

(registered charity No. 264873 UK)

Established in 1972 to provide funds for research, diagnosis and treatment of eye diseases. Examples of contributions made are: —

A Children's Assessment Unit at Moorfield's Hospital, London.

•

Twin operating theatres at the Western Ophthalmic Hospital, London.

•

A Chair of Ophthalmology at the Royal Australian College of Ophthalmologists.

•

The Ulverscroft Children's Eye Unit at the Great Ormond Street Hospital For Sick Children, London.

You can help further the work of the Foundation by making a donation or leaving a legacy. Every contribution, no matter how small, is received with gratitude. Please write for details to:

THE ULVERSCROFT FOUNDATION,
The Green, Bradgate Road, Anstey,
Leicester LE7 7FU, England.
Telephone: (0116) 236 4325

In Australia write to:

THE ULVERSCROFT FOUNDATION,
c/o The Royal Australian and New Zealand College of Ophthalmologists,
94-98 Chalmers Street, Surry Hills,
N.S.W. 2010, Australia

EXCEPT FOR ONE THING

Many criminals have often believed that they'd committed the 'Perfect Crime', and blundered. Chief Inspector Garth of Scotland Yard is convinced that modern science gives the perfect crime even less chance of success. However, Garth's friend, scientist Richard Harvey, believes he can rid himself of an unwanted fiancée without anyone discovering what became of the corpse. Yet though he lays a master-plan and uses modern scientific methods to bring it to fruition, he makes not one but several mistakes . . .

Books by John Russell Fearn in the Linford Mystery Library:

THE TATTOO MURDERS
VISION SINISTER
THE SILVERED CAGE
WITHIN THAT ROOM!
REFLECTED GLORY
THE CRIMSON RAMBLER
SHATTERING GLASS
THE MAN WHO WAS NOT
ROBBERY WITHOUT VIOLENCE
DEADLINE
ACCOUNT SETTLED
STRANGER IN OUR MIDST
WHAT HAPPENED TO HAMMOND?
THE GLOWING MAN
FRAMED IN GUILT
FLASHPOINT
THE MASTER MUST DIE
DEATH IN SILHOUETTE
THE LONELY ASTRONOMER
THY ARM ALONE
MAN IN DUPLICATE
THE RATTENBURY MYSTERY
CLIMATE INCORPORATED
THE FIVE MATCHBOXES

JOHN RUSSELL FEARN

EXCEPT FOR ONE THING

Complete and Unabridged

LINFORD
Leicester

First published in Great Britain

First Linford Edition
published 2008

British Library CIP Data

Fearn, John Russell, *1908 – 1960*
Except for one thing.—Large print ed.—
Linford mystery library
1. Detective and mystery stories
2. Large type books
I. Title
823.9′12 [F]

ISBN 978–1–84782–144–7

Published by
F. A. Thorpe (Publishing)
Anstey, Leicestershire

Anstey, Leicestershire
Printed and bound in Great Britain by
T. J. International Ltd., Padstow, Cornwall

This book is printed on acid-free paper

1

The musical comedy was over. Valerie Hadfield stood before the stage curtains, her left hand raised to still the applause.

'Thank you so much, ladies and gentlemen.' Her voice seemed tiny in the swelling quiet, yet every word was distinct. 'You have been very kind. I hope I shall continue to please you.'

She had recited this line countless times, bowing with easy feminine grace at the close of it — then she stepped back between the curtains. Her allure and air of modest reserve disappeared. She became cold, hard, and unprepossessing.

She crossed the stage amidst shirt-sleeved property men, half-clad chorines, and so into the vista of whitewashed brick labelled 'No Smoking!' which went into the dressing rooms.

Nobody congratulated her upon her fine soprano singing or delicious sense of comedy. Once the uninitiated had praised her unstintingly but no longer.

Entering her dressing room she sat down before the mirror. Shimmering blonde hair, straight fleshless nose, pointed chin. She was definitely good-looking — except for the hard light in her blue eyes.

Valerie looked beyond her reflection to her maid at the back of the dressing room. She tugged the paste jewellery from her slender bare arms and threw it in the lacquered box before her. 'What are you *doing*, Ellen?'

'Just setting out your clothes, m'm.'

'You should have done that hours ago! Give me a hand out of this strait-jacket!'

Ellen set to work with nimble fingers. The girl pulled herself free of her dress impatiently, then, when she had creamed away her stage make-up and applied instead a shadowy mask of rouge and mascara, she began donning her normal clothes.

'Nobody called while I was out front, I suppose?'

'No, Miss Hadfield. Nobody ever does, do they?'

'No,' Valerie admitted bitterly. 'Except those confounded reporters who can't keep their noses out of anything.'

'I'm puzzled, Miss Hadfield,' Ellen reflected. 'An attractive lady like you, and famous too, yet nobody ever seems to come — '

'Shut up! When I want an analysis of my affairs I'll ask for it! Now help me on with my coat!'

Valerie left the dressing room and walked swiftly down the stone-walled corridor to the outdoors.

''Night, Miss 'Adfield,' the stage doorman called from his warm little cubby hole.

''Night,' Valerie answered briefly. She wondered how the myopic old fool even recognised her — or anybody else for that matter.

In the main street beyond the short alleyway leading from the stage door stood a black Daimler limousine. The moment Valerie appeared a liveried chauffeur snatched the rear door open for her.

'Home,' Valerie ordered, and clambered

onto the soft upholstery.

'Hello!' said the average-sized man in the further corner of the car.

'This is like your nerve, Ricky!' Valerie exclaimed angrily.

'Don't blame that poor devil of a chauffeur of yours. I told him I'd take the responsibility for being here.'

The car glided forward.

'Why did you risk it?' Valerie demanded at last.

'Why not? We're engaged, aren't we?'

'But suppose somebody had seen you getting into my car?'

'They didn't. I took good care of that.'

The man's face was partly in shadow, but without seeing him in detail, Valerie knew his eyes were grey, always seemingly secretly laughing at her misanthropic attitude towards life; that the mouth was broad and the chin square. She knew he was a research chemist, mainly on his own account but working for the Government or Scotland Yard now and again. She knew a lot about Richard Harvey, except why he was now lounging beside her analysing her as a doctor might his patient.

'I suppose,' he said presently, 'you're a perfect example of dual personality, Val — schizophrenia. I saw you on the stage tonight for about the twentieth time in the two-year run of this show and I thought, 'That's Valerie Hadfield, believe it or not! To see her laughing and singing, making love, you just wouldn't credit she's the same woman you are officially engaged to!' One carefree and joyous — and the other cold, hard, and carved out of a glacier . . . '

'Just what are you getting at, Ricky?'

'I'm summing you up as dispassionately as I can. I find it easier than telling you to your face that you're really a stinking piece of femininity.'

'Ricky! You've no need to be so vulgar! And you promised to keep away from the theatre. You could have just telephoned and I'd have met you or — '

'I decided on the spur of the moment. I came to the show tonight with the full intention of visiting your dressing room afterwards; then I decided against it in case it upset things for you. I don't suppose that short-sighted doorman would have even seen me, but then I remembered your maid Ellen.'

Valerie gazed out of the window on the bright lights of London. It was a damp, raw night in late autumn. The chauffeur brought the car to a sighing halt at last outside a modern block of flats in South Kensington.

'Garage the car, Peter,' Valerie instructed the chauffeur briefly, alighting. 'Same time tomorrow morning — and don't be late. I have shopping to do.'

'Very good, Miss Hadfield.'

Valerie crossed swiftly to the bright glass-panelled entrance doors of the building. Richard Harvey stood up thankfully.

'I appreciate good driving, Peter,' he said rather dryly, slipping money in the chauffeur's palm. 'And I *also* appreciate sealed lips. Thank you — and good night.'

'Good night, sir — and I quite understand.'

Richard followed the girl into the building and across a soft-carpeted expanse of entrance hall dotted with dried palms, and so to the self-service lift. He stood beside Valerie inside it and smiled crookedly as she pressed button 4.

The lift halted at the fourth floor. Together they stepped out into a deserted corridor with polished doors set at regular intervals all the way down it.

'Ellen not home yet, I suppose?' Richard asked casually, as she searched her handbag for a bunch of keys.

'She'll be here in an hour, but only to bring some stuff in from the theatre. She lives out, don't forget — and I prefer it that way.'

Valerie swung the door of flat 7 open, switched on the light, and walked inside. Richard followed her, closed the door, then stood looking round the familiar room while Valerie went across it to be rid of her hat and coat.

Richard laid his gloved hands on the central heating radiator and warmed them. He knew the place well enough — the definite air of femininity that hung about the cosy furniture. All of it so soft and sleek, so mathematical in its orderliness it was nearly as unapproachable as its owner.

Valerie returned from her bedroom, slender in her pale green gown, her pallid beauty showing to perfection. Richard looked at her analytically.

'Drink?' the girl asked him, going over the sideboard.

'Thanks, no.' He took his gloves off and strolled over to her.

'On the water wagon?' she questioned dryly, squeezing the siphon jet into her half-filled glass of whisky.

'I just don't want to feel muddled.'

The girl shrugged, swallowed the drink down steadily, then began to prepare a second one. To her surprise Richard's lean, strong hand closed on her wrist.

'Hold it,' he said quietly. 'Hear what I have to say first. Come and sit down.'

They crossed the room, settled on the divan.

'You're not going to like this, Val,' he said. 'I'll give it to you neat so you'll get it down quicker . . . I'm breaking our engagement!'

'Oh you are, eh? *Why*?'

'You're not a woman — you're an iceberg! You drink too much, you go about as though the whole world owes you something. As far as I can trace you've never done one really decent, unselfish act in your life. And it won't do for me.'

Valerie gave an acid smile. 'Stop clowning and come to the point!'

'It was the girl on the stage with whom I fell in love, two years ago,' Richard mused. 'I decided to discover the places you frequented — the cafés, the salons, and so forth. And so, gradually, we got to know each other. All the time, Val, I was looking for the girl I'd seen on the stage. I thought perhaps you were tired and overworked and that it accounted for your hard outlook. I sent you flowers; I wrote you letters: took you everywhere I could when we could be sure of not being seen together — because of the publicity. But it dawned on me finally that the granite was just you yourself and that the adorable girl of the stage was just a dream, something I could never possess . . . ' Richard sighed. 'During this current musical comedy I have been thinking that Valerie Hadfield, the actress, and Valerie Hadfield, the woman, are totally distinct . . . Tonight I realised it as never before. And I made up my mind to end our association.'

Valerie went to the table in the centre of the room. From it she picked up a small silver box, opened the lid.

' 'To Val, from Ricky, with all my love',' she quoted dryly. 'Remember?' She took a cigarette out of the box, lighted it, and then stood contemplating the box in her hand.

'Of course I remember it!' Richard rose and came over to her. 'I gave that to the girl I once thought I loved. It doesn't mean a thing any more — not a thing!'

He snatched it from her abruptly and hurled it across the room. It struck the far wall and dropped, scattering cigarettes. The lid had snapped from the hinges and lay a little distance away.

'You idiot!' Valerie reproved. 'All right! You've told me your side of the story: now I'll tell you mine! I'll sue you for breach of promise.'

'I thought your sort preferred a cash settlement.'

'My sort!' Venom came in the blue eyes. 'I don't need the money! You've made me smart tonight, and I'm going to make you smart in return. I refuse to break the engagement, and later on I shall inform the Press, and whom ever else it may concern, that I shall be marrying Richard Harvey, the wealthy and distinguished chemist, in the near future.'

'I'll deny it, Val. The whole thing will descend to the level of an alley fight.'

'*Perhaps!*' Valerie drew quickly at her cigarette. 'Let me remind you of certain things, Ricky. I have all your passionate letters to me — I have that inscribed cigarette box you've just smashed; I have the diamond ring you gave me and which I do not wear in public just yet. If you persist in denying our engagement I shall sell your letters to me to the editor who offers the highest price. I'll start a scandal, an intimate exposure of your feelings towards me, which will embarrass you in every club and scientific association in town. There is nothing a man of your position values more than his prestige. I know. I haven't lived for nothing.'

'That,' Richard said, 'I am inclined to question.'

'Are you?' Valerie's smile looked painted. 'On the other hand, Ricky, I am prepared to admit that you have not perhaps had the chance to judge me properly. We have seen so little of each other with both of us having been so busy.'

'I'm not busy any more — except for my own research. My Government contract finished three days ago.'

'Look, Ricky — we both have a certain fame and position: we both have money. Our marriage would simply mean a union of our — our respective arts.'

'You mean that you want to triumph over everybody as Mrs. Richard Harvey, wife of the celebrated chemist, don't you? You mean you *have* to stick to me because no other man will even bother with you? It's me — or nothing. Right?'

'My God, Ricky, what a gift you have for being a pig!'

'Face facts!' he snapped. 'I'm the only man you ever hooked. Other men may have looked at you, with you being a famous musical comedy star with a perfect stage manner, but I'm the only one who went far enough to fall for you completely. It's desperation that makes you want to stick to me! You know you can't nail anybody else!'

'*Who* can't?' she blazed. 'If men don't run after me it's because I don't give them any encouragement. Didn't that ever occur to you? I've found the only man I want — you!'

'So you've got a lot of useful weapons on your side which I hadn't reckoned you'd be rotten enough to use . . . ' He faced her, unsmiling. 'I can't afford to have my career smashed up just to gratify your spite. I shouldn't have written those letters.'

'I intend to marry the man who has been secretly engaged to me for the past two years. But if — '

'I think,' Richard interrupted, thinking, 'I'll accept your proposition. We'll marry — and live happily never afterwards.'

Valerie went to the sideboard and took up the whisky decanter again. 'Have a drink on the strength of it?'

'No thanks.'

She shrugged, siphoned the soda water. 'I only wish I dared let the public into our secret. Nobody knows as yet that I *am* engaged, and it's most annoying.'

'That's your own fault!' Richard's voice was cold. 'You said you couldn't announce it for fear of your stage career.'

'That's right.' Valerie drained the glass. 'My contract insists that I remain single, but it expires in about the next ten days when the present show ends. Then I can tell everything to the world — and *shall* I tell! Be a relief to me, too. Even my maid keeps pointing out that there are no men in my life and — well, I don't like being thought of as a kind of social leper. My contract for the new show for which I'm rehearsing doesn't contain any marital clause. I took care of that. I'll be able to do as I like.'

'So because of your contract you've refused ever to see me in or near the theatre? How do you think I've felt about that?'

'I just don't care.' The girl's fine brows

were raised insolently. 'I had my career to think of, but soon now it won't matter any more.' An expression close to satisfaction crossed her features.

'I'll actually be able to wear the engagement ring you gave me instead of having to keep it hidden! It seals our bargain, remember, and I've got it neatly tucked away. And incidentally, Ricky, *your* selfishness isn't exactly a negligible quality, you know.'

'Okay, announce your engagement when your contract's expired and we'll be married as soon as you like after that.' He glanced at his watch. 'Now I've got to go. It's gone eleven and we don't want that maid of yours to arrive and find us together. Maids talk — sometimes.'

'But not Ellen,' Valerie declared. 'She knows when she's well off.'

'That chauffeur of yours? Can he be trusted not to reveal our association? It occurs to me that he's the only one who knows of it.'

'He can be trusted implicitly,' Valerie assured him. 'You've developed a sudden concern for my security, haven't you?'

'I'm thinking about your contract. I wouldn't like your career to be cut short at the eleventh hour. I tipped Peter tonight. I'd better do it again next time just to seal his lips entirely.'

As Valerie said nothing, Richard added, 'I'll see you again tomorrow night or maybe the night after. You know me: I come and go.'

'You're certainly a man of surprises,' she acknowledged, opening the door for him. Without a sound he crossed the soft carpet to the lift.

Deeply preoccupied, he left the building and walked into the stiffening wind. He walked on steadily, only subconsciously aware of his direction and his need to reach the Underground station.

The realisation that he was passing a telephone box halted him. Quickly he turned into it and dialled a number from memory and waited, listening to the eerie call sign burring through the night. He pictured it impulsing along dark wires through the biting winds and finally ringing a dove-grey telephone in a comfortable residence near Belsize Park.

He imagined an auburn-haired girl with a bright, intelligent face coming to answer it. Or perhaps it would be her father, or the housekeeper . . .

It was Joyce Prescott herself. 'Hello! You're late, Ricky.'

'It took me longer than I expected, Joyce,' he answered. 'I didn't keep you up, did I?'

'Why, no.' Joyce Prescott laughed. 'I was waiting for you. You promised to ring, and I know you always keep your promises. Well, how did things go?'

'They didn't! She won't release me. I've got to go through with it and marry her.'

There was a long silence. 'And are you going to?'

'It takes thinking about, dear. Tell you what: I have to leave early for the city tomorrow — so why not meet for lunch at the Blue Shadow? We can talk the thing over. There *are* more ways of killing a cat than hanging it!'

2

The Blue Shadow restaurant lying off the Haymarket, was one of Richard Harvey's favourite haunts.

Alberti, the head waiter, was standing in his usual position as Richard entered at twelve-thirty the following day.

'Gooda morning, Meester Harvey! You like for a table, eh? Thees way . . . I show you . . . '

'Just a moment! I'm looking for a lady — a Miss Prescott. You know her . . . auburn hair . . . '

'Ah, Miss Prescott!' Alberti beamed. 'Eef you come thees way, Meester Harvey, I fix you good, eh?'

He led Richard to a table in a far corner, where Joyce Prescott was seated.

'There! Everything all right, eh?'

'Hello, Joyce,' Richard greeted quietly, settling into a chair opposite her.

'Hello, Ricky.' The girl's voice sounded listless.

Alberti hovered. 'What ees it to be, Meester Harvey? Ees it to be — '

'The usual,' Richard said, glancing up.

Richard watched Albert vanish behind swing doors. Then he looked back at the girl. 'You've taken it hard, Joyce, haven't you?' he asked.

'After what you said last night, everything sort of — broke up for me.'

'Perhaps I put it badly,' Richard mused. He noticed that her usually bright face *was* sombre. The firm, full mouth was dragged down at the corners; the brown eyes had lost their sparkle. He was looking at a youthful, twenty-six year old face with its normally clean-cut features blunted by despair.

'Since she won't release you,' she said at last, 'that's the finish of everything for us. Are you afraid to risk a breach of promise suit?'

'I'd risk fifty of 'em, though for your sake I'd rather settle it out of court. Trouble is she has letters of mine, and other mementoes. She can use those to wreck my social and professional position — and she's vicious enough to do so.'

Richard tightened his lips. He wanted Joyce Prescott more than anything else on earth.

'I suppose, Ricky, you won't tell me who she is? Perhaps I could reason with her and explain the position.'

'I'd as soon let loose a child in the den of a lioness, darling. She'd tear you in pieces!'

Alberti was back with a tray. In silence he set out cold chicken sandwiches and a bottle of champagne.

'Thanks, Alberti. Just leave us alone now, please. We're in the middle of an important conversation.'

As Alberti went off the girl said: 'Why champagne? We've nothing to celebrate this time.'

'To even be with you is a celebration!' Richard unfastened the wire and exploded the cork ceilingwards. 'Drink, my darling, and banish dull gloom!'

Joyce smiled faintly and obeyed with the simplicity of a child.

Richard caught her hand. 'If I deliberately cut this woman out she can make things so unpleasant for me that I'll be

When he left Joyce he did not return home to finish his latest work. Instead he walked through the frosty autumn afternoon and turned the problem over in his mind. If Joyce kept her word and *did* commit suicide — !

'Hell no!' Richard whispered. 'Anything but that!'

He looked up as the full realisation of her threat pervaded him, noticing that he was on Waterloo Bridge. He rested his arms on the parapet, and pondered again.

He saw Joyce's slender youthful figure poised beside the stonework, saw her glance quickly round. She clambered quickly on to the parapet and then . . . He closed his eyes and the sound of splashing water smote him like a blow and sent deadly ripples through every nerve.

'It might benefit society if Val did it,' he whispered. 'But not Joyce . . . She's fine and decent.'

His thoughts seemed to come to a sudden stop. If Val did it! If it were made to *look* as if Val had done it . . . Here was an insidious thought . . .

With a sigh he resumed walking, back

towards the city, in no mood to return to the rigours of laboratory work.

So he went to the Stag Club, lying just off the Mall, where perhaps he might find seclusion to think things out.

But as he stepped into the cosy warmth of the clubroom he knew he would not get that opportunity. The three men lounging in the broad overstuffed armchairs by the fire satisfied him on that. He smiled resignedly to himself and went forward towards then, across the soft carpet.

'Hello, Dick!' one of them greeted him. 'Still kicking around in the stinks department, I suppose?'

Richard strolled between the seated men and stood for a moment with his back to the fire. The club was otherwise deserted at the moment. Softly lighted, it expanded away in polished tables and heavy armchairs to the dark panelled walls with their armoury and brass plaques. In the distance a waiter glided soundlessly.

'Crime must be quiet, I take it?' Richard commented at last, looking at the man who had addressed him.

Chief Inspector Garth of the C.I.D. shrugged heavy shoulders. 'My last case finished and I've a bit of time to draw breath — as much as I can with my damned indigestion.' He thumped his broad chest.

'Did I interrupt something?' Richard asked.

'We were talking about crime!' Garth looked momentarily severe. 'As a chemist with a few Yard dabblings to your credit you may be able to contribute something useful . . . Sit down and let's hear from you.'

Richard moved to an armchair near the fire. He watched Garth as he frowned over his thoughts.

Mortimer Garth was reputedly a brilliant analytical thinker. His face was thin to the point of emaciation with high cheekbones and then sunken hollows that gave the thin, tight lips an illusion of fullness. The fleshiest thing about the face was the jaw, bulging with taut muscle on each side. His face was generous when it smiled, inhuman when it didn't. His brown wiry hair was becoming scanty at the temples, making Garth look a good deal older than his factual forty-seven.

'You were saying, Garth, that a murderer's hardest job is to rid himself of the body . . . '

Richard turned his gaze to the fat man on his left. He knew him vaguely — a retired merchant with a morbid penchant for harrowing crime details.

'So I was,' Garth agreed. 'A criminal may think of all kinds of ingenious ways of killing a person, but it's the *body* that usually gets him down. It's impossible to be rid of a corpse so completely that nobody can find it.'

'That shouldn't trouble modern criminals much,' commented Colonel Melrose, directly opposite Richard. 'I mean — dammit, there are acids for one thing.'

Garth smiled. 'You can't entirely do it with acids, Colonel. I was on such a case a few years back. The murderer managed to dissolve most of the body but he forgot the gold and platinum in the teeth of his victim. A dental surgeon identified the stuff which had resisted the acid and the murderer was caught.'

'All of which destroys, I suppose, the possibility of a perfect crime?' asked the retired merchant.

'There isn't such a thing,' Garth said. Criminals like Crippen, Mahon, Fox, Ruxton . . . All the lot of 'em found the corpse still speaking no matter how carefully they tried to shut it up. Probably Sheward of Norwich was the most thorough. He dismembered his wife into such small pieces and strewed them over so wide an area it took the police thirteen days to prove there had even *been* a murder, and even then they couldn't identify the victim. Sheward got away with it for eighteen years until his own conscience finally got him down and he confessed.'

'One would hardly think such a man would *have* a conscience,' said the Colonel, brooding.

'He had, anyway.' Garth mused. 'And he was thorough enough to clip the woman's hair into fine dust and scatter it about the streets of Norwich as he walked. That was clever. Hair is hard to hide. It smells if you burn it, and if you don't you can never be sure of some strands haven't blown away somewhere.'

'Nice cheerful sort of talk for a dull autumn afternoon,' Richard observed languidly, proffering his cigarette case to the Chief Inspector. 'And I don't see what it proves, either. Perfect crimes do exist, and because they're perfect we never hear of them.'

'I admit' — Garth lighted his cigarette — 'I admit there may be crimes so perfect they've never been solved, but in the vast majority of cases over-confidence or else pure idiotic bungling has legged down the killers.'

For instance?' prompted the merchant.

'Well, take Crippen.' Garth sat back. 'The damned fool was infinitely thorough in cutting up the victim, yet he made the glaring mistake of wrapping the grisly pieces in his own pyjama jackets which had *his* laundry mark! Then there was Voirbo, the French killer, who threw the remains of a victim down a well from which a famous café drew its drinking water. The acidity of the water led to arrest. Then take Kate Webster and Henry Wainwright. They carried their gruesome parcels of remains about London until Wainwright hired a boy — a boy, mind you! — to look after the remains of Harriet Lane while he called a cab. On the other hand, Kate Webster also had a boy to help her. Both boys, with the inquisitiveness normal to their age, were suspicious — and there you are! Then there was Greenacre who carried the head of Hannah Brown in a cardboard box on top of a 'bus and later threw the box in Regent's Canal. Unfortunately for him the head jammed the lock gates! There it is! Perfect crime always coming unstuck.'

'You mean 'nearly always',' Richard murmured from the depths of his chair, 'In all the cases you have quoted, Garth, it wasn't police work that did it. It was chance, circumstance, Providence. It wasn't sheer deduction.'

'Admitted,' the Chief Inspector agreed. 'We're not magicians, Dick, after all. Though of course science and police methods have improved so much in these latter days since the war that I'm willing to gamble that in this age of nineteen-forty-nine crime — of the perfect variety — could not exist.'

'That's a big gamble,' commented the Colonel.

Richard stared into vacancy. He was in a world apart. There was a feeling of security about the room, a pleasurable realisation of the fact that Chief Inspector Garth was only human like the rest of people . . . He had known Mortimer Garth intimately for many years, usually in the line of chemistry business or else at the club here. He had come to look upon him as a machine . . .

Yet he could make mistakes! He had said so himself.

3

'Well, Dick, what's your opinion?' Garth asked. 'You're a first class chemist. I don't have to tell *you* that chemistry plays a major function in solving crime. Do you think that in these days a murder could be so cleverly committed as to defy solution?'

Richard threw his cigarette into the fire. 'Yes, I think it could. I believe that criminals, like Scotland Yard, have improved their methods. The days of Dr. Crippen have gone. What science has placed before Scotland Yard it has *also* placed before the criminal. So, the two will keep pace — or so I think. I cannot see why a perfect crime should not exist even today.'

'That,' said the merchant, 'puts a spoke in your wheel, eh, Inspector?'

Garth smiled. 'I have the advantage of knowing the mind of a killer,' he said. 'Murderers as a rule possess colossal vanity — egotism. What *they* think is original the Yard found out about years ago . . . However' — Garth got to his feet — 'I've got to be going. I've an appointment with Assistant Commissioner Farley at five-thirty. When the perfect crime blows in, gentlemen, I'll be glad to let you in on it!'

He turned away, and Richard watched him pass beyond the panelled oak doors. Then his eyes returned to the Colonel and the merchant once more.

'Damned clever fellow, Inspector Garth,' the Colonel said.

Richard wasn't even listening. He had relapsed into introspection again, his eyes on the fire. Garth had mentioned fire. Fire — water — burial — dismemberment — concealment. But all the killers Garth had cited had been limited by the point of advancement to which their period had attained. Today, in 1949, it was different. Science had walked with seven-leagued boots between and especially during the two World Wars. None of the early murderers had been first-class chemists with modern equipment; none of them had had a father with supreme chemistry knowledge such as Richard had had. In fact they had been motivated by only one thing in common — hatred for a particular person, or persons. Just as he hated Valerie Hadfield.

Abruptly he got to his feet and turned to face the two elderly men.

'If you'll pardon me, gentlemen . . . I too have an appointment.'

He took his coat from the attendant in the hall, tipped him, then went out into the darkening cold of the autumn afternoon.

Buttoning up his collar Richard walked down the street until he reached a telephone box. Inside it he dialled the same number as on the previous evening. It was Joyce Prescott who presently answered him.

'Something happened, Ricky?' she asked quietly.

'Yes. Something that is going to make all the difference in the world to you and me. It may mean that I shall be less regular in seeing you than I have been — but promise me you won't do anything rash on that account.'

'You mean you can do something about . . .?'

'Yes. I mean just that. My only worry now is that you may think I've deserted you or something with my being less punctual than usual — '

'I understand — completely. I'll wait for whenever you call again . . . ' Joyce hesitated. 'Ricky, you're not going to do anything rash, are you?'

Richard laughed. 'Bless your heart, no!'

* * *

Richard's home was in the Belsize Park neighbourhood — a massive detached residence with the grounds thick with plane trees. He liked the privacy they gave to the house, the leafy shield they formed in summer for the modern brick laboratory at the back of the residence.

Building was Richard's hobby, and he had built the laboratory himself — a low brick annex with a flat concrete roof and broad ground-glass windows to give both maximum daylight and absolute secrecy.

For some time now he had been thinking of building a garage at the side of the house, where a driveway led straight up to an empty part of the grounds. An architect friend had drawn up the plans for it long ago, and had obtained Council approval. Only somehow Richard had never got round to it. He used his car — a black Jaguar saloon — very little, and most of the time it lay dust-sheeted in a public garage.

Tonight, however, as he walked slowly home the idea of a garage had a new appeal for him.

When he entered his scrupulously polished hall old Baxter came forward as usual to meet him. He was a tired, crumpled man who had used up his energy and youth in the service of Richard's parents. Richard kept him on because of his trustworthiness and his uncanny knowledge of where everything lay in the rambling old place. His wife Sarah did the cooking and the housekeeping.

'Good evening, Mr. Richard, sir . . . ' Baxter took Richard's coat in shaky hands. 'Cold again . . . '

'Yes, Baxter — very cold.'

'Everything's ready, Mr. Richard, sir,' Baxter added. 'I'll just tell the wife to serve dinner — shall I?'

'Er — yes,' Richard agreed pensively. 'No callers, Baxter?'

'No, Mr. Richard, sir. Nobody at all.'

Richard nodded and went on into the firelit room. After he had switched on the electric light he stood looking round on the huge Regency pedestal sideboard, the William and Mary walnut escritoire, the Queen Anne walnut angle chairs, the antique glass cabinet, the old-fashioned armchairs . . . All of them would have to go when he married Joyce. She had modern ideas and her coming into the Harvey residence would mean the opening of a new chapter in furnishings, hangings, in life itself in fact.

Richard settled down at the table and watched the advance of Mrs. Baxter's ample, bustling figure. Eight years younger than her husband, she was grey-haired, spotlessly clean, a superb cook and house-manageress.

‘I have a surprise for you, Mrs. Baxter,’ Richard said. ‘I’m going to be married.’

‘That’s *wonderful*! Who’s the lady, may I ask?’

‘At the moment,’ Richard said, smiling oddly, ‘it’s a secret. We’re planning to spring a big surprise, and you are the only person so far who has even a hint of what is coming. I thought I’d just warn you,’ Richard explained. ‘My wife-to-be will very probably turn this rambling ancestral pile into a bear garden in an effort to convert it to modern standards.’

‘And I’ll be glad too!’ Mrs. Baxter declared surprisingly. ‘The place is never as clean as I’d like with all this heavy furniture about.’ She brightened suddenly. ‘An’ when’s it to be?’

‘I’m not sure yet,’ Richard answered, commencing his meal. ‘First, I have to attend to a little matter of a garage on the premises. You see, my fiancée likes a car far more than I do, so I think I’d better get some contractors to send along a few bricks, cement, and a small-sized concrete mixer.’

Mrs. Baxter’s expression changed. She

had memories of the dirt and confusion attending the building of the laboratory annex.

'You're not going to build a garage yourself, Mr. Richard?'

He grinned. 'Why not? I built the laboratory annex, didn't I?'

'Ye-es, but . . . How will you be able to spare the time when you're going to be married?' It was a hopeful if futile effort.

'Oh, I'll wedge it in,' Richard decided calmly. 'Anyway, should a few loads of bricks and timber and things arrive while I'm in the city you'll know what it's all about.'

'Yes, Mr. Richard,' Mrs. Baxter agreed sadly. 'Will there by anything more now?'

'Not just now, thanks. I'll be going into the study afterwards. I've a few things to work out.'

Mrs. Baxter went out. Richard smiled faintly to himself: he felt a curious elation at having made the first move in what he knew was going to be a deadly gamble in wits. So a perfect crime could not exist, eh? The body was always the stumbling block, was it?

Preparation! Faultless preparation upon which to build a master plan . . . Letters. Check up on the letters Valerie Hadfield had sent him from time to time during the first flush of their acquaintance. He recalled that she had rarely put a date — and usually put the day instead.

From his safe he took the half dozen letters Valerie had written in the last two years and read them through carefully beneath the desk lamp, smoking and pondering as he did so. Odd how the innate coldness of the woman flowed even from her written words.

Tuesday.

Ricky, my dear,

Of course I'll meet you at the Silver Grill tomorrow! In fact I consider it a privilege to which your future wife is entitled. Frankly, I cannot understand your constant reiterations of love for me. I know you love me, just as I love you. Tomorrow then at 12:30 in that nice, quiet café.

Always,
Val.

'Funny she didn't finish it 'Yours faithfully',' Richard muttered, tossing it down and selecting another.

Thursday.

Ricky, my dear,

All right. I can spare time for a little tête-à-tête tomorrow. Thanks for keeping away from the 'phone. It might make things difficult for me and I must think of my career.

Always
Val.

Richard took a pair of rubber gloves from the desk drawer and snapped them on his hands; then with a soft indiarubber he went over the letter carefully, back and front, erasing all trace of fingerprints. That the surface 'mashed' a little in the process didn't signify.

This done he put the letter carefully away in an envelope, sealed it, and put it separately from its fellows. Then he replaced the whole bundle back in the safe. Coming back to the desk he wrote 'Friday' in block capitals on his note pad, tore the leaf off and put it away in the desk-drawer, locking it. Then he tore away the next five blank leaves until he was satisfied no indent of the word remained on the clean pad. The five blank leaves he tossed into the fire.

'You don't get *me* with your iodine spray, Mortimer Garth!' he said slowly, pulling the gloves off and putting them away again.

He switched off the lights, left the study, and went along the hall into the laboratory annex. The lights came up at his touch and he drew the bolt over the door behind him.

The laboratory was ultra-modern: his unlimited money and love of the work had seen to that. Three centre tables on the concrete floor contained test-tube racks, beakers, retorts, and a good selection of electrical equipment. On the side, benches held microscopes and racks of modern instruments — and above them shelves lined with orderly labelled bottles and culture-jars. Against one wall stood heavy X-ray equipment on a rubber-wheeled base, and against the opposite wall a liquid air compressor with its quiescent electric dynamo.

Richard strolled the length of the laboratory until he came to three large bellying Dewar flasks, stoppered with cotton — actually giant vacuum flasks containing a pale blue mobile fluid. Richard contemplated them, then he turned and looked at the second door of the laboratory which led into the driveway and thence down to the road outside the gates.

Next, he studied the ground glass windows — six wide ones — the three on the 'drive-side' wall carrying his shadow from the low hanging lights as he walked along deliberately to see the effect.

'Alibi?' he mused. 'That's what I need — I might create an artificial image of myself and make it cast a shadow on the window — a mechanical model perhaps . . . '

Then he shook his head. A mechanical model though possible, cut out of aluminium and actuated by a motor, might develop a fault and stop. A motionless image of 'himself' if seen in shadow form on one of the lighted windows would bring Mr. or Mrs. Baxter, or both, running to find out what was wrong.

On the other hand, if he simply left the laboratory lights on and did not bother about a shadow or any other proof of his presence in the laboratory, there was no reason to suppose but what Mr. and Mrs. Baxter would accept the fact that he *was* there. They would not pry: they never had.

'Never gild the lily,' he muttered. 'Right! Lighted windows and nothing else. Good!'

He switched off the lights, left the laboratory, and locked it behind him. The great house was silent. A dim electric glimmer showed along the hall. The Baxters had retired to bed at eleven. This Richard permitted as a regular thing in deference to their ages and his own erratic nocturnal work upon research.

He switched the light off, and went up the broad, familiar staircase in total darkness — and so to his bedroom. Entering, he switched on the small single lamp on the table by the big old-fashioned armchair and sat down in it.

He was planning cold-blooded murder, working it out beforehand with the relentless logic of a chemical formula. Murder — destruction of life — the slaying of a living woman no matter how coldly cynical she might be. Planning for her total disappearance, for his own unshatterable safety and future happiness with Joyce Prescott. She would never even guess. In fact *nobody* could ever know or guess. When finished the plan would be foolproof . . .

But still murder!

Richard's mind went racing back over the events of the day, to the point where this monstrous, glorious idea had first occurred to him . . . The vision of Joyce leaping into the river; the cold shock to his nerves as in imagination he had heard the sound of her body striking the water. Yes, it had begun there — gently, insidiously . . . Then Inspector Garth with his macabre anecdotes of the blunders of past criminals, his colossal faith in his own and Scotland Yard's ability . . .

A chemist with modern equipment against Scotland Yard's merciless array. Somehow it had all acted on Richard like a catalyst and at the same time had offered a solution to his own dilemma.

If Valerie did not die Joyce would probably do so!

Here, Richard felt, was an excuse for his actions. He wasn't destroying life: he was saving it. And still he did not see how deeply he had assimilated the toxin of selfishness, how it had grown by subtle mutations from a plain earthy desire to discard one woman and possess another, into an implacable ego-mania which insisted he *destroy* one woman completely to prove his mastery over an otherwise intolerable situation.

At last he got into bed and lay in the darkness, not dwelling any more upon the rightness of his behaviour but upon the next moves he must make. Tomorrow he must call on Rothwell, the builders' merchant; buy a cheap car; find a small house in a village if he could, preferably a good way from Belsize Park. Perhaps in the quiet Sunbury-on-Thames district . . . Yet not *too* quiet. Enough people about to notice him coming and going.

He went to sleep deciding that he would travel to the Sunbury district on the morrow.

4

Next morning Richard told Mrs. Baxter he would probably not be home until evening, and then left the house about nine-thirty.

After walking to his bank and withdrawing a hundred pounds, which he insisted be in one pound notes, he went on to Rothwell's, the builders' merchants.

Old Rothwell looked at the specification sheets Richard had handed him as they sat together in the little shack with its reek of fumes from the paraffin stove. 'Yes, we c'n do that easy enough.'

'One thing I want added — a small concrete mixer,' Richard said. 'It will save me a lot of trouble.'

'No problem, sir,' Rothwell assured him. 'I expect we'll deliver the stuff today sometime.'

Richard next made for the bus stop, and waited for a bus to take him to Camden Town. Here he sought an emporium where he purchased a ready-made suit, raincoat, cap, shirt, socks, shoes, and gloves, all of them below the grade of his normal attire.

Then on to Camden Town Underground. Here, still hugging his brown paper parcel, he disappeared into the gentlemen's waiting room. A man in a cap and raincoat, with blue trousers showing beneath it, and clutching a brown paper parcel emerged again some minutes later. He walked with a pronounced limp of the left foot, stooped, and sported blue wool gloves on his hands. Dimly visible where his raincoat collar had fallen open was a print shirt and collar and somewhat glaring tie.

With the cap pulled low down over his eyes Richard limped along towards the platform, entered the train when it arrived and alighted again finally at Euston. Here he deposited his parcel in the luggage office to be called for later, and then set out into the city to find a second-hand car depot.

After considerable searching he finally alighted upon the kind of firm he sought, loaded with cars of all ages and types.

'I just want a plain good goer,' Richard explained, hardening his mellow voice into a decided Northern intonation. 'Nothing fancy.'

'Quite, sir,' the young salesman agreed politely. 'About what price?'

'The price doesn't matter — within reason — as long as the car's what I'm looking for. How about that one over there?' Richard limped towards an old saloon.

'Reliable enough, sir — a good engine,' the salesman said.

Richard pulled open the doors and peered inside. That the car was a saloon was the chief attraction. He knew right away it was exactly what he wanted but he didn't wish to appear too eager. Internal metalwork was very rough, he noticed.

'All right, it'll do,' he said finally. 'How much?'

'Sixty-seven pounds, sir — ready licensed. I can make out a cover note for the insurance while you wait. Third party or comprehensive?'

‘Third party,’ Richard said; and he waited until the salesman turned aside before he pulled out his wallet and extracted seventy pound notes; then he limped across to the glass-topped counter where the salesman was scribbling on a printed cover note.

‘And the name and address, sir?’

‘The name’s Rixton Williams, spelt with an ex. I haven’t an address yet — or rather I don’t know exactly what it will be. I’m going to see about a place — Sunbury way.’

‘Sunbury, sir? Pretty spot . . . Well, as long as the car is recorded in your name we’ll use this address for the moment. You can let us have it when you’re settled and we’ll let the insurance company know.’

‘All right,’ Richard agreed.

He took the slip handed to him, paid his money in one pound notes, and studied the receipted bill and log book. The driving licence he had decided he would risk. Then with the salesman preceding him he went back to his car and clambered inside with deliberate awkwardness.

Somewhat jerkily he started forward and so out into the street. He drove slowly, getting the feel of the relic, until he felt safe enough to put on speed and so began a swift journey which eventually brought him to grey, drab, vaguely commercial-looking Twickenham.

Just beyond Twickenham Green he pulled up sharply outside an estate agent's office and went inside, shambling and limping.

'Good afternoon, sir . . . ' A girl of perhaps eighteen with blonde hair obscuring one eye came to the enquiry desk.

Richard glanced at the various auction sale bills. 'Is Mr. — er — Hardisty about?' he asked. 'It's about a house around here. I want to buy one.'

'If you'll just wait a moment, sir?'

The girl turned aside and went into an adjoining office, then she came back and lifted the counter flap to let Richard through. He limped into a small room with a desk laden with papers and files. Behind it sat the shirt-sleeved Amos Hardisty, round-faced, and beaming.

'*Good* afternoon, sir!' He shook Richard's hand. 'Take a chair.'

Richard sat down, and failed to remove his cap. Never do to show he had rich dark wavy hair and that his face was really young.

'I'm looking for a small house,' he explained. 'What have you got?'

Hardisty closed his eyes and thought; then he opened them and said, 'I've got one, three up and three down with the usual appointments. But maybe it won't do. It's detached, good garden back and front.'

'Sounds all right to me. What sort of people live around it?'

'Oh, mostly retired old folks. One or two houses in a bunch if you follow me. It's on this very road, which leads through to Sunbury. Open country situation with a few small shops nearby.'

'But there *are* people about?' Richard insisted; then he added casually 'I don't want to feel lonely you see.'

'I think,' Hardisty said, 'you might find it the very thing. It's going at sixteen hundred. Would be more only it wants a bit of painting. And the fact that, though detached, there is not enough room at the side to bring in a car, is another drawback. Maybe you'd like me to show it to you?'

'No need for that. Give me the key and I'll look for myself.'

Hardisty summoned the girl with the waterfall hair and had her make out a receipt for the small key charge; then when the exchange was complete and Richard had the key in his pocket, Hardisty added:

'You can't miss it, Mr. — er — ?' He frowned at the receipt.

'Williams — Rixton Williams, spelt with an ex.'

'Oh! Well, follow the main road outside and on the way you'll see the house with four others. People are away next door to you. You'll let me know soon?'

Richard nodded and departed. Ten minutes of driving brought him to the house. He went inside it, glanced round, and came out again to survey. The narrow side path with bordering wall *was* a drawback, certainly. Have to leave the car at the front that was all. On the other hand the next house was far removed. In all directions around the houses there seemed to be open fields.

At the next but one house a bald man in an alpaca jacket, smoking a pipe, was supposed to be tending chrysanthemums, but he was looking at Richard at the same time. Richard moved towards him, limping along the pavement.

'Good afternoon, sir . . . '

The elderly man pretended surprise and glanced up with a round, pink face. ''Afternoon. Thinking of taking the house?' The childlike blue eyes were inquiring.

'I might,' Richard mused. 'That is if it isn't too dead-alive round here. I'm used to a busy Lancashire town, you see. Industrial district — but I'm looking for somewhere quiet. I've had quite enough of noise. I'm Williams, by the way — Rixton Williams.'

'Glad to know you . . . '

The man said he was Timothy Potter, a retired paper merchant, and for nearly half an hour Richard stood talking to him deliberately — allowing curiosity on the part of other neighbours to have its fling — most of whom seemed to find it necessary to suddenly come outside or else clean windows or arrange curtains from inside — and also gleaning a full-scale picture of the local colour.

When he took his leave of Timothy Potter and climbed back into his car it was already becoming drab evening. He turned the car round and headed back for Hardisty's estate office.

'It'll do,' he told Hardisty. 'Here are five pounds to hold it for me. Tomorrow you'll get a cheque. I'll be down to fix it up.'

'Good!' Hardisty enthused. 'You'll like it there.'

'Who is a good house furnisher around here?' Richard asked. 'Somebody who can do the job from top to bottom?'

'Draycott's, in the main street,' Hardisty replied promptly. 'They'll do all that's necessary.'

Richard thanked him briefly, and left. He called in Draycott's, gave them the house key and told them to look over the place and decide what it needed to be furnished just enough without elaboration. Then with the promise to be back on the morrow for the estimate he began the trip back to London.

It was dark when he arrived. He garaged the car in a public garage near Euston, reclaimed his parcel from the luggage office, reappearing from the waiting room as himself with the brown paper parcel under his arm. Next he took the Underground back to Belsize Park and emerged into the dim lights of the gloomy street leading from the station.

Next he detoured to the public garage where he kept his Jaguar. Into it he put his brown paper parcel, behind the movable part of the back seat, relocked the doors, nodded to the garage owner whom he knew intimately, and then set off for home. A vague sense of elation was upon him as Baxter took his coat and told him that the building contractors had delivered the necessities for the impending garage.

* * *

As Richard ate his dinner he reflected that he had created the character of Rixton Williams from Lancashire with entire conviction, and far enough away from Belsize Park to escape all possibility of connection with himself.

Ending his meal he went outside to see what the contractors had brought. The light from the kitchen doorway streamed out on to a hill of clean new bricks, neatly stacked timber beams and planks, sacks of concrete powder and sand, and grey and battered amidst the array stood the concrete mixer with its generator waiting to be plugged into the power supply.

Richard went back inside to his study. Here he drew the plans of the garage from his desk and studied them. It was to have a concrete floor, brick walls, a properly slated roof, and a plaster ceiling after the fashion of a room in a house. It was to be a perfect garage.

He rolled the plans up again, put them back in the drawer, and sat thinking.

'Next, the bank. Take out two thousand and deposit it in a Twickenham bank under the name of Rixton Williams. Must be in one pound notes though. Simple enough. Then generally convince people around that place in Twickenham that I am living in their neighbourhood . . . Have to think up an excuse for the Baxters. Urgent business to keep me away should do.'

Richard went back to the desk, made several notes for his own personal guidance, memorised them, then threw them away in the fire along with the five blank sheets of the scratch-pad immediately under them. Glancing at his watch, he decided there was time for a walk before an early retirement . . .

5

He returned home towards half-past eleven. As usual the Baxters had gone to bed.

He went to sleep happily, was untouched by dreams, and climbed out of bed again at seven-thirty the following morning.

'I shall be away until evening,' he told Mrs. Baxter, after breakfast 'I have some business to attend to in the city. Dinner at the usual time.'

Then, smiling genially, he departed with a small attaché case and made the local bank his first stopping place.

'In one pound notes, if you please,' he told the clerk, presenting his cheque made out to 'Self'.

The clerk looked up in vague wonder after he had scrutinised the 'Two thousand pounds . . . '

'Just a moment, please.'

Richard waited impatiently, trying to appear civil when the bank manager invited him into his private office.

'Nothing wrong, Mr. Harvey,' he explained. 'It's just you're here early and we haven't that much cash in one pound notes on hand at the moment. It'll be here in a few minutes. I thought you'd prefer to come in and sit down.'

'Oh . . . I see.' Richard tried to look mollified, and took the cigarette from the case proffered him.

'Business good, Mr. Harvey?' the manager asked him, with that polite detachment usually shown to a wealthy client.

'Good enough,' Richard answered briefly. 'But I'm likely to lose a good deal of it if your clerk doesn't hurry up!'

The manager gave up the effort at small talk and turned to his morning correspondence. Five minutes later the clerk announced that everything was in order now. How would it be taken?

'In this case,' Richard answered, handing it over.

'Yes, Mr. Harvey, with pleasure.'

The clerk went, and returned, waited while Richard checked the amount.

Finally he nodded and snapped the case shut, got to his feet. Nodding a farewell to the manager he strolled out of the bank and commenced the short walk to the garage where he kept his Jaguar.

'Fill her up, George,' he said to the mechanic, busy repairing a Ford. 'And check the oil. I've a good bit of travelling to do.'

'Right you are, Mr. Harvey!'

Richard drove out by way of Haverstock Hill to the city centre. When he reached Charing Cross he garaged the Jaguar in an underground park, took out his parcel and attaché case, and went into Charing Cross Station to change into Mr. Rixton Williams. Thus attired, and again with parcel and attaché case he collected his old car and drove it to the nearest florists.

'I want a bunch of those pink roses,' he told the girl who hovered amidst the steamy warmth and exotic perfumes. 'And give me a card, will you? I want to write a few words.'

'With pleasure, sir.' She handed a blank piece of pasteboard across the counter and, bending his hand round so it completely altered his normal style of handwriting — and wearing his woollen gloves too, to the secret amazement of the florist's assistant — Richard wrote laboriously:

To that lovely actress Valerie Hadfield from a man who admires her from far off and whose name is Rixton Williams.

He slipped the card amidst the roses as they were handed to him in a dunce's cap of tissue paper, paid for them, and went out. In another ten minutes he was drawing to a halt a block away from the stage door of the Paragon Theatre.

Clasping the roses he made his way limpingly through a familiar alley and entered the stage doorway between two posters proclaiming VALERIE HADFIELD in JINGLE BELLS.

The doorman stopped him, just as he'd expected.

'Hey now, where do you think you're goin'? Bit early with your flowers, aren't you?'

'Maybe I am,' Richard acknowledged, aware that those short-sighted eyes were peering at him through the dense spectacles. 'I don't want to go in, anyway. Just see that Miss Hadfield gets these, will you?'

'Well, I — '

'And here's a tip.'

The doorman took the roses, looked at the money in his palm, squinted at the man who had given him both, and then he nodded.

'Right, y'are, sir. I'll see to it.'

Richard mused as he walked haltingly back to his car. 'That short-sighted old fool will verify that there is such a person as Rixton Williams but he'll only remember a hard voice and a raincoat maybe. Good enough . . . '

He drove to a restaurant for lunch, and then afterwards repeated the journey of the previous day. By late afternoon he had completed most of his business — deposited his two thousand in a branch bank in Twickenham under the *alias* of Rixton Williams, which signature he gave in his backhanded style; signed the conveyance for the house and paid out the cheque; approved the furniture estimate right down to the draperies and paid for these by cheque also, leaving the key with the furniture company so they could put the stuff in as quickly as possible. Then he finished the afternoon off by arranging for the water and electricity to be put on.

His return trip merely repeated the previous day's actions, changing from one personality to the other, using the same garages again. He had got his plan moving without a soul suspecting that Richard Harvey and Rixton Williams were one and the same person . . .

On his way home he called on Joyce Prescott and found her, after the housekeeper had allowed him in, in the midst of helping her father in the preparation of one of his periodic lectures on philosophy.

'I didn't think I'd be disturbing you,' Richard said with a smile as the girl clasped his hands eagerly in the brightly lighted study. 'Only I thought I'd let you know I'm still in the land of the living . . . Hello, Doctor, how are you? Hope I'm not taking your valuable time.'

Dr. Howard Prescott, Ph.D., got up

from his desk and smiled cordially. He was a venerable looking man of perhaps fifty, retired now from University lecturing, wealthy through inheritance, and with the fate of orphans his main concern in life. His once red-brown hair was grey now.

'Of course I can spare time for a future member of the family . . . And I suppose,' Prescott finished, 'that is what you will become?'

Richard grinned. 'No doubt of it!'

'So everything's all right now?' Joyce sank down on the edge of an armchair.

Richard glanced at her, then back to her father.

'Yes,' the Doctor said, interpreting Richard's look, 'I know all about your difficulty. Joyce tells me everything that worries her.'

'I suppose,' Richard said with a dubious smile, 'you think I'm pretty unethical?'

'You are only answerable to yourself, Richard,' Prescott smiled. 'If you prefer Joyce to a woman with whom you know you can never find happiness then by all means remove the opposition, amicably of course. My own married life, up to the death of my dear wife, was extremely happy — but in the beginning I had a similar trouble to yours. I was in love with another woman. Fortunately for me she switched her affections to another man and left the way clear. Your case, I understand, isn't quite so easy as that?'

'No,' Richard sighed. 'It isn't.'

'Still keeping her identity a secret?' Joyce asked with a touch of grimness.

'Yes,' Richard agreed; then he brisked up a little. 'As a matter of fact, Joyce, I dropped in to tell you personally that I'm liable to fade out of sight for about a week.'

'So you said over the telephone.'

'I only said I'd be irregular in seeing you. Now I know it will be for a week. I've business out of town. If I come home at all it will only be very late at night. I'll ring you if I think you'll not have retired.'

'All right,' she said somewhat indifferently, and he patted her hand.

'Incidentally, Richard,' Howard Prescott said, 'I went past your place this morning on a trip from a sick friend. I see you're having some building done, or else are going to. Bricks, timber, and stuff . . . What's it for? New lab?'

'It's for Joyce's special benefit as a matter of fact. Material for a garage I'm intending to build myself. I built my own laboratory, you know.'

'I'm more of a believer in every man to his trade, I'm afraid. For instance, I should hate to start doing chemical experiments the way you do, just as you'd be at sea, I expect, in preparing a lecture on philosophy.'

'Well,' Richard said, 'I'd better be on my way.'

'See you again,' Prescott acknowledged — and the girl saw Richard to the door. He kissed her and went down the path to his car parked in front of the house.

He drove homewards, had dinner in the usual way and then drove back to London again, drawing up finally in Kensington outside Valerie Hadfield's apartment building. Here he sat waiting for the time when her big black Daimler would appear round the corner.

'It's her last chance,' he muttered. 'If she'll let me go for the sake of the unknown Rixton Williams and a monetary consideration, all well and good. But if she won't . . .'

The girl's Daimler glided round the distant corner, drawing up outside the building in front of his own car, bonnet to bonnet. He got out to the pavement and stood waiting as the girl alighted.

'What's the programme this time? Another string of insults like the night before last?'

Without giving him a chance to reply she hurried up the steps towards the glass panelled doors. Richard turned to Peter as he closed the Daimler's rear door.

'As usual, Peter, you know nothing,' he said, parting with a Treasury note. 'Whoever asks you — at any time, anywhere.'

'You know me, sir,' Peter said, grinning, and put the note in the breast pocket of his uniform.

Richard turned and hurried up the steps into the building, across the hall, and into the lift. Richard and Valerie's actions were a repetition of the night before last — the lift, the corridor, the door of flat no. 7; then they were in the apartment with the lights on.

'Ellen following on?' Richard inquired.

'Naturally.'

Valerie went through to the bedroom, came back presently in a creation of black and gold that clung faultlessly to her curves. She went to the drinks on the sideboard, prepared one, then raised questioning eyes.

'Not for me,' Richard said. 'I'm still keeping my head clear. I thought I'd see if you've changed your mind about us. There's been time for reflection since.'

'I've no need to reflect, Ricky. We're going to be married and we announce the fact immediately my contract expires a week tomorrow, Saturday, October twenty-second . . . Give me a cigarette, will you?'

Richard opened his case, flicked his lighter. 'You haven't thought any more kindly about a cash settlement and a parting with a handshake, then?' he asked, lighting his own cigarette.

'You can't buy me off, Ricky. I don't *need* the money, only the position you can give me as my husband. And if you want to break with me because you have some other woman in tow, then forget it. I saw you first, and I'm sticking to you!'

Richard sighed. 'I suppose I'm something unique really — the only man you ever had, or are likely to have . . . '

The girl blew smoke through her sensitive nostrils. 'You are the man I want because you have the right position for an actress like me — but don't think you're unique! I had flowers from an admirer only this morning.'

'Nothing unusual for an actress to receive flowers, is it? It doesn't necessarily mean anything . . . '

'This did! He wrote a note . . . I liked it well enough to keep it!' She hurried through into her bedroom. She returned to hand Richard the pasteboard upon which he had written in the florist's shop that morning.

' 'To that lovely actress Valerie Hadfield from a man who admires her from far off and whose name is Rixton Williams',' Richard murmured, taking care to hold the card edgewise. Then he handed it back.

'What does he look like?' Richard asked casually.

'I don't know, nor can I tell you from the stage doorman's story whether the man who brought the flowers was a messenger or the real sender. He appears to have been stooped-shouldered, dressed just so-so, and having a hard voice.'

Richard smiled. 'If *he* was the real thing I should forget him. If, though, he was only the messenger and the real Rixton Williams is somewhere around, waiting to give you his address, what are you going to do?'

'Absolutely nothing! He can send all the letters he likes . . . '

'But surely you'll inform the police if he becomes a nuisance with his loving notes?'

'Why should I? Loving notes are useful sometimes. Look how they've tied me to you, for instance! I've merely produced this card to show you you are not so unique as you think. But I'm going to marry *you*.'

Richard thought: *Valerie has just signed her death warrant!*

Valerie turned away from him, went back into her bedroom and parted with the visiting card. When she came back she found Richard by the door.

'Going?' she inquired in surprise. 'But we haven't discussed anything yet.'

'I only came at all to find out if you'd suffered a change of heart. Now I know that you haven't there's nothing more to be said. I can make my arrangements from here on.'

'Arrangements? *What* arrangements?'

'Marriage changes the life course of a bachelor,' he explained dryly. 'I'll have to cancel a lot of things. For the next week, until your contract ends, you'll probably see nothing of me. I've a lot to do.'

The girl shrugged. 'All right, but do you *have* to be so infernally judicial about it?'

He kissed her painted mouth, looking for a moment deep into those faintly mocking blue eyes. Then he went off down the corridor to the lift.

'The fool!' he whispered, as he left the lift and strode out into the night to his car. 'The damned, over-painted little fool! If only she realised what she's *done* . . . '

6

On reaching home he went straight to his study, locked the door, slipped on his rubber gloves, and then on plain paper wrote three letters, each in the cramped backhanded style of Rixton Williams. The first one said —

Saturday.

Dear Lady,

I sent you flowers to show admiration for your lovely acting. Now I want you to know that I want to meet you sometime. I'll be waiting outside the theatre on Monday night. I wear glasses and a fawn raincoat.

Rixton Williams.

The second —

Tuesday.

Dearest Valerie,

What a wonderful time we had last

night and how fine it is when two people love each other as much as we do. There is nothing to stop us going away in secret if you want.

Rixton

And the third —

Wednesday.

Dearest Val,

We must have tea together on Friday at my home. I'm sending you this letter because of the danger of 'phone calls upsetting you. Say you'll come to my home to tea on Friday.

Rix.

He put each one in an envelope of cheap quality and addressed them back-handedly to 'Miss Valerie Hadfield, c/o The Paragon Theatre, Central Street, W.C.', and in the left top corner he wrote 'Strictly Confidential.'

For his own edification he put 1, 2 and 3 on each one in pencil, and after that the intended day of posting. Next, he went to the safe and took out the letter of Valerie's he had placed in a separate envelope. He read it again to make sure, put it with the three letters he had written — after stamping the envelopes — and then transferred all of them to his wallet.

Snapping off his gloves he put them back in the desk drawer.

'Chauffeur,' he muttered. 'Don't quite like him knowing so much — but since the tie-up between Williams and me will never be traced I can't see that it matters. I paid him well and I think he'll keep quiet. Anyway, nothing to prove murder; just a disappearing act, and it will even look voluntary . . . What else? Engagement ring and cigarette box — and letters! Must find all those and remove them.'

Switching off the light he left the study and went to bed.

* * *

After breakfast Richard called the Baxters to him as he put on his coat in the hall, his travelling case standing beside him.

'I'll be marrying soon,' he told them,

'and my arrangements are likely to keep me out of town, on and off, for about a week. I shan't be home tonight, but I may return for a few hours tomorrow. Anyway, don't either of you prepare anything for me and just expect me when I arrive. Right?'

'Of course, Mr. Richard, sir,' old Baxter agreed.

Richard picked up his bag and departed. In fifteen minutes he was putting the bag in the Jaguar, and from here on began his routine performance of change of identity. Towards early afternoon he reached his newly-acquired house near Twickenham and brought the old car to a halt. The furniture men were there with the pantechnicon.

Richard surveyed the men going in and out; then he got out of the car, strolled further down the road to a pillar-box and sorted the letters from his wallet. With the soft rubber head of his pencil he removed the guiding marks and posted letter number one — Saturday — and then he strolled back to watch the men at work.

'Everything all right?' he asked the foreman.

'Be finished in an hour, sir,' the man answered.

Richard glanced up as he saw Timothy Potter strolling up and down his front garden in his alpaca jacket. He limped towards him.

'So you decided to take it, eh, Mr. Williams?'

'Yes,' Richard acknowledged. 'But now I have taken it I don't know whether my fiancée will like it. She'll be coming to see it next Friday.'

'She should like it,' Potter reflected. 'Quiet about here. Most people mind their own business.'

In every house, as far as Richard could see, there were faces dodging behind curtains. Everything he was doing was being noted — which was exactly the way he wanted it . . .

For perhaps twenty minutes he went on talking to Potter, then he turned away again to see how the removal was progressing. In another half-hour the job was finished and Richard retired inside the place to find it furnished, the hangings at the windows, everything ready — even to the electric current having been switched on. It appeared that the meter-man had called during the morning and had been admitted by the removers.

'So it begins,' Richard murmured, pulling off his cap and sitting down. 'The creation of somebody who is already familiar in the immediate neighbourhood, and who has yet to become known in various other directions as well . . . All the time I am here I must wear gloves, waking or sleeping. Come to think of it, I'll sleep down here and not upset the upstairs at all, except for washing. I can rub away any prints I might leave behind.'

And from this moment onwards he began the strangest adventure of his life. After a meal from some of the tinned provisions he had brought wrapped up in the pyjamas in his suitcase, he went out, cap pulled down and leg limping, and made his way to the little block of stores a half-mile further down the road.

A grocers-cum-post office, a news-agents, the usual little huddle of essential tradesfolk were all there. Richard talked with the shopkeepers at length and gave time for every detail about himself to be absorbed; then he returned to his hideout, drew the curtains, and satisfied himself that the light showed through them in a glow. Everybody knew the place was occupied.

He slept at the house — putting the light on upstairs for a brief while towards half-past ten — in an armchair in the front room. During the following morning he put himself on view in the unkempt front garden, inspecting the weed-strewn chaos. He had lunch in the house, then towards mid-afternoon slipped his packed suitcase in the car and drove off down the road on the start of the return trip which brought him to his Belsize Park home in the Jaguar.

The Baxters merely greeted him and left it at that. He spent half an hour in his study, another half in the laboratory — for no other reason than to seem occupied in business — then at four-thirty he went outside with the blueprints of the garage and considered the layout of the site for it. For two hours, until dusk, he pottered round with the concrete mixer, getting the floor of the garage laid so it could set in the night. That it was Sunday and that the concrete mixer made plenty of noise did not even seem to occur to him . . .

So, alternating his behaviour between Twickenham and his own home he passed the days between building the garage and living a reserved life as Mr. Rixton Williams of Twickenham. He found it nerve-racking work, but not once did anything unexpected cross his path. By the following Wednesday, after he had posted the last of the letters to Valerie from Twickenham, he felt he could return safely to Belsize Park with the illusion of Mr. Williams complete in the minds of his inquisitive Twickenham neighbours.

During this time the garage had grown from a concrete floor to having its walls half up. All day Thursday he added but little to it, preparing instead considerable amounts of concrete and then, for reasons best known to himself, he stopped working on the garage and retired to the laboratory.

On the Friday morning at breakfast Mrs. Baxter found Richard entirely genial and smiling at her.

'Going away today Mr. Richard?' She asked him, setting the meal down before him.

'Only until five o'clock,' he answered. 'Then I shall be working on a very important laboratory job at home here until after midnight. High explosive test. But you needn't worry; I shan't blow you up!'

Mrs. Baxter smiled. 'I think you're working too hard lately, Mr. Richard. What with your business trips, your laboratory work and trying to build that garage too . . . '

'Yes, I've done as much as I can do so that the garage will be ready for the car when I bring the wife here; but now I've found out I've got to make the floor two inches higher! That's the worst of these amateur builders,' he added, grinning. 'Anyway, I'll finish it in readiness for when my intended wife comes here even

would do. He had calculated on that.

After she left he he ate the sandwiches and drank the tea. Was there any point he had missed? No — apparently not. He looked in his wallet to be sure he had that letter of Valerie's to him. Very essential. No, there was nothing wrong at all so far, unless it was that infernal chauffeur of Valerie's. It was a nuisance him knowing so much . . . Perhaps later, if he showed signs of talking . . . At first, though, Valerie's disappearance wouldn't look like murder. There would be time to turn round.

At half-past-five he finished the sandwiches and then went across the hall to the annex. Darkness was just commencing to pale the daylight.

He switched on the laboratory lights and went to the big storage cupboard, emptied it completely of its contents and then locked it up again.

Twenty minutes later he went out into the gloom of the drive and looked at the lighted ground glass windows. That old Baxter himself would see them at about eight o'clock was tolerably certain for at that time every evening he went past the laboratory to the woodhouse and coal shed to get in his fuel supply for the following morning. And at eight o'clock, all being well, Richard planned to be in Twickenham.

He turned aside and inspected the cloying, soggy mass in the concrete mixer amidst the jumble beside the partially erected garage. Then he looked in the sacks containing the lime, sand, and other ingredients intended for the plaster of the ceiling when he had progressed that far. Satisfied, he went back into the laboratory, took an overcoat from a peg on the wall, made sure once again that the door to the house and all windows were securely fastened, then he left the laboratory by the drive door, closed it carefully.

The plan was reaching its climax.

7

He went silently down the drive, passing the side of the house where lay the domestic regions, blinds drawn down over the big kitchen window. The Baxters were unaware that he was leaving the house.

Beyond the gateway the street was deserted and faintly misty. He crossed to the opposite side, dodged down side streets, and so came at length to a bus stop. From here he went into the city. By the time he had claimed his old car from the garage, parked it in a quiet alley while he changed into his Williams outfit in Charing Cross Station, and had returned to the car again it was six-thirty. Perfect timing so far.

He drove to the second alley near the Paragon Theatre, which he had singled out in the afternoon. Here he spent ten minutes with a duster, rubbing the smooth parts of the old saloon inside and out. This done he returned the duster to the cubby-hole, donned his blue wool gloves, and then walked to the corner of the next alley which contained the theatre's stage-door. Pressing himself in the shadows he stood watching.

There was a light shining over the stage door. Now and again as he waited Richard saw figures appear and go in at the stage doorway. He glanced at his watch: six-forty.

The sleek bonnet of her Daimler had just appeared at the opposite end of the entry. In desperate anxiety he glanced about him. The entry was quite empty. He stole forward, keeping close to the wall. He heard the car door slam and Valerie's elegant figure in a fur coat, her blonde hair streaming, a big handbag under her arm, passed beneath the single lamp at the end of the alleyway. The car, as he had hoped, moved on.

He fled past the stage doorway and from the lightning glance he gave saw there was nothing to fear. The stone-walled vista was deserted except for the doorman browsing over a newspaper in his little office with its glass sides.

'Just a minute, Miss Hadfield!' Richard caught her arm and swung her round as she was about to pass him.

'What the — ?' she demanded blankly; then before she could say a thing further Richard's hand clamped tightly across her mouth. He impelled her forward through the gloom, his strong hands keeping an iron hold over her. They went past the stage-doorway, round the corner, and then the girl found herself being shoved violently into the saloon's front seat.

'What do you think you're doing?' she shrieked. 'Who are you? What are — ?'

'I'm your admirer, Miss Hadfield — Rixton Williams. You got my notes, didn't you — ?'

'You impudent swine!' the girl spat at him, clutching her handbag. 'Let me out of — '

'Shut up!' he snapped, as she tried to push her way out of the car again. 'Be quiet or I'll use chloroform. Just shut up a minute!'

She stared at him bewilderedly, and rather than take the risk of her slipping out while he went round to the driving seat he climbed in over her and slid into position under the steering wheel. Then he started the car up and swung out of the alleyway into a long, dark street.

'What are you doing?' Valerie shouted. 'Where are we *going*? Don't you realise that I've got to be on the stage in — '

'You're coming with me, on a little trip!'

'This is abduction!' She pounded his shoulder with her fists.

'Not exactly,' Richard said, relapsing into his normal voice. 'Since you want me as a husband I thought I'd do a bit of old-fashioned stuff!'

She stared at him fixedly. 'Ricky!'

'We're going to elope,' he said calmly. 'Think of the publicity we'll get — or you will, anyway. Picture the headlines — 'Musical comedy actress deserts show to marry man of her dreams!' You want it known from one end of the country to the other that you're marrying me, and by God you shall!'

'But my *contract* . . . '

'To hell with your contract! It expires

tomorrow night in any case. If you are sued for it, we can pay it easily enough. You've another contract in the bag, anyway. As for tonight, the understudy can go on for you. She looks enough like you to be your twin.'

Valerie stared at him as he began to thread carefully through the London traffic. 'What on earth are you doing in this awful get up? And in this ancient car?'

'I'll explain it to you later. Believe me, I've thought of a wonderful publicity stunt for us both. You will hug me for it . . . Didn't think I could turn into a gallant, did you?'

'I've always known you to be crazy in some things, but this caps them all.' Valerie was calming a little. 'So *you* are Mr. Rixton Williams! What's the idea of it? How does it fit in?'

'All part of the surprise,' he said, grinning. 'You got my love letters? Didn't throw 'em away?'

'Well, no,' she answered, hesitating. 'Like the visiting card, I kept them in case I needed to convince you that somebody else was interested in me. And you've had the laugh of me all the time . . . '

'All in the game,' he said again.

'*What* game?' she implored. 'Where are we going now?'

'Twickenham.'

'Twickenham! Now I *know* you're crazy!'

He drove on for a while in silence, then once he drew out of the area of speed limit he stepped up his speed. Valerie sat beside him, lost in thought, staring at the road with the glare of headlights upon it.

'There's an awful lot about this which I don't understand,' she said.

'Just trust me until we get to the house I've bought in Twickenham.'

'You bought a house?'

'Yes. Wait until we get there, and if we should meet anybody and I start talking in a hard northern voice don't be surprised. It has been essential to keep my identity a secret for your sake, but the elopement is all planned out. That's what you want, isn't it? A gigantic publicity build-up?'

'Yes, of course. I want everybody to

know that I am marrying Richard Harvey — but this Rixton Williams business seems queer in some way . . . I've been suspicious about it ever since I got the first letter. Yes, I remember now, it had the Twickenham postmark,' Valerie added with a vaguely startled glance.

Richard's forced grin somewhat reassured her. She subsided into silence, evidently deciding to wait and see what happened. She had not got to guess his real purpose until they were in the house, then . . .

Richard sped along the dark country roads, now thoroughly familiar to him. He passed the lane, down at the end of which lay his Jaguar, and drove on swiftly, pulling up noisily outside his hideout.

Valerie climbed out into the night. 'Now what?'

He alighted from the other side and waved a hand to the dark detached house standing in the gloom.

'That's it,' he said briefly. 'Our little hide-away for when we come back from our honeymoon and elopement — '

'*This?* Not if I know it! I don't want to

be buried alive!' Valerie declared. 'You've done all this to humiliate me, haven't you?'

'Honestly, Val, no!' he insisted, gripping her arm. 'Come along in anyway and see for yourself.'

She submitted to being escorted up the front pathway. He opened the door and switched on the hall globe. Valerie followed him into the now lighted drawing room with its sparse new furnishings. Richard hurried over to the curtains and drew them, then switched on the electric fire.

He turned to find the girl looking at him peculiarly in his raincoat and cap. She moved uneasily, put her handbag on the table. She noticed that his face was peculiarly strained and deadly pale . . .

He took off his woollen gloves, put them down near her handbag, and then came over to her.

'Your manners are improving,' she commented cynically. 'Is that beastly cap glued to your head, or what?'

'No — nothing like that.' His voice had cold patience in it. 'You see, my hair is pretty distinctive.'

'But whom is there to see? We're alone, aren't we?'

'At the moment,' Richard agreed. 'But I have inquisitive neighbours.'

Valerie turned away from him impatiently and appraised the small room.

'Hang it all, Ricky, you don't think this will ever suit *me*, do you?' she demanded.

'It might for the moment,' he answered.

Baffled, she gave up trying to argue. Instead she turned aside and pretended an interest in the square, modernistic clock on the mantelshelf.

'I'll get some drinks,' Richard said, and turned to the door. 'Take a seat and I'll explain everything while we have them. They are in one of the outhouses somewhere. I haven't got the place straight yet . . . '

Frowning, Valerie went to one of the easy chairs and settled in it, crossing her shapely legs. Richard smiled at her, glanced at the clock and saw it was ten minutes to eight.

Leaving the house he hurried next door but one to Timothy Potter's and hammered on the front door. Potter himself who opened it, in his usual alpaca jacket.

'Oh, hello Mr. Williams!' he greeted. 'Something I can do for you?'

'I'd like you to come and meet my wife-to-be. You've been so decent to me since I got here, I feel you should. She's just got here. Come and have a drink with us.'

'Well, I . . . All right,' Potter agreed. Then he called back into the house: 'Just going to give Mr. Williams a hand, Mother. Be back soon.'

Together they walked the short distance past the next house and so entered the hall. Richard hurried through into the kitchen to sweep up a tray containing three glasses and a bottle of champagne, which he had bought in London and arranged specially for the occasion — then he motioned Potter into the front room.

Valerie, still seated, gazed at the newcomer in silent astonishment.

'This is Mr. Potter from the next house but one, dear,' Richard said, setting down the tray. 'He's been so kind to me I thought you ought to meet him, and we can all have a drink together.'

Valerie listened to the change of voice in troubled wonder and then looked at Potter's round and genial form, his pink face, and eyes like a child awakened in the middle of the night.

'How are you,' she acknowledged briefly.

'Glad to know you,' Potter said. 'You and Mr. Williams here will make a grand couple. He's told me about you, how you plan to marry and settle here . . . Just a minute.' Potter broke off in amazement. 'I've seen *you* somewhere! You look just like — Valerie Hadfield, the musical comedy star.'

'Considering I *am* Valerie Hadfield that isn't surprising,' she answered curtly, getting to her feet. 'Didn't Ricky here tell you?'

'Ricky? Oh — Mr. Williams! No, he didn't give me your name.'

'Well, you know it now, eh?' Richard asked, grinning, holding the tray forward with three filled glasses upon it. 'Drink, Val — and you too, Mr. Potter. Just to celebrate!'

Potter nodded and drank the champagne off quickly. Valerie did the same and then fell to musing, her brows knitted. Potter coughed uncomfortably.

'Well, maybe I'd better be off,' he said, hesitating. 'I'm glad to have met you, Miss Hadfield. I hope both of you will be happy.'

'Thanks,' Valerie said laconically, her lips tight.

Richard saw Potter to the door and closed it upon him. He locked it and then came back into the drawing room to find Valerie looking at him fixedly.

'Suppose you get the surprise off your chest and let's get out of here?' she suggested in impatience.

Richard only gave a stony smile, which made her take a step back.

'I've — been linking things up,' she went on hurriedly, as though she were afraid to stop talking. 'The name of Rixton, for instance. Abbreviated, it would sound like Ricky, which is the name I have for you . . . '

'I know,' Richard answered. 'That's why I invented the name of Rixton.'

'I have the awful feeling that there's something terribly wrong about all this — that I should never have come here!' Valerie tried and failed to sound at her ease. There was plain, naked fear on her sharply chiselled face. 'Everything's so timed — so arranged — even to that man Potter ... I think you're planning something more than an elopement.'

'I am,' Richard agreed.

'Why do you stare at me like that?' she demanded, clenching her fists. 'Ricky, why *did* you bring me here? What *is* this surprise?'

'I brought you here, Val, to kill you,' he answered quietly. 'I've planned a perfect crime,' he went on. 'And incidentally a perfect answer to your damned selfish decision to cling to me! I've tried every way to be rid of you and you wouldn't let me go — so now I'm going to *make* you! I've arranged it so beautifully that nobody will ever know I did it or what has become of you. Potter is a witness to the fact that you and I were here at eight o'clock tonight. At home Baxter will be a witness to the fact that I am in my laboratory making experiments!'

'You're mad . . . ' Valerie's blue eyes dilated.

'No — subtle,' he corrected. 'Fortunately nobody in the city knows you and I are even acquainted — thanks to your love of isolation. Only that chauffeur, and maybe he'll keep quiet.'

'Ricky, you fool!' Val screamed suddenly, and her blind panic exploded. She hurled herself at him, fought to thrust him on one side and reach the door, but his powerful hands dragged her back, tore the fur coat from her shoulders and then flung her across the room on to the divan. She lay half across it, her costly gown shimmering.

'Ricky! In God's name . . . Ricky! *Don't!* No . . . NO . . . '

The words ceased tumbling from Valerie's lips as Richard's strong, knotty fingers clenched deep in her throat. Merciless, he watched colour flow into her ashen face, a glassy brightness steal over her starting eyes. Not a sound escaped her. Her limbs threshed madly, her hands tore at his arms and tried to gouge his face. He forced her down hard, squeezing tighter and tighter, perspiration trickling from his forehead . . .

At last she relaxed and lay staring at him blankly with those fixed blue eyes. Her tumbled hair streamed out in flowing waves across the upholstery at the divan end. Her tongue had forced itself between her teeth.

He stood straight and drew his sleeve over his face. His heart slamming so violently he thought he would faint he went to the table, poured out some champagne with a shaking hand and drank it off. It was flat and tasteless, but it steadied him.

Going back to the girl he held the pulse of the limply dangling left wrist. There was no beat: life had ceased. Deliberately he closed the lids over the staring eyes, closing the gaping mouth. The suffused colour of suffocation was changing slightly to a vaguely purplish hue. Deliberately he raised her limp form and draped the fur coat about her shoulders; then he propped her up against the back of the divan so that she seemed to be sitting there in a trance.

Working methodically now he put his woollen gloves on again and then removed Val's own letter from his wallet, pulled it out of its plain protective envelope and left it folded up on the mantelpiece. The envelope he returned to his wallet. Next he opened her handbag and searched through it until he found the bunch of keys he had seen her use so often. He smiled at them in his gloved palm, thrust them in his hip pocket, then stuffed the bag inside his coat out of view.

He turned to the tray holding the bottle and three glasses and inspected them, then he raised each in turn in his gloved hand and polished them assiduously with his handkerchief, including the bottle. The tray itself he also rubbed over thoroughly and then carried the whole lot back into the kitchen and set the tray down on the table.

Still holding the handkerchief he polished the knobs inside and outside the kitchen and drawing room doors, then moved over and wiped the woodwork of the divan carefully. As far as he knew he hadn't touched it, but it was better to be sure. This done he heaved the girl's body on his right shoulder, switched off the light, then walked under her weight to the front door. In the dark he rubbed the inside of the doorknob and bolt, then opened the door carefully, closing it by drawing the door to with his handkerchief tugging the knob. A final rub over the knob and then he began to move down the path with his burden.

To his alarm a tubby figure was just approaching along the pavement. Instantly he lowered Valerie from him, put an arm round her waist and leaned her head on his shoulder. Thuswise he dragged her along with him as he advanced down the path.

'Well, well, what's this?' Timothy Potter exclaimed blankly, pausing in the gloom. 'What happened to — *her*, Mr. Williams?'

Richard forced a laugh. 'That champagne,' he explained, and thanked God he had had prevision enough to supply champagne as an excuse for anybody seeing him removing the body. 'She had a couple more drinks and they went right to her head. She's dead out . . . '

Potter stared at her, her hair faintly gleaming.

'Can't hold her liquor like a gentleman, eh? Well, I'd better go back home then. I was bringing along a bottle of port to drink your health from *my* point of view. Never mind though . . . '

'Decent of you,' Richard said. 'But you see how it is. I'll run her into the country air; it'll help her a bit. Y'know' — he dropped his voice to a whisper — 'we're eloping, but don't you go telling everybody!'

'As if I would!' Potter exclaimed. 'All right, I'll go. Unless I can help you?'

'Not a bit,' Richard assured him, and he heaved the slipping body more tightly to him and again shuffled down the path.

Potter did not go, however. He helped to lift the girl into the back seat of the car where Richard propped her up in the corner.

'My word, she *is* out!' Potter declared. 'Sure she isn't ill?'

'Not she,' Richard answered, going round to the driving seat. 'I should have remembered she can't stand much drink . . . '

Potter stood in the starlight and Richard muttered things under his breath. Then he got the car going and drove off down the road with ever-growing swiftness, the dead girl swinging over on her side as at last he turned down the lane at the bottom of which his Jaguar should still be hidden.

It was. The moment he saw it in the headlights of the saloon he put the lamps out and drew the car to a standstill. Going over to the Jaguar he unlocked it, then returned and dragged the body into his arms, carried it to the Jaguar, deposited it on the floor at the back and threw the motor rug over it. This done he went back to the saloon, took out the brown paper parcel of clothes and dropped them beside Valerie, then he came back yet again, climbed into the old car and started up the engine.

Jerkily he drove into the uncultivated field bordering the lane, changed into second gear and then began to ease himself out on the running board, fixing the throttle-control so the speed was maintained. By dint of manoeuvring he closed the door, holding the steering wheel through the open window . . . Then suddenly he leapt clear and felt the underside of his forearm scrape viciously on the worn metal of the frame. Bumping and bounding, the old-fashioned car went chugging on into the night.

He looked about him in the dim light. He had jumped away just in time, still on the coarse grass round the edge of the field. There would be no footprints. Returning to the lane he peered at his injury just above the underside of his wrist between shirt cuff and glove top. Faintly visible were smears of blood. Irritably he bound up the wound with his handkerchief and then returned to the Jaguar. Clambering into it he backed up to the end of the lane, stopped again, and then returned on foot down the lane until he came to the spot where the Jaguar had been standing.

Masking the full glare of the torch he was carrying he searched for and found two lots of prints — one from the Jaguar's tyres and the other from the saloon's. With his foot, as he walked backwards, he scraped out the Jaguar prints, and particularly the deep indentations where it had been standing in the wood. His own footprints he also eliminated.

So he came back to the roadway, but before he climbed into the Jaguar's driving seat he put the handbag on top of the girl and then slipped his own trousers, overcoat, and scarf over the Williams outfit and took off the cap. Since he was usually hatless he now looked his normal self. Besides, in the Belsize Park neighbourhood plenty of people knew his Jaguar.

With a sigh he settled at the steering wheel and drove swiftly into the night. The clock on the dashboard said eight-thirty-five. When it had reached ten-ten, after an almost uninterrupted journey — apart from traffic signals — he had gained the road where his own home stood. He drew the car up a few yards from the driveway gate. Now came the supreme risk, unless the Baxters had gone to bed.

Glancing up and down he satisfied himself that nobody was in sight — as there rarely was in this select residential district — then he got out of the car, put the parcel of clothes and handbag firmly on top of Valerie, drew the rug well over her, then heaved her already stiffening body into his arms.

Without a sound he relatched the car door and carried the dead girl up the driveway, past that drawn kitchen blind with the light chinks down the sides — the Baxters still hadn't gone to bed — and past the still lighted laboratory windows.

He opened the driveway door of the laboratory and stole silently inside. Immediately he went to the storage cupboard, unlocked it and propped the girl up inside it, closing and locking the door upon her.

He picked up the parcel of clothes that lay in the fallen rug along with the handbag and for the moment pushed them away under a bench. Then he glanced down at his cut arm. It was only a flesh wound and the blood was drying, but it looked and felt messy. Going over to the antiseptic he poured some on a puff of cotton wool, wiped the wound clean and threw the small bloodstained swab into the bin under the bench.

He frowned as he put an adhesive self-sealing plaster over the cut. Have to be very careful nobody saw it: it was no part of his plan . . . He had the plaster to his liking finally and continued with his moves in the prearranged order. Pulling off scarf, overcoat, and suit coat, he donned his laboratory smock, which covered him high up in the throat, and his Williams' collar and tie.

With a critical glance about him he went to the door leading into the house, unlocked it, and stepped into the hall. Since the Baxters *were* still up he might as well make his alibi more solid than ever.

'Oh, Mrs. Baxter!' he called, and after a moment she came out of the kitchen.

'Yes, Mr. Richard? Something you want?'

'You might fix me a sandwich, please,' he said. 'I'm getting hungry.'

'I'm sure you must be,' Mrs. Baxter sympathised. 'My hubby was saying how you've been hard at it all evening. When he went out to get the coal and wood in . . . The lighted windows, you know.'

'Oh, yes indeed!' Richard assented, smiling and inwardly congratulating himself. Then: 'I'll wait here for the sandwich. Too many fumes in the lab for you to risk going in.'

He hung about the hall for a moment or two until the sandwich was forthcoming; then, satisfied that he had conveyed the impression of never having left the house during the evening, he returned into the laboratory and locked the house door again securely.

He ate the sandwich, looking at the storage cupboard broodingly as he did so. Then he began to change his clothes, ridding himself entirely of the Williams outfit, transferring the articles in the pockets — particularly Valerie's bunch of keys and his own wallet — to his own suit. The entire set of old clothes he stuffed away in a cupboard for the time being and then looked at his watch. It was ten-twenty-five and there was much yet to be done.

Slipping a pair of rubber gloves in his overcoat pocket, he went outside and closed the driveway door after him, locking it. Without being seen he reached his Jaguar and drove off silently into the night.

8

At quarter to eleven Richard drew up his Jaguar a few yards from Valerie Hadfield's apartment building. One or two people were passing up and down the street, mere passers-by and of no significance. He drew the rubber gloves from his pocket, slipped them on, got out of the car, locked it, then walked briskly along the pavement until he came to the steps of the building.

The usual entrance-hall light was shining through the glass of the doors. He felt for the keys he had taken from Valerie's handbag, clenched them in his palm, then hurried up the steps quickly and across the hall. It was as deserted as usual and the lift took him up to the fourth floor.

The thick pile carpet deadened noise as he went along to Flat 7. Since the maid lived out the chances were that she was nowhere on the premises, but to make certain he knocked lightly — enough for anybody in No. 7 to hear him but not enough to attract anybody in the neighbouring flats. There was no response, and as far as he could tell no light either under the small space below the door.

He slid the key in the lock, and glided into the dark room beyond. Then he paused, took off his shoes, and put them together edgewise on the carpet by the door. They were slightly muddy; they could leave prints in the carpet pile and maybe even enough deposit for a spectrograph analysis.

In stockinged feet he went with complete sureness to the windows to make certain that the draperies were over — and they were; heavy velvet which would show no light outside. Since Valerie had left the flat for the theatre after nightfall they were just as he had expected to find them.

Turning, he took his scarf from about his neck and laid it along the bottom of the door; then he switched on the light and looked about him. There was nothing changed, no obvious signs of anybody having been in the room, though he guessed it was quite possible that the maid had been present some time during the evening — and possibly the chauffeur too.

First he went through to the bedroom, searched the dressing table, his rubber gloves still on, until he found the securely locked ornamental metal box which he guessed contained trinkets and jewellery, though whether the costly diamond ring he was looking for was inside it or not he did not know.

Selecting the right key from the bunch he had appropriated from Valerie he turned it in the lid catch. To his exasperation there were only paste jewels and odds and ends of stage adornments; no sign of the ring he wanted. He closed the box up again and returned it to the table, stood thinking with his lips compressed.

'Safe, I suppose,' he muttered.

He strode back into the drawing room and went across to the hinged landscape painting behind which, as he had seen several times, was the wall-safe. He contemplated it for a moment or two, searched for the right key by trial and error and finally had the heavy door open. In the circular well beyond there were papers and documents neatly tied up in red tape, a wad of Treasury notes amounting to some three hundred pounds — and there, at the extreme back of the safe, lay the thing he wanted . . . a small plush box. He took it out, snapped back the lid, studied the engagement ring he had given the girl, then thrust it quickly in his pocket.

He was about to close the safe when he hesitated. Letters! That was the next thing he wanted — those impassioned letters he had written to her before he had learned better sense. They might be in the locked bureau — but equally they might be here. He began to sort the documents quickly and suddenly came upon what he wanted. They were bound up separately in red tape. He leafed through them quickly. Every one of them was there. He stuffed them in his pocket and relocked the safe door, swinging the picture back into place.

'Ring . . . letters . . . ' he muttered. 'That only leaves that inscribed cigarette box.'

He went across to the table to look for it; then he stopped, frowning. It was not there! A faint stirring of panic went through him. This was not the first snag that had revealed itself in the unfolding of his plan. Suddenly haggard, he roved about the room, looking on the sideboard, on top of the bureau, even on the floor where he remembered he had thrown the box when the lid snapped off. There was no sign of it — nor in the bedroom, or bathroom.

He opened drawers and cupboards and searched them from top to bottom. For fifteen minutes, with ever mounting anxiety, he pried into every place he could think of and the box was not to be found. Slowly he came back into the drawing room, perspiring freely. A flaw. A terrible flaw with which he hadn't reckoned. What the devil *had* Valerie done with it? He thought for a wild moment of finding the maid's address and asking her; then he knew he couldn't do that.

‘Think it out,’ he told himself, forcing calmness down on his mind.

He switched off the light, put the scarf back round his throat and got into his shoes again. He left the flat silently and closed the door behind him.

As he turned to move towards the lift the grille slammed back. His heart jumped as it had done when he had failed to find the cigarette box. He glanced up and down. In the long corridor there was no chance of concealment — so he took the only other alternative and stood waiting, fighting to appear calm. His hands, with the rubber gloves still on them, he plunged abruptly into his overcoat pockets.

To his inward horror it was the plum-liveried figure of Peter, the chauffeur, who stepped out into the corridor. He took a few urgent steps, the light gleaming on his polished leggings and boots, then as he saw Richard he slowed a little and took off his peaked cap.

‘Hello, Mr. Harvey!’

Richard nodded but he did not speak. The man hesitated, put his cap back on again and gestured to the door of No. 7.

'Miss Hadfield come back yet?' he asked.

'Apparently not.' Richard kept his voice steady. 'I came along to have a few words with her but she doesn't seem to be in; so I decided to hang about and wait. I think I must have missed her at the theatre. I was delayed and — '

'But you don't understand!' Peter interrupted. 'She's disappeared! I've just come now to see if by some chance she's got back — from wherever she's been,' he finished ambiguously.

Richard frowned most convincingly. 'Disappeared? What the devil do you mean?'

'It sounds so idiotic — and yet it happened! I drove her to the theatre as usual — to the alley where the stage door is . . . You know it, sir?'

'Of course I know it,' Richard agreed.

'Well, she set off for the stage door — only a few yards' distance — but she never got there! She hasn't been seen since. She's vanished utterly, just as though into thin air.'

‘But — it isn’t *possible!*’ Richard declared blankly.

‘It happened, sir, and that’s all I know. I didn’t find out about it until ten-thirty when I went as usual to pick her up after the show. I found the theatre staff in a ferment — stage manager raving, producer having grey hairs, audience grumbling about the understudy — whom they’d guessed *was* an understudy despite her uncanny resemblance to Miss Hadfield . . . That is, the latecomers. The others were told about it before the show opened, of course. Well, there it is — or was. Miss Hadfield gone. Completely!’

‘Naturally the police have been told?’ Richard demanded.

‘I don’t think so, sir. Not until tomorrow if she hasn’t returned by then — ’

‘But why not?’ Richard cried. ‘Dammit, something serious may have happened to her!’

‘The stage manager thought of that, then decided that was hardly likely since I’d actually seen her set off for the stage-door. Now he thinks she's gone off on some jaunt of her own. She's an erratic woman, Mr. Harvey, if I may say so — full of odd little notions. Likes to keep to herself a lot and gets sudden impulses . . . Anyway, the police will be told tomorrow if she hasn't come back. The chances are that she'll return and laugh right in everybody's face — maybe even married or something. That would be just about like her.'

'Married?' Richard repeated slowly. 'To whom?'

'A Mr. Williams, who has been writing to her a lot lately.'

'Oh?'

'It was Ellen, the maid, who told the stage-manager about it. Seems Miss Hadfield has been having letters from an admirer and the latest letter asked her to have tea or something with him today, so they must have been pretty intimate.'

'She never told me about that,' Richard said, musing. 'And I don't really see why she confided the fact to her maid.'

'As I understand it, sir, Miss Hadfield is quite proud of her conquest with this unknown Mr. Williams. Anyway, it's pretty clear that she may be able to explain the thing herself. I've had the evening off, of course, after leaving her at the theatre — but ever since I returned to pick her up I've been driving to all the spots in town she frequents, but I've drawn blanks. Then I came back here to see if she'd returned. I called at Ellen's room on the way here but she'd had no news either . . . If this goes on, the police will *have* to be told, naturally.'

'I should damned well think so!' Richard declared. 'If nobody else does it, I shall! I have the uneasy feeling this may be more serious than it looks . . . Miss Hadfield wasn't very popular, was she?'

'*Wasn't*, sir?'

Richard hesitated. '*Isn't*, then! Show's how this thing's getting on my nerves. I'm already thinking of her in the past tense.'

The chauffeur reflected briefly, his keen blue eyes studying Richard's face.

'No, sir, she's not too popular,' he admitted finally. 'In private life, that is. You think maybe some enemy of hers — '

'It's possible. In her position as an

actress an enemy would know just where to find her . . .'

There was silence for a moment or two. The corridor was still deserted except for the two men. Richard pondered the two mistakes he had made — one, the fact that this damned chauffeur was here at all; and the other the slip in grammar, which had momentarily aroused the man's suspicions. He was no fool, and Richard realised it.

'This may look awkward for me before long, I suppose.' Richard took up the thread again, frowning. 'I'm Miss Hadfield's closest acquaintance and if anything *has* happened to her — which I hope to God it hasn't — the first person to draw a load of grief on top of himself will be me!'

Peter nodded; then he shrugged. 'Naturally you'll be questioned if the police are called, Mr. Harvey — same as I shall. Same as all of us will be.'

'But don't you realise the adverse effect it will have on my career and position to be involved in such a business! I've got to keep my name out of it, Peter. You are the only one who knows of my association with Miss Hadfield.'

The chauffeur waited, keen blue eyes watching.

'I'll pay you well to keep quiet,' Richard added. 'I've got to have your co-operation.'

Peter reflected. 'Well, sir, without meaning to sound disrespectful, I have a career too in a manner of speaking. In fact since I am a chauffeur, police are more keen on me than they are on people in a less exacting job. If I were found to have been telling lies I'd probably lose all chance of ever being a chauffeur again . . . '

'To keep me out of this, should it become necessary, I'll give you enough money to make up for years of employment at a good salary,' Richard said tersely. 'It's worth it to me.'

Peter still held back, a quizzical expression on his strong-jawed face.

'I'd rather not, Mr. Harvey. Thanks all the same.'

Richard fumed inwardly, wishing he could decide how much the man had guessed — whether the offer had been so lavish it had appeared suspicious for that very reason. He was gripped now by the inner conviction that he had already said too much.

'I still think we can perhaps hammer out some sort of compromise,' he said finally. 'And look here, this is no place to talk. Where do you live? Rooms?'

'I live with my widowed mother, sir, about a mile from here. We happen to have a garage on the premises, which just suits Miss Hadfield since there isn't one for this apartment building. She rents it from us, of course.'

Garage? Private house? Dim, unexpected thoughts stirred in Richard's desperate mind. This was no part of his plan: it was an addition and it had to be dealt with right away before this blue-eyed man with the agile mind put two and two together.

'Suppose I go home with you and we'll have a chat?' Richard suggested. 'We may be able to work out something suitable for both of us . . . '

'Okay,' Peter agreed. 'But I can't see it'll make much difference. The car's at the front, sir . . . '

Richard kept beside him as they went down in the lift and then outside. The passers-by had thinned considerably with the lateness of the hour.

'Your mother won't object to you bringing home a visitor at this hour, I hope?' Richard asked, as Peter opened the front door of the Daimler for him to sit next to the steering wheel.

'She'll be in bed by now, Mr. Harvey.'

In bed! Richard reflected that perhaps things were going to work out in the way he wanted them, after all.

To get into the car he had to use his hands, but in the dim street lighting the tight-fitting rubber gloves were indistinguishable from natural skin. Peter slammed the door and hurried round to the driving seat. In a few seconds he had the powerful car gliding away from the kerb.

'Only a short distance,' he said. 'How about you, sir? Have you got your car?'

'Just down the road,' Richard replied. 'I'll walk back.'

Peter nodded and drove along for a few

minutes, then he swung right down a side road. The glimmer of lights revealed to Richard a sudden change in the style of property. The residential goliaths of the main road had given place to smaller houses, mostly semi-detached and of the middle-class residential variety. Halfway down the road, between two sets of street lamps, Peter swung the car's big bonnet leftwards and swept gracefully through an open gateway. The headlights blazed upon the green doors of a brick garage. Peter halted the car, climbed out, opened the garage doors, then returned and drove the car into it. It just fitted in the space.

'One advantage of not living far away from your work, Mr. Harvey,' Peter said, grinning, and switched off the ignition and headlights, leaving only side and rear on.

Richard climbed out, saw an ordinary door leading to the yard and house. Then he looked about him quickly. The first thing he noticed which came anywhere near what he wanted was a tool-rack on the whitewashed wall, and in it, among other things, were a pair of heavy tyre-levers; he took one of them in his gloved right hand and strolled round the back of the car.

Peter had got out now and was busy throwing a rug over the car's bonnet, stooping towards it. Silently Richard moved up behind him, jaw set hard, eyes measuring the man. Up went his hand — then down again. The heavy steel tyre-lever struck Peter at the base of the skull and slumped him helplessly over the car's offside wing.

Silently Richard dragged him up and then laid him down so that the back of his neck was exactly along the edge of a nearby sand bucket. On the floor he put a bulb-handled screwdriver from the tool-rack, about an inch from the man's out-thrust foot. The impression given was that he had slipped on the screwdriver and struck the base of his skull on the bucket edge.

Returning to the tool-rack Richard replaced the tyre-lever in it, then he closed and bolted the double garage doors on the inside. Getting inside the car he switched on the engine again and adjusted the throttle control until there was a mere whisper and the exhaust was puffing out in faint blue clouds at the rear.

He opened the door of the driver's seat, left the side and rear lights on, then climbed out again and closed his own side door as quietly as he could. Turning, he moved to the ordinary door in the wall leading out towards the house and let himself into the darkness of a small flagged yard. Pushing the door to behind him he heard it click into place.

Around him everything was silent. Cautiously, quivering from the strain of this second and entirely unrehearsed murder, he fled into the drive, out through the gateway, and walked swiftly along the deserted street and so to the main road. Here he slowed his pace, breathing hard.

'Had to be done!' he said to himself as he walked. 'He'd guessed — no doubt of it. But it'll look like an accident. It's *got* to!'

Reaching his own car, he stripped off his rubber gloves. Getting into the car he reversed it and drove back swiftly down the street, finally sweeping into the night-and-day garage where he normally kept the Jaguar. He manoeuvred it into its accustomed position, locked it up, then with a nod to the night mechanic on duty he departed. Shortly afterwards he was back again at his own home, entering the laboratory where the lights were still on.

He closed and locked the outer door, made sure the house door was also secure after he had satisfied himself that the Baxters had gone to bed — then he pulled off his overcoat and scarf and hung them up. For a moment he pressed finger and thumb to his eyes, his head throbbing with strain and weariness . . . But there was still a hard night's work ahead of him.

He mixed a stimulant for himself, felt better after he had drunk it, then he got into his smock. Next he recovered 'Mr. Williams'' clothes from inside the cupboard and tossed them, brown paper as well, into the sink. Over them he poured nitric acid and there left them; the tart, lung-tickling fumes setting him coughing for a moment . . .

His eyes moved to the big, cotton-stoppered Dewar flasks by the wall with their pale blue liquid contents — then he glanced at the selection of tools in the rack over by the nearby bench. Finally his eyes went to the dissolving parcel in the acid . . .

He walked across to the steel storage cupboard.

* * *

Richard went to bed at four o'clock — but couldn't sleep. His nerves were too taut, his brain too active. He was discovering gradually that he was not devoid of conscience, a calculating schemer well satisfied with his handiwork. He was instead in the same awful plight as murderers before him . . . He realised what he had done, and however perfect the plan had been so far, he was secretly appalled by the immutable fact that there was no way back, no way of untying the knot.

He turned over again, enduring the

anguish of killers gone before — the pitiless awareness that life has been destroyed. He sat up, sweating, and prayed for the dawn.

It came at last and somewhat soothed his aching nerves. Sore-eyed, weary, he clambered out of bed. Shuffling in his slippers to the dressing-table mirror he surveyed himself. His face was ashen and unshaved, eyes bloodshot both from insomnia and the chemical fumes in the laboratory. To appear downstairs like this would raise questions.

He went along to the old-fashioned bathroom, took longer than usual shaving and washing, using plenty of cold water afterwards to bring a little colour into his cheeks. Then he dressed in a pin-stripe suit, brushed his hair carefully, and feeling a trifle better in mind and body went downstairs to breakfast, pressing the bell for Mrs. Baxter as he entered the dining room.

He went over to the table and picked up the folded morning paper from the silver clip by his serviette. He half expected to see the mystery of Valerie

Hadfield spread in glaring headlines, but instead the latest political wrangle took pride of place. Then he noticed a column on the right topped with the words — MUSICAL COMEDY STAR VANISHES!

''Morning, Mr. Richard, and how are you this morning?'

He forced a smile at Mrs. Baxter as she came hurrying in with her loaded tray. It wafted an aroma of bacon and coffee.

'Oh, good enough,' he answered quietly.

'But you're looking a bit tired,' she said in concern. 'Only to be expected when you worked all night . . . Or did you? I know you were at it when Mr. Baxter and I went to bed.' She set the plate down in front of him and started pouring out the coffee.

'It was four o'clock when I retired. But I finished my experiment and now I'm free to do as I like. I can divide my attention equally between my fiancée and finishing that confounded garage.'

'You and your garage, Mr. Richard!' Mrs. Baxter laughed. 'Why don't you let the contractors do it?'

He smiled. 'I started the job, as I did the lab, and I'll finish it.'

'And you've cut yourself too!' she exclaimed, as his cuff drew back to reveal the plaster above the inside of his wrist as he reached for the toast.

'It's nothing — just a scratch from the laboratory.'

She picked up the empty tray and bustled out. Richard propped the newspaper up before him and read:

> Miss Valerie Hadfield, the famous musical comedy star, who has been appearing for the last two years in 'Jingle Bells' at the Paragon Theatre, disappeared in mysterious circumstances last night. She is known to have left her car to enter the stage door of the theatre, but has not been seen since. The probability is that she went of her own volition and further details are awaited.

'I'll bet they are,' Richard muttered, and folded the paper up again; and in so doing he exposed the stop-press column.

> Peter Cranston, chauffeur to Valerie Hadfield (see page 1), was found dead in the garage adjoining his home this morning. Carbon monoxide poisoning following a fall is suspected.

Richard put the paper down and turned to his neglected breakfast. He felt much more comfortable now. Instead of things hanging in mid-air they were coming down to earth and fitting into place as he had expected them to do. He felt satisfied that his plan was not showing any serious deficiency yet. There was only one flaw in the whole business that he could see: that inscribed cigarette box. Again he thought of calling on Ellen and trying to find out about it discreetly, and again he decided against it. From now on the less said the better. The thing to do was to forget all about Valerie Hadfield and Peter Cranston and become the normal Richard Harvey, chemist, anxious to marry Joyce Prescott.

After breakfast he called for his Jaguar in the usual way and drove round to the Prescott home. Both the girl and her father were in.

'It's wonderful to see you again, Ricky!' Joyce kissed him as he embraced her in the hall. 'I've missed you a good deal these past days . . . '

His arm about the girl's waist they went into the study where Howard Prescott was busy at a portable typewriter.

'Hello there, Richard!' he greeted genially. He got up, came over and shook hands.

'I've cleared up all outstanding business and there's nothing to stop Joyce and me being married as soon as convenient,' Richard told him.

'You really mean you are free of the encumbrance?' Joyce asked, her dark eyes shining.

'Free as air! I had a bit of a job to disentangle myself but she finally listened to reason. Cost me a good deal, but if it had taken all my money I wouldn't have minded — just as long as I have you.'

Richard sat down as the girl motioned to a chair and she settled on the divan close to him. Dr. Prescott remained half seated on his desk.

'Poor Joyce here's been thinking you'd deserted her,' he chuckled.

'But I told you I'd be out of town for a week, dear.'

'You haven't been away *all* the time. Dad here noticed how the garage has grown when he's been coming from seeing that sick friend of his. You said you are building it yourself so surely you could have spared a few minutes to come along and see me rather than do a job like that?'

Richard was silent. Damn the sick friend!

'I thought I'd use what bit of time I'd got at home to get the garage nearer completion,' he said finally. 'I'll have it done by the time we're married. It never occurred to me that you'd notice it, sir.'

'Ordinarily I wouldn't have . . .' Howard Prescott said. 'Only I'm more than naturally interested in that garage because you are building it . . . And I still can't think *why*!'

Richard looked up sharply, trying to see if there was any hint of suspicion in those small, shrewd dark eyes.

'Labour of love,' Richard said smiling. 'Joyce likes the Jaguar and I want it on the premises. So I am building the garage myself to be sure it will be ready by the time we move in together as husband and wife. Contractors might take a long time.'

'But, Ricky, it isn't all *that* important!' Joyce protested, vague wonder on her face. 'I'd much sooner you'd spend the time with me than on that messy job.'

'Sorry,' he said. 'I'm going to finish it now I've started. I'll have to; can't leave it like that . . . Anyway, you don't want to be with me *all* the time! What about being your father's secretary?'

Prescott laughed. 'I'm thinking we'd better drop the subject. And incidentally, Richard, you're going to take away a first-class secretary! But you'll be getting a first-class wife. I know. I think I shall either have to remarry myself or else advertise for another secretary.'

A thought was banging in the back of

Richard's brain. Dr. Howard Prescott had seen that garage increase its size while he, Richard, had said he would be out of town! Didn't mean anything of course; quite a natural occurrence with nothing profound attaching — yet it would have been better if it had not have happened.

Then Joyce said: 'Are we going to lunch in town, Ricky? And maybe a show later on?'

'Why not? I simply came along to show willing and see what plans you'd made for the day . . . Get your things on and we'll nip in to the city to celebrate our first free day . . . Oh, but first let me give you this!'

Richard took a small case out of his pocket and snapped it open to reveal a costly engagement ring — not as costly as Valerie's had been certainly, but then Joyce had none of her avarice. She glanced at it as it lay in Richard's palm, then she got to her feet. Richard looked at her in surprise.

'Look here, Ricky, before you give me that I want to ask you something. Who *is* this woman who has been holding us apart? Now you're free of her it doesn't signify any more if I know, does it?'

'You're still worrying over that, eh?' Richard got to his feet, the ring in its case clenched in his palm. 'Did you ever see such a girl, Doctor?' he asked, laughing. 'Not content with having me she still wants to know who the other woman is.'

Howard Prescott said nothing. He remained looking at his daughter and Richard.

'I've the right to!' Joyce snapped. 'I think we ought to start fair and square, Ricky — with no secrets. In fact, I insist on it. Who *is* this woman? What difference can it make now if you tell me?'

'What difference can it make if I *do*?' he countered. 'The thing is over — finished with. Why dig it up again? I know why — because you are still hankering after seeing her yourself and telling her what you think of her. Just for that I shan't tell you anything — and that's because I love you, Joyce, believe me.'

'You're sure it *is* that?'

'Of course it is!' he answered briefly. 'Why not? Do you think I'm trying to hide something?'

'I don't want to think so, Ricky, but surely you realise that, as a woman, I want to know exactly how we stand — assure myself we shall never be interrupted by this — this shadow. I know so *little*, Ricky,' she pointed out. 'You said she wouldn't let you go for money, for anything at *all* apparently . . . Then you said you had a plan, and now . . . She's no longer an obstacle. Tell me what happened. I don't like mysteries!'

Richard rose, a hard glitter in his grey eyes. He thrust the ring case back in his pocket.

'The contrariness of woman!' he breathed amazedly. 'I've been to all this trouble to smooth the path for us and now you won't have me because I'm not prepared to explain every little thing! If that's the way it is, Joyce, maybe we'd better not go any further.'

'Oh, come now!' Howard Prescott protested. 'It isn't as bad as all that, surely.'

'I think it is, dad,' the girl objected. 'I want a clean breast of everything. Marriage is a serious business.'

Richard smiled wryly. 'And to think you said that if you didn't get me you'd commit suicide!'

'She said what?' Dr. Prescott asked blankly; then he laughed heartily. 'Good Lord, man, you don't think she *meant* it, surely? Oh, my poor boy! How little you know of Joyce as yet! She's always joking, wangling things, changing her moods . . . All in good fun, of course.'

'All in good fun, eh?' Richard repeated sourly; then he looked at the resolute girl. 'You actually mean you were only joking when you said that?'

'Of course I was,' she assented, surprised. 'Anyway, it takes courage to commit suicide, and I haven't got much of that . . . That's one reason why I want to be sure of our marriage. I only said it because there seemed to be no other way of bringing you up to scratch in ridding ourselves of this unknown woman. And now you have got rid of her I'm wondering if I did right in prompting you.'

Richard turned from her abruptly. From the doorway he looked back.

'I can tell you the answer to that right now, Joyce! You did *not* do right. I believed you, and deception in a woman is just one thing I can't stand. Good*bye*!'

He saw her look of blank amazement, but no more than that. Furious, white-faced, he stalked through the hall and strode out to his car.

'Ricky . . . Ricky, listen to me . . .'

Joyce's fading voice reached him frantically as he drove off — to where he didn't know, or care.

Women! He glared through the windscreen in bleak fury. He had made a master plan, taken all those deadly risks, committed two murders, all to be sure of having Joyce Prescott — only to realise now that he had misjudged her character, only to find she was decent woman enough to want to know the facts before entering into the solemnity of marriage, only to find she had never had any intention of taking her own life, anyway!

'You fool!' Richard breathed to himself. 'You Goddamned fool!'

9

Towards noon Richard found himself in London without much conscious realisation of how he came to be there — or why. His temper had cooled now into an icy resentment against all women. He felt he had been made to look a fool, that Joyce, with her deceptions, had driven him into a desperate dilemma. He would not have another thing to do with her! But deep in the back of his mind he knew his emotions towards her might yet undergo revision. He couldn't overcome the inescapable fact that he really loved her — that everything he had done had been on that account alone . . .

He parked his car in the city centre, lunched, and then strolled moodily into the Stag Club, to try and think things out. To his relief there were only two members present, strangers to him, and both of them were absorbed in newspapers and gave him nothing more than courteous nods when he strolled over to an armchair and sank into it. Lighting a cigarette and ordering a drink he sat down and brooded, staring into the fire.

Should he tell Joyce that the woman had been Valerie Hadfield and say that she had fled? Too risky, and unconvincing. Well, invent some woman who didn't exist and get round it that way? No — Joyce might quite easily try and seek the woman out, find she did not exist, and then the fat would be in the fire properly.

'Damn!' Richard swore aloud, and noticed his drink had arrived on the table while he had been preoccupied.

'Why, is it that bad, Dick?' asked a gruff, leisurely voice.

He looked up sharply to a short, immensely powerful figure, hands in jacket pockets, hollowed face grinning genially.

'Well, Chief Inspector Garth!' Richard exclaimed, forcing himself to smile back. 'We seem to have a habit of meeting here, Garth. Or are you following me?'

Mortimer Garth laughed and settled in

the armchair opposite.

'No coincidence about it, Dick,' he said. 'When I'm not nosing around after some crook I spend an hour in here most days at dinner-time — more if I can spare it. I like the quiet. Gives me a chance to think.'

'I agree with you there,' Richard said. 'Have a cigarette?'

'No — the old cheroots for me, thanks.'

Richard watched in silence as a short cheroot was selected from a leather case by the strong hands, and presently the fragrance began to drift on the warm air. Richard realised that he must tread warily from now on.

'So, there's nothing occupying your attention at present, Garth?' he asked at length.

'Nothing much,' Garth assented. 'But I almost forgot! You're looking for the perfect crime, aren't you? And some hopes you have of finding it!'

Valerie Hadfield! Valerie Hadfield! Richard wanted to pop her name out, but he didn't. Instead he wondered why Scotland Yard didn't seem to be concerned about her.

'What were you cussing about when I came in?' Garth asked presently.

'Oh . . . just a thought. Having a little girl-friend trouble.'

'Which of us isn't?' Garth asked, grinning. 'Wouldn't surprise me if girl-friend trouble wasn't the cause of that actress running away as she did . . . What was her name now? Er . . . Valerie Hadfield. Maybe you saw about her in the paper this morning?'

Richard could not be sure if he was being tricked into talking or whether this was sheer genuine conversation on Garth's part.

'Yes, I read something about it,' he admitted. 'Bit queer really, her getting out of her car and then not being seen at all.'

'Oh, I dunno . . . Women have done that many a time — and walked out on shows for a purely emotional reason. Not necessarily love: might be other psychological causes.'

'Then you don't think she has perhaps met with foul play?'

Garth shrugged and smiled. 'Why should I? Anyway, it's nothing to do with me. I understand that Divisional-Inspector Whiteside for the Kensington district has been asked to look into the business, chiefly because of the death of the woman's chauffeur. Did you see about that in the stop-press this morning?'

'Why, no . . . ' Richard feigned surprise.

'Queer thing . . . Almost suggests a tie-up. Missing woman — dead chauffeur . . . But there I go!' he broke off, grinning. 'Judging without evidence! It doesn't do.'

Richard remained silent, studying those cruel features, the scowl of concentration as unuttered thoughts went through the brain . . . Then a waiter glided over the soft carpet and stopped at Garth's side with a note on his salver.

'For you inspector. I was asked to say it is urgent. The message came over the telephone.'

'Eh?' Garth glanced up. 'Oh — thank you.'

He took the note up and read the message through. A faint grin came to his thin-lipped mouth.

'Well, well, talk of the devil!' he exclaimed. 'Or maybe it should be she-devil. A call from the indefatigable Sergeant Whittaker. Will I come at once. Somebody wishes to see me with regard to . . . Guess?'

Garth got to his feet as Richard speculated.

'Valerie Hadfield,' Garth finished. 'So maybe I'm going to get mixed up in it after all — or else I'll end up telling my visitor to relate his story to the Divisional Inspector and stop bothering me . . . Feel like coming along with me?'

'I?' Richard repeated vaguely. 'What have I got to do with it?'

'Nothing, only you're interested in crime and especially in running down us poor devils at the Yard. Maybe you'd like to see a thing or two. The man's only got a statement to make: no harm in you hearing it. Come on.'

Richard rose. The last thing he wanted to do was set foot in Scotland Yard, but to refuse might look a trifle odd.

Ten minutes later they were climbing the worn flight of stairs leading to Garth's office overlooking the Embankment.

When they entered the drab, electric-lighted interior with its broad, paper-littered desk and metal filing cabinets two people glanced up. One was Sergeant Whittaker, Garth's right hand man, and the other . . .

Richard swallowed hard. The other was Timothy Potter, his pinkish round face concerned and his bald head shining in the light.

Quietly Richard settled in a chair at the further side of the office and Garth put his hat and coat on the stand. Then he advanced with extended hand.

'Well, sir, good afternoon . . . You want to see me?'

'You're the Chief Inspector, I understand? Criminal Investigation Department?'

'That's right. What's the trouble?'

'I — I was directed to come to you when I entered the building. I'm Timothy Potter, of Twickenham. I've come about Valerie Hadfield, the actress who has disappeared . . . '

Garth smiled. 'Actually this business is being handled by Divisional Inspector

Whiteside of the Kensington District . . . However, what news have you got?'

'I know for a fact that Miss Hadfield eloped last night from Twickenham with a man called Rixton Williams, a Lancashire man who has bought a house next door but one to me.'

The sergeant made a movement. 'That part about Rixton Williams is correct, sir,' he put in. 'You'll see from the Divisional Inspector's report here' — he nodded to the papers on the desk — 'that Miss Hadfield's maid has stated that her mistress had some sort of connection with a Rixton Williams.'

'So the affairs of Miss Hadfield are coming to roost here, after all, eh?' Garth murmured, picking the report up and studying it pensively. When he had finished reading it all the easy cordiality had left his face. It was hard and keen, definitely interested. He looked back at the tubby Timothy Potter as he sat bouncing a bowler hat on his knees. 'They eloped, Mr. Potter? How do you know that?'

'He told me they were going to — Mr.

Williams did, I mean — when he was carrying the girl out.'

'*Carrying* her out?' Garth settled back in his chair in readiness for a long session. 'Do you mind explaining?'

'She was blind drunk! Williams had to haul her down the front pathway, his arm round her waist. I helped put her in the back of Williams' car.'

'You are sure of the woman's identity, Mr Potter?' Garth asked pensively.

'Definitely! You see, I went into the house, at Williams' request, and had champagne with them. I gathered it was a sort of celebration drink — '

'Was she intoxicated then?'

'No. Stone cold sober.' Potter reflected over this and then went on. 'I recognised her from photographs I'd seen, and when I said she looked like Valerie Hadfield she confirmed the fact. Then I left, but I went back later with a bottle of port to add my share of a celebration drink. It was then that I saw Williams helping the girl down the front path.'

'And what happened next?' Garth questioned.

'Williams drove away down the road and that's the last I saw of either of them . . . '

Silence. Garth sat thinking. Sergeant Whittaker straightened up from taking shorthand notes at his table in the corner. Richard looked at Timothy Potter across the desk. Timothy Potter looked back at him, a faint trace of puzzlement coming into his wide blue eyes.

'You say this Mr. Williams is a Lancashire man?' Garth asked. 'The cultured or uncultured variety?'

'Oh, just ordinary. Never seemed to take his cap off. I can't understand a woman of Miss Hadfield's obvious style eloping with him. It seemed to me — well, unnatural.'

'I think,' Garth said slowly, 'you had better give me full details of everything you know about Mr. Williams — where you met him, how he behaved, what he did — everything. Sergeant, take it down.'

'Yes, sir.' Whittaker turned the leaf of his notebook and waited.

'Carry on, Mr. Potter,' Garth invited.

Richard listened also to that chirpy,

eager voice. The fat little know-all was obviously determined to tell everything, was clearly proud of his offerings to the gods of Scotland Yard. Richard had foreseen all this — that Potter would be almost bound to speak. The only thing he had not foreseen was that chance would put him in the office to hear it all and watch Garth's reactions.

At last the story was told. Garth looked at Potter keenly.

'So Williams is about five feet nine, broad shouldered, and powerfully built, and has a limp of the left foot, eh? Well, thanks very much, Mr. Potter. You've been very helpful, and if we need you again we'll get in touch.'

Potter rose and moved towards the door. Garth got up too and accompanied him.

'Oh, my manners!' Garth sighed, catching sight of Richard. 'I'm so sorry, Dick . . . Mr. Potter, meet Mr. Harvey, research chemist, friend of Scotland Yard and the brains behind some of our analyses.'

Richard smiled and rose, shook the

chubby hand. Timothy Potter stood looking at him.

'Y'know, Mr. Harvey,' he said slowly, 'that chap Williams would be just about your build . . . And similar features, too.'

'So?' Garth looked at Richard and grinned. 'You'll do as a stand-in then, eh, Dick?'

'Can't say I like the idea,' Richard laughed.

Potter did not laugh. There was a blank look in his eyes as he went out, fumbling his bowler hat on to his head.

'Apparently,' Garth said, 'we're booked on this case, Dick . . . Care to see it through, or maybe you're too busy?'

'But you don't want me hanging around, surely?'

'Don't I though! I want you if only to drive some reason into your damned obstinate head! I haven't forgotten how you disparaged the Yard in the club the other day. You said that all the great murders had been solved by coincidence or else the conscience of the killers . . . '

'Why should this murder be any different?'

'Has anyone said it *is* murder?' Garth asked.

'Not as far as I know,' Richard answered easily. 'Only with you mentioning murders I sort of assumed — '

'And naturally,' Garth said, grinning. 'But I'm not *sure*! The whole damned thing may be a publicity stunt for all we know. Stage artistes live and die by publicity, remember. Anyway, I have a desire to make you eat your words in regard to Scotland Yard, Dick, so if you'd like to tag along, merely observing and not interfering, you're welcome . . . At least I'm going to look into it. Whiteside has plenty on his plate sorting out the problem of the dead chauffeur. Who knows? This may even turn out to be that perfect crime which you insist can occur.'

'Well, I'll tag along until I get bored,' Richard agreed, smiling. 'After being cooped up in the laboratory for weeks on end the exercise will do me good. What are you going to do first?'

'Nothing very exciting. Simply study this report.'

Garth seated himself at the desk again and Richard took the seat opposite him. For several minutes Garth brooded.

'Whiteside has been thorough,' he admitted at length, 'but he seems to be getting out of his depth. He's questioned Valerie Hadfield's maid and it seems that she — Valerie Hadfield — has had three letters from this mysterious Mr. Williams, and one message on a card in a bouquet of roses. None of the letters was dated but marked 'Saturday', 'Tuesday' and 'Wednesday' respectively. No address given, though the maid did see one of the envelopes when she herself got it before her mistress arrived in the morning at the theatre. She noted it was postmarked 'Twickenham'. The doorman at the theatre has described a man tallying with the description of Williams given us by Potter . . .'

Garth wrinkled his forehead. 'Mmm . . . don't seem to have been any other men in Valerie Hadfield's life, and she gave no hint that she intended to depart so abruptly. Her chauffeur was found dead early this morning by his mother

— apparently an accident, though Whiteside hasn't completed his inquiry yet. Anyway, chauffeur died from either a head injury or carbon monoxide poisoning. Doctor's report isn't complete yet. Be an inquest later, of course. At the moment Whiteside is trying to trace the girl and her northern-accented lover. Certainly they haven't been seen at Gretna — or anywhere else for that matter. Nor has the car they went in.'

'Sort of into thin air, eh?' Richard asked casually.

'People and cars don't go into thin air, Dick. I think we might . . . Excuse me.'

Garth turned as the telephone rang. Sergeant Whittaker picked it up.

'Yes? Chief Inspector Garth's office . . . ' He listened, then handed it to Garth. 'For you, sir. Inspector Whiteside.'

'Hello, Whiteside? Eh . . . ? Yes, of course we'll help. Yes, I judged you wanted us to by sending your report on here. Eh . . . ?'

Garth sat clenching the instrument and Richard saw the gaunt face slowly become taut. Garth ceased commenting as the Divisional Inspector talked; but at last he said:

'All right, get off right away. We'll join you at Twickenham Green.'

Twickenham Green? Richard sat waiting.

'Perhaps,' Garth said, hanging up, 'you weren't far wrong when you said 'murder', Dick. The Yard's in on this now; Whiteside has asked for it. It's no ordinary disappearing act, apparently. Realising the significance of the Twickenham postmark Whiteside has had the Twickenham police investigating. It seems that Williams and his old saloon car are both familiar to the local inhabitants near where Williams lived. Anyway, P.C. Hanthorne has found the missing car and Whiteside has just received the news. Fortunately we are saved the trouble of sending out a description of Valerie Hadfield and Williams. Whiteside has done it already. The police in all parts of the country are on the watch.'

'He'll be found all right, then,' Richard said.

'Mebbe. Anyway, I'm going to join

Whiteside at Twickenham Green and we'll look the car over. Hanthorne says the car is empty and standing at the edge of a ditch bordering on an uncultivated field. He makes some vague reference to bloodstains that will want checking on. Sergeant, contact the fingerprint boys at Ipswich and the photographers at Weston. Tell them to get to Twickenham Green as soon as they can and they'll be directed from there. And the pathology department had better send a man down to look at these bloodstains.'

'Right, sir.' Whittaker picked up the telephone.

Bloodstains? Richard sat thinking. Yet another of those things he had not reckoned with. There had been no blood about Valerie; he had made sure of that. The only explanation was that the blood had come from his own cut on the wrist when he had jumped from the car after starting it off on its final journey. Gently he drew his cuff down lower over the injured forearm, then he turned as he realised Garth had got into his hat and overcoat and Sergeant Whittaker had finished giving instructions over the telephone.

'Feel like imbibing the air of Twickenham, Dick?' Garth asked.

Richard nodded and rose from his chair. A few minutes later they were in an official car, Whittaker taking the wheel and Garth and Richard seated next to each other in the back.

'Why,' Richard asked presently, 'do you think it's murder, Garth? Just because of a few bloodstains?'

'No; because, for one thing, the girl's chauffeur has died. I'm sure the two things are definitely connected. And I'll lay evens that an experienced chauffeur wouldn't let himself get mixed up with carbon monoxide fumes. There's another thing, too. According to Potter a bottle — *one* bottle — of champagne was split between Valerie Hadfield, Williams, and Potter. I cannot conceive of a girl becoming incapably drunk on that amount, particularly as there is mentioned in the maid's statement that her mistress was — or is, if still alive — a hard drinker. Unless there was a drug in her drink, of course. More I think of it the more I incline to the possibility of murder.'

'Possible,' Richard admitted, thinking.

'On the other hand,' Garth proceeded, 'Valerie and Williams haven't been seen since, so what *did* happen? In lonely country, as it is around Twickenham, murder suggests itself — or else kidnapping. Purely a theory, Dick . . . ' Garth thumped on his chest. 'Blast my indigestion!' he added irritably. 'Come on, Whitty, get a move on, can't you? We want the best of the light for this job.'

'Yes, sir,' Whittaker said, and increased the speed to the limit of safety. In forty-five minutes flat they had reached Twickenham Green where a constable, police sergeant, and local superintendent were standing beside a car, waiting.

'Afternoon, sir.' Superintendent Chalfont of the Twickenham police saluted sharply. 'I'm Superintendent Chalfont. If you will follow my car — '

'Does the sergeant there know where the spot is, too?' Garth questioned.

'Yes, sir. We've all seen it, for that matter — '

'Have the sergeant wait here to direct Divisional Inspector Whiteside when he comes along; and you, Constable, will direct the fingerprint men and photographers, and a man from pathology. You'd better get another constable to help you. They'll be coming separately, I expect.'

The constable nodded, saluted, then hurried back across the road to the police station. Garth sat back and Whittaker began to follow the car ahead. Richard gazed about him in fascinated interest. It was exciting to travel in a police car over the very route he had covered so many times in the battered old saloon. He was filled with a deep curiosity, too, wondering where the old wreck had finally finished its bumpy course after he had set it off. Been a clever move, that. It would have Valerie's fingerprints on it and show she *had been* in it. Much cleverer than ditching it in the bottom of a river or setting fire to it . . .

Presently the leading car turned off down the fatal land and went on towards the small wood at the bottom. Here it stopped and Whittaker, too, applied the brakes. Garth alighted stiffly and jerked his legs up and down, sniffing the dank, countrified air. Richard came climbing out beside him, then Whittaker.

Superintendent Chalfont came back towards them.

'You notice the tyre tracks going down this lane, sir?' he asked, pointing. 'They go right back to the main road.'

'Uh-huh,' Garth agreed, looking.

'I'm having the licence-holder traced. Soon hear about that.'

'Good,' Garth acknowledged. 'Now where's the car?'

'This way, sir.' Chalfont nodded to the field on the right. 'We can't get a car along it — not all the way. Better walk.'

He led the party across the field for about half a mile, all of them plunging in soft earth and following the car's distinct tracks. Presently they went through a smashed area of hawthorn hedge, along the contiguous field for perhaps another half-mile; then the old car loomed upon them, tilted on its side but not completely overturned, its offside wheels embedded in a ditch and its bodywork supported by the strong hedge branches.

Beside it were two constables who came to attention as the party approached.

'Just as Hanthorne found it,' Chalfont said, and motioned to the constable in question who promptly saluted. 'When we got the call to investigate the neighbourhood I sent my men off on a search. Hanthorne found this in the course of his travels.'

'No footprints?' Garth questioned.

'No, sir. Not a trace. A bit odd that. I came to look for myself and make sure. It doesn't matter how many we make. As you see there's nothing but the tyre tracks. Hanthorne and I both walked in them at first to avoid disturbing the ground.'

'No footprints,' Garth repeated pensively. 'Hmmm . . . this gets interesting. Now, let's see . . . '

He prowled forward, surveying the car from every angle without actually touching it.

'The inside hasn't been examined yet,' Chalfont said, presently. 'Have to be fingerprinted first, of course.'

'They're on their way, and the photographers,' Garth told him; then he disappeared round the back of the car, made his way through the gap in the hedge and then stared at the door nearest the driving seat.

'There are the bloodstains, sir.' The Superintendent pointed to three brownish red spots on the pale blue of the car's worn cellulose. 'Hanthorne thought at first they might be rust marks, but I'm pretty sure they're blood, and not very old either.'

Richard looked on with interest at the three nearly insignificant spots he had left behind. He could see now how he had done it — snatched his wrist across the rough metalwork inside the lowered window. *Nearly* insignificant, yes — but there just the same. He began to wonder if it would not have been better to have sunk the car in the river after all . . . Useless now.

Garth glanced at Chalfont. 'Any ideas, Super?'

'Well, apparently the car was sent off on its own from the land and after a brief career finished here. That's more or less proved by the absence of footprints. Nobody was in the car. It was just ditched, like this. The lowered window suggests that somebody stood on the running board, probably held on to the steering wheel for a while, and then jumped clear on to the grass bordering the field. Not much impression of footprints on the running board, you notice. It's that infernally dirty there hardly could be.'

Garth looked at the running board, then surveyed the landscape.

'Yes, I think your hypothesis is right,' he admitted. 'So, whither went Valerie Hadfield and Rixton Williams? And to which of them — if either — do these bloodstains belong?'

He turned aside and then glanced up as a tall figure with a lesser figure beside it came into view in the neighbouring field.

'Divisional Inspector Whiteside and Sergeant Clair,' Garth murmured, and nodded genially as the lanky, fox-faced Divisional Inspector for Kensington came up.

''Afternoon, Inspector,' he greeted Garth, and nodded to the others. 'The car, eh? Tell us anything?'

'Only that it is ditched and that the birds have flown,' Garth sighed. 'We're waiting for the fingerprint boys and photographers. Can't do much until then. How about you? How are things regarding that chauffeur?'

'More I see of the business, sir, the more I suspect murder,' Whiteside answered, pulling out a notebook and studying it for a moment. 'The odd thing to me is that Cranston, the chauffeur, had covered the car's bonnet with a rug, presumably for the night, and yet he must have done it while the engine was running otherwise he'd never have been poisoned by fumes. It seems queer to me . . . Why leave your engine running on a slow tick — we checked on that by filling the tank and starting the engine up to see what speed it was going at — and *then* cover the bonnet? It's sort of cart before the horse. Then again, there is some doubt in Dr. Lewis's mind about the wound the chauffeur sustained. He thinks it's broader than it should be if Cranston hit his head on the edge of the sand bucket. And why, in a garage so neat you could eat off it, did Cranston have a screwdriver lying on the floor, which presumably threw his foot from under him and caused him to fall and strike his head?'

'Any fingerprints?' Garth asked, reflecting.

'Quite a few. I had the boys on the job right away, of course. Chiefly there are two sets . . . One set of the plain arch variety with ten ridges — showing age over fourteen, of course — definitely belong to the chauffeur; and the other, mainly in the back of the car, are of the twinned loop type with nine ridges. There is no doubt that they belong to Valerie Hadfield. They checked with prints found in her flat and especially on a fan at the theatre that she used a lot in her act . . . There are also,' Whiteside finished, frowning, 'traces of a third set of prints, ten ridged, and of the exceptional arch type. A man's. Can't quite place to whom they belong as yet.'

Richard took out a cigarette and lighted

it, watching the smoke drifting into the windless air. *Other* prints? A *man's?* He had ridden in that Daimler himself, of course, but he had been wearing rubber gloves . . . But had not been wearing them when he had been *with Valerie* in the rear of the car! He stood with his cigarette motionless as he suddenly realised the fact. He had clean forgotten that he had ridden with the girl at previous times and no doubt had left prints in various places in the car back — on the polished parts and even on the door latch, parts which had evidently escaped Peter's duster. And since he, Richard Harvey, had been the only man ever permitted to ride with Valerie Hadfield . . .

10

'It is possible,' Garth said at length, 'that the prints not yet identified may belong to our elusive friend Rixton Williams. We'd better take a look at that house he bought. Anywhere near here, Superintendent?'

'Yes, sir — not far down the main road. I've been over the place casually myself. Thought I'd better leave the details to you or the Divisional Inspector here.'

'You come with me, Super,' Garth said, 'and you, Whiteside, and you, too, Whittaker. You others had better wait for the fingerprint and photograph brigade and tell them to follow us on to Williams' house. You know where the place is?' Garth asked one of the constables.

'I do, sir,' said P.C. Hanthorne, nodding.

'Right.'

The four men turned and Richard followed them at a slight distance, caught up with them again when they had reached the official cars in the lane.

'Gets better as it goes on, eh, Dick?' Garth asked, smiling. 'Any notions?'

'Afraid not,' Richard answered quietly.

'Nor I, dammit — not yet.'

Richard clambered in the car's rear and Garth dropped beside him. Whittaker took the wheel and Superintendent Chalfont sat next to him. Whiteside went to his own car and drove it in the wake of Garth's. So, one behind the other, they emerged from the lane, turned left, and headed down the main road towards the house the Superintendent presently indicated. Outside the front door a constable stood on duty, his bicycle propped against the front garden fence.

'You certainly covered everything, Super,' Garth remarked. 'Nice work . . . '

Chalfont smiled in satisfaction; then he climbed out of the car and went up the house's narrow front pathway. Garth, Whiteside, and Sergeant Whittaker followed him.

Richard glanced about him. If there had been faces behind curtains when he had taken the place they had been mere ghosts compared to now. Curtains had been abandoned as shields and for quite a distance men and women stood in doorways or found interesting things to do in their front gardens.

'Nobody called?' the Superintendent asked the constable.

'No, sir. Nothing's happened since I came on duty.'

Garth led the way into the front room and stood gazing round him. Presently his eyes moved to the folded letter on the mantelpiece. He went closer to look at it but did not touch it,

'Everything just as I found it, sir,' the Superintendent said. 'Or nearly. Light was switched off and the curtains drawn. I used a piece of string round the light switch to put it on and so save blurring any prints—'

'And door handles?' Garth questioned.

'This door here was open, sir, and there was no need to smear the front door. A master key opened the lock and we just pushed the door forward. No disturbance.'

Richard felt uneasy as he looked the

room over. The air was heavy, musty from enclosure. The small, modernistic clock ticked steadily on the mantelshelf and showed four-twenty.

Garth looked at the clock casually, then back again with sudden intentness. Richard frowned, wondering what the attraction was. Garth went over and surveyed the clock from different angles. Presently he turned round with a grin.

'What a lovely set of fingerprints!' he whistled. 'On the glass face and polished wood sides . . . '

Fingerprints? *There?* But why should there be? For a moment cold dread gripped Richard, but he fought it back. Probably from the furniture removers anyway . . . Yes, that would be it! The furniture removers!

Garth went to the windows and flung back the curtains, then he nodded to the Superintendent who pulled the piece of thin string wrapped round the light switch. The lights went out. Dull grey afternoon daylight made the small, newly-furnished room pale and sombre, filled with a vague suggestion of dread and things unexplained.

Coming to the divan, Garth paused and knelt beside it, looking but not touching anything. Sergeant Whittaker came to his side.

'Hair,' Garth said, pointing. 'Long hair too — blonde . . . In fact *several* hairs. Evidently our lady friend had a lie down on the divan here amongst other things.'

'Maybe when she was tight,' Richard suggested.

'Maybe.' Garth stood up again. 'Which reminds me — what about the champagne?'

The Superintendent looked vaguely surprised. 'There *is* an empty champagne bottle in the kitchen, sir, as it happens — standing on a tray with three glasses. This way.'

Garth grinned a little. 'I'm not dazzling you with a piece of Holmesian deduction, Super. I just happen to know about the champagne from one Timothy Potter. Whittaker, let the Super see Potter's statement, will you?'

'Right, sir.'

Richard followed into the hall and

stood leaning idly in the kitchen doorway as Garth went and looked at the glasses and Chalfont stood reading the notes Whittaker had given him. Divisional Inspector Whiteside prowled round the kitchen meanwhile, peering everywhere and touching nothing.

'Odd,' Garth said, raising each of the glasses in turn with his fingers straddled inside them. 'Don't seem to be any fingerprints . . . not even a blur. What do you make of it, Whiteside?'

'How about the tray?' Whiteside asked, and Garth pressed his palms against the tray's thin edges and took it to the light. 'Clean!' he said. 'And the same goes for the bottle.'

Garth peered into the glasses, sniffed at them. Champagne dregs in each glass apparently. No smell of any drug. 'Now why the devil should all the prints be wiped off?'

'Off-hand,' Richard said, 'I'd say it was to conceal identity by fingerprints.'

'But *why?*' Garth turned his death-mask face. 'Everybody around here knows Mr. Williams, and Potter has testified that he was present when Valerie Hadfield and Williams drank the champagne. So where was the point in wiping away the fingerprints afterwards?'

'Mr. Harvey may not be so wrong, sir,' Whittaker said, musing. 'Perhaps Williams isn't that chap's genuine name and he knows — or knew — that fingerprints would prove his identity to the hilt, so he wiped them away. An alias, sir, if you see what I mean.'

Richard stared at the sergeant in snake-like coldness for a moment, astounded that the actual truth had been dropped upon so neatly. In fact too neatly for Garth didn't accept it — not in its entirety.

'Mebbe,' he said, pondering. There came a sudden noise in the hall and two men entered, one carrying small camera equipment and the other a black attaché case.

'I'm Smithers, sir, from Ipswich,' said the one with the attaché case, cuffing his trilby up on his forehead. 'Oh good afternoon, Inspector Whiteside. Second time today, eh?'

'Have you got specimen prints of Valerie Hadfield with you, Smithers?' Garth questioned.

'Yes, sir. From her flat. Fixed them up this morning and got some good photo-enlargements.'

'Right. Check on this house for prints. When you want me I'll be seated on the stairs out of your way . . . Come on, Dick.'

Richard followed to the staircase and sat two steps below Garth as he squatted down with a sigh and tugged forth another of his fragrant-smelling cheroots. It was gloomy here in the hall. Inspector Whiteside and Superintendent Chalfont stood waiting, the Superintendent still reading Whittaker's notes. Whittaker remained in the kitchen, watching the fingerprint men as they got to work with the insufflators and varicoloured powders. The man with the camera weighed up the surroundings pensively . . .

'Still sure that Scotland Yard doesn't work hard for its living, Dick?' Garth asked presently.

'I grant that, Garth — but what have

you found? An abandoned car with three bloodstains on it; a man who might really be somebody else and who has vanished into thin air, and a musical comedy actress who has done likewise. A chauffeur who dies from an accident. And not an atom of proof that murder was done . . . '

'It's looking mighty near to murder,' Garth said, suddenly grim again. 'F'rinstance, those champagne glasses have no trace of foreign element in them, so Valerie Hadfield was not drugged. And I defy anybody, much less one accustomed to drinking, to get hopeless on a third of a bottle of champagne.'

'Unless Williams slipped her some kind of poison separately,' Richard said slowly. 'Maybe he forced her down on the sofa and did it. Remember the hairs.'

'Why?'

'God knows! You're the detective . . . '

'Which reminds me, I'd better go and take a look upstairs.'

'No need, sir,' Superintendent Chalfont interrupted. 'I've had a look already and there's nothing of interest. Whatever happened seems to have happened down here.'

'Hmm, that's a relief,' Garth settled down again. Then he peered through the banisters, 'I say, Whiteside!'

The Divisional Inspector looked up from the notebook. 'Sir?'

'About those notes Valerie Hadfield received from Williams. Have you got them with you?'

'Not with me, no; they're at headquarters.'

'Then bring 'em along to my office this evening. I want to see them. A lot depends on whether Valerie made this trip here of her own free will or not. Maybe we can get somewhere when we can handle that letter on the mantelpiece in the front room. Hey, Smithers, how much longer are you going to be?'

'Just finishing, sir . . . ' Smithers came out of the kitchen.

'Well?' Garth questioned.

'Plenty of prints about, but none of them check with the prints we've got. From the depth of most of them, and the smudges, I'd say the furniture men made them.'

'And the tray, glasses, and bottle?'

'Polished like mirrors.'

'Blast! What did you find on the car?'

Smithers went back for his notes and his colleague went through into the drawing room to start work.

'Prints in various parts of the car, sir,' Smithers said. 'Mostly inside as though somebody sat next to the driver. The 'somebody' was undoubtedly Valerie Hadfield. Her twinned loop, nine-ridged variety is all over the place. No others worth bothering with. Only smudges.'

Garth nodded. 'Had that chap from pathology got there before you left?'

'He'd just arrived — Doc Winters himself. The photographers and he were busy as we came away.'

Smithers turned into the front room as nothing more was said. For a time Garth sat thinking, elbow on the step above him. Richard too, was lost in thought.

There were sounds on the macadam pathway outside and the photographers came in. Behind them trotted a small, middle-aged man in a bowler hat and overcoat too long for him, carrying a neat bag.

'Not much for you boys,' Garth said to the photographers. 'No body, no work, as far as you're concerned. Anyway, photograph those glasses and bottle in the kitchen and then get three angles on the front room, including the clock. That'll be all for you. Send in your findings with the car photographs to my office.'

The men nodded and went through with tripod and equipment to the kitchen. Richard glanced at the little man in the bowler hat. He knew him fairly well — Dr. Eustace Winters, the Home Office pathologist, by no means the top man of his department but relentlessly thorough all the same. Not that there was anything to fear from him; Richard knew exactly how far the man's knowledge extended.

'Anything?' Winters asked briefly.

'Not here, no,' Garth answered him. 'No sign of a body and even less sign of your beloved stains. Nothing gory about this job. One of the 'thin air' breed . . . How about the car? Any luck?'

'Undoubtedly bloodstains,' Winters

said. 'No telling whether they're human or animal until I've given the residue the precipitin test. I've got the deposit off the car and I'll let you have my report as soon as I can.'

'Good,' Garth approved. 'Make it some time this evening if possible.'

Richard smiled and looked up at Garth.

'He can prove whether it's human or animal blood,' he said, 'but he can't prove whether it's man or woman's. Research hasn't got things narrowed down that far yet.'

'I know,' Garth growled. 'Never know what you might find, though.'

He rose, went into the front room where the electric light was now on and the curtains drawn. The fingerprint men were busy with the clock. It was on the table, smeared in powder. Garth remained silent, watching.

'Several Valerie Hadfield prints, Inspector,' said the man with the camera finally. 'They're on the arms of that chair by the fire, on the top of this table here, and then there are these beauties on the clock

. . . Lots of other smudged prints, but again from the position of them I think the furniture removers may be responsible.'

'And the letter?' Garth asked. 'That's the important thing.'

'Very faint smudges, useless for identification.'

'Hmmm . . . ' Garth reflected. 'Okay, turn in your report to headquarters in the usual way. Better see what there is upstairs.'

The men nodded, gathered up their equipment and left the room. Garth picked up the letter, unfolded it and brooded over it as the photographers came in from the kitchen with camera and flashbulbs. Richard stood pondering, recalling Valerie's interest in the clock. While he had been out fetching Potter she must have picked it up and examined it.

'Sent on Thursday,' Garth murmured. 'Or at any rate the letter says Thursday . . . ' Whiteside and Whittaker moved up to look over his shoulder. ' 'Ricky, my dear. All right. I can spare time for a little tête-à-tête tomorrow. Thanks for keeping away from the 'phone. It might make things difficult for me and I must think of my career. Always, Val . . . ' Hmm, it looks normal enough but I think we'll put it under the ultra-violet later and see if there's anything fishy about it. We'll give those letters you've got the same treatment, Whiteside.'

'Right you are, sir. I'll bring them along this evening.'

Garth put the letter away in his wallet 'Bit odd,' he mused, 'using the phrase tête-à-tête to a man who apparently was not remarkable for his culture. Isn't convincing somehow.'

'But surely,' Richard put in, 'if that be Valerie Hadfield's natural way of expressing herself she wouldn't think of descending to her — er — lover's level?'

'For a lover one is prepared to sink most things — even culture — sometimes,' Garth answered briefly. 'It's queer, like this whole infernal business. Motive, for instance? Damned if I can find one yet, unless it's publicity.'

He gave his chest a thump and went over to the divan, carefully lifted three or four of the golden strands of hair in a pair of small tweezers and dropped them in a cellophane envelope out of his wallet. Sealing it up he returned it to his wallet.

'Might as well have them mounted and checked with any hairs we can find in Valerie Hadfield's flat or dressing room.'

'Supposing after all this she isn't dead?' Richard asked dryly. 'Make all of you look fools, wouldn't it?'

'No, Dick, I think she is dead — and I think she has been murdered . . . Anyway, she *has* disappeared and the police have been asked to look for her, so we're doing it . . . Okay, I think we can get out of here now.'

'Back to London?' Richard inquired.

'Why? In a hurry to go home?'

Richard shrugged. 'Not at all — but what more is there around this neighbourhood?'

'You'd be surprised,' Garth chuckled. 'I'm going to the post office — or sub-post office rather. It just occurs to me that there's no sign of an envelope for this letter Williams left. I'd like to know the date it was sent. 'Thursday' might be any time. Be a help to find out when it was delivered.'

When it was delivered! For the second time during this initial investigation Richard felt cold shock. Of course! A *postman* should have delivered it, and none had. No postman had ever been since he'd bought the place . . . He got a grip on himself as he followed Garth and the others out of the room.

Superintendent Chalfont gave his instructions to the constable on duty and then came down the front path to where Richard and the others were standing.

'The sub-post office for this district is just across the way, sir,' he said to Garth. 'About half-a-mile down the road amongst a group of shops.'

'Okay!' Garth gave a nod. 'I'll go over . . . Care to come, Dick?'

Richard fell into step beside the Chief Inspector's square, overcoated figure. It was nearly dark now and the countryside was smothering gently in a dank autumnal mist.

'Whoever this chap Williams is — or was — he seems to have covered up his tracks beautifully,' Richard commented. 'Not left a single print — not even any footprints on the pathway to his house or on the pavement outside.'

'He may have left some tell-tale dust in some of the carpets, though,' Garth answered thoughtfully. 'We'll have them inspected and any residue checked by spectrograph if need be. Depends what else we find . . . '

For a while there was only the sound of their footsteps in the quiet road.

'This letter of Valerie's to Williams baffles me,' Garth sighed. 'Apart from 'tête-à-tête' I can't imagine why a woman so high in society and such an artiste — I've seen her, by the way, in that revue at the Paragon Theatre — should be so intimate with a very ordinary Lancashire man as to call him 'Ricky' . . . Yes, 'Ricky',' he repeated slowly, and Richard felt his pulses quicken. 'Would you call 'Ricky' the short for Rixton, Dick?'

'I might. 'Rixy' would be more appropriate but not as easy to say. I think it's normal enough.'

The lighted fronts of the shops loomed

up ahead of them. Garth entered the grocery-shop-cum-post office and glanced about him. A man wearing a soiled apron was affixing a ticket beside the postal counter.

''Evening, gentlemen . . . ' He turned — shrewd, dark, smiling.

Garth displayed his warrant card and the man's expression changed.

'Scotland Yard? Why, what have *I* done?'

'Nothing — I trust,' Garth answered dryly. 'Don't excite yourself, Mr. — er —?'

'Spalding, Inspector. Douglas Spalding.'

'Well, Mr. Spalding, I merely want a little help. You're aware of the business going on at the Williams house, I suppose?'

'Yes,' Spalding admitted. 'But how can I help?'

'What about the mail for this particular district? From where is it sent out? Here?'

'Yes. We get it from Twickenham main office and this branch office handles the immediate neighbourhood. As a matter of fact my brother is the postman — '

'He is? Good! Family affair, eh? Is he in?'

Spalding nodded and called to somebody in the house part of the building. A man some years Spalding's junior came in.

'I understand you are the postman around here?' Garth asked. 'How many times have you delivered letters to Mr. Rixton Williams at number forty-seven, down the road?'

'Never. If it matters.'

'This is Chief Inspector Garth of Scotland Yard,' the postman's brother said quickly, and the younger Spalding's expression changed at once.

'Oh! I beg your pardon, sir, I didn't know . . . But that's the truth. I've never delivered anything to Williams.'

'Today is Saturday. How long has he occupied that house? Any idea?'

'A week, as far as I know. I remember that this time last week the removers were taking the furniture in.'

'I see. And you have seen Williams himself at times? What does he look like?'

'Oh, about what you'd call average

height, Inspector, limps with the left foot, and always seems to have his cap on. Never been able to place his age properly.'

Garth nodded. 'Thanks very much. You've been quite helpful. Good night.'

Richard followed Garth out into the gloom. He mentally cursed the slip he had made. He had gone out of his way to avoid correspondence and overlooked that the move had defeated its own purpose. It struck him as peculiar that Garth did not even refer to the letter when he presently spoke again.

'The description of Williams checks up with Potter's, anyway. Which is a help. Checks, too, with the descriptions obtained by Superintendent Chalfont . . . But where is the man now? If this *is* an elopement it's about the most secretive one I've ever encountered. It begins to look as though Williams left that letter on purpose so it could be found. Obviously it didn't come through the mails. Have to check up and be sure if Valerie Hadfield did write it . . . '

So the subject had come round to the letter again, after all. Richard made no comment and in silence they reached the cars. Garth singled out the Superintendent in the gloom.

'Super, find out from whom the house furniture was bought, and all details about the buyer; also find the name of the agent who sold the house. Get all the facts about Williams that you can — the bank upon which he drew, everything. In detail. Send your report in to me at the Yard.'

'I will, sir, as soon as possible,' Chalfont promised.

Garth nodded. 'Fingerprint boys and photographers finished yet?'

'They left five minutes ago,' Sergeant Whittaker said. 'No sign of anything upstairs, beyond removers' finger marks. They'll send in their stuff in the usual way.'

'Good!' Garth took a deep breath. 'Well, I think my indigestion will permit of a good tea, then we'll go into a huddle in my office, boys. We may need to work fast in this business before the trail goes stale. Come on . . . You follow us, Whiteside.'

Richard took his customary seat in the back of the car next to the Chief Inspector.

'Any ideas?' Garth asked, as the car got on the move.

'Not the vaguest, but I might have if you'd let me come to that conference tonight. I've nothing else to do . . . '

'Come by all means,' Garth smiled. 'I'll stand the whack for our tea and maybe this evening we'll *really* learn something!'

11

By seven-fifteen that evening the group in Chief Inspector Garth's office overlooking the Embankment was complete.

Garth sat browsing through reports, studying them carefully, rechecking everything.

At right angles to him Sergeant Whittaker was leafing through his notebook. By the window, Divisional Inspector Whiteside sat by the window, and Richard sat in the deep hide armchair by the door, contemplating Garth as he studied the reports.

'Not a trace of Valerie Hadfield or Rixton Williams anywhere . . . ' Garth sat back in his swivel chair. 'There are reports here from all over the country, collected during the day, but no results.'

'Maybe the missing pair are in hiding,' Richard suggested.

'Even to hide, though, you have to get there first,' Garth remarked. 'And according to these reports nobody has even had a glimpse of our elusive friends. I'm sure now it isn't an elopement, but something deeper . . . Anyway, let's get down to a few concrete things. Here is Dr. Lewis's report on the chauffeur, Peter Cranston . . . ' Garth cleared his throat and read: ''Post-mortem report. Deceased was stunned by a blow from a blunt-edged instrument, which fractured the base of the skull at the occipital bone, which of itself did not cause death but loss of consciousness. Death was caused by inhalation of carbon monoxide fumes. The Pathological Department's Gasometric Test reveals the blood-extract of Peter Cranston as having carbon monoxide content of twenty-five c.c. to one hundred c.c. of blood' . . . '

'Then it wasn't the sand bucket which did it?' Divisional Inspector Whiteside mused. 'I'll take another look round the garage tomorrow. Pretty plain we're dealing with murder.'

'Exactly,' Garth assented. 'We want everything we can find concerning Cranston, Inspector. If we can trace *his* killer we also stand a reasonable chance of discovering what happened to Valerie Hadfield — and to Williams. Unless Williams is the man we're looking for.'

Richard was silent, reflecting on the rubber gloves he had been wearing when he had struck down the chauffeur. He had not cleaned the tyre-lever, which had been a mistake. But then there had not been time. It could only prove to be the instrument of death, but would yield no clue as to who had handled it.

Garth glanced up as the door opened and Dr. Winters of the Home Office came in, a white card in his hand. He laid it on the desk in front of Garth.

'There you are Garth — precipitin findings on the bloodstains on the car. Group AB human blood, and fairly recent. Not more than fifteen or sixteen hours old, I'd say. It answered readily enough to test.'

'Thanks,' Garth acknowledged. 'Nothing odd about it in any way, I suppose?'

Winters shrugged. 'Not particularly — except that AB is the rarest of the blood groups, and can only be agglutinated by groups O, A and B. Don't know if it is a man's or woman's, of course. Anyway' — Winters shrugged as he went back to the door — 'it's all yours. I'm going home. 'Night.'

Garth looked at the report and sighed. 'Might equally well belong to Valerie Hadfield, Rixton Williams, or an unknown entirely. Only thing in our favour is that it is in a rare group if we ever get the chance to match it . . . '

He turned to the mass of papers on his desk and drew forth the three letters that Whiteside had brought. To them was clipped the letter from the house in Twickenham.

'None of these letters is forged,' Garth said. 'The ultra-violet has shown that. Concerning the three letters from Williams to Valerie, there are only her fingerprints on them. The letter found in Twickenham has a 'mashed' surface where prints have been erased. Valerie definitely wrote the letter found in Twickenham, but she wrote it *some time ago* — some other Thursday.'

'What makes you think that?' Richard asked curiously.

'The age of the ink. Infra-red tells us this note is over a year old, but the others from Rixton Williams are quite recent. So it seems as though Williams got hold of one of Valerie's old letters somehow and left it behind in Twickenham, maybe in an endeavour to prove that Valerie came to see him of her own accord. As for the card in the roses — only Valerie's prints.'

Richard sat pondering. Good job he'd held that card edge-wise. But the infrared! The age of the ink! Yet another point he had overlooked.

'The more I study these letters from Williams to Valerie the more puzzled I get,' Garth muttered, 'For a whirlwind courtship it sets an all-time record. First this card — 'To that lovely actress Valerie Hadfield from a man who admires her from far off and whose name is Rixton Williams . . . ' The confounded thing sounds like a ritual!'

Garth tossed it down, picked up the letters and brooded.

'Last Saturday — a week ago today — he sent his first letter and called her 'Dear Lady', signing himself 'Rixton

Williams',' Garth went on. 'On the following Tuesday he called her 'Dearest Valerie' and remarked on what a wonderful time they had had on the previous night. Signed himself 'Rixton'. Notice the slight improvement in relations? Then on his Wednesday letter — we're in this week now, don't forget, he arrived at 'Dearest Val' and signed himself 'Rix'. 'Rix'! Mark that! *Not* 'Ricky,' which is what she called him in that Twickenham letter . . . Incidentally, Whiteside, did the maid verify that her mistress *was* out on the Monday night of this week?'

'No,' the Divisional Inspector answered. 'It seems that the maid goes off to her own rooms after leaving some theatre stuff at the flat. Nothing to prevent Valerie doing just what she liked once the maid had gone. Blind alley lead there, I'm afraid.'

'And the maid has never seen this man Williams?'

'No. Only the doorman seems to have done that, and his description is identical with the one we've got.'

'Mmmm . . . But I wish I could

understand this relationship between Valerie and Williams. He's only a recent arrival, I'm sure of it. In other words, since infra-red cannot lie as to the age of ink, Valerie knew somebody called 'Ricky' over a year ago!'

Garth put the letters down and scratched impatiently among the papers, finally yanking yet another report into view.

'Calligraphy department,' he said. 'According to the experts, the letters Williams wrote were written with the right hand bent at an angle, or else the person had writers' cramp or some form of paralysis.'

'Unless,' Sergeant Whittaker said slowly, thinking, 'somebody with a hand familiar to Valerie wanted to disguise the style?'

'Possible,' Garth acknowledged, and fell to reflection.

Richard became aware of the Chief Inspector's cold, deadly eyes fixed on him — not in suspicion; merely absent-minded interest as he weighed up Sergeant Whittaker's suggestion. Twice now Whittaker had revealed a disturbing sagacity.

'I don't think that angle has much to it,' Whiteside commented. 'I gave that maid a thorough cross-examining and one fact emerged quite clearly — namely, that this Hadfield woman had no men friends whatever. Outside of this Williams chap, that is, and it seems she positively gloated over his letters when they turned up. As for the chauffeur, his mother told me that he never revealed any of his mistress's activities. Conscientious, of course, but infernally awkward for us.'

Richard smiled faintly and his thoughts strayed back to the earlier part of Whiteside's statement. Of *course* Valerie had gloated. She had admitted it herself — that she had been proud of the fact that there was another man interested in her. What had she said now? Hadn't it been — ' . . . you are not so unique as you think! There's great power in black and white, Ricky . . . ' Something like that . . .

'Ricky!' The name stilled Richard into grim reflection again. That name must never have been seen or heard within the Chief Inspector's sight or hearing or the fat would land in the fire with a vengeance. Garth was already suspicious of it: he had revealed that much . . .

'Well, Inspector,' Richard said presently, 'from the expression on your face you actually look as though you're up against a brick wall.'

'I admit it. I can't even decide what the *motive* is. For the time being I think we have done all we can,' he added, glancing at Whiteside. 'A lot will depend on what you find out in the garage tomorrow, and also upon what Superintendent Chalfont discovers on Monday about the furniture and purchase of the house. Tracing backwards, we'll probably get to know a good deal about Mr. Williams, and then . . . '

Garth rose from his chair and shrugged. 'Time we were getting home. It's past eight o'clock now and I've a crossword puzzle I want to finish. Let's be moving.'

'Can I give you a lift?' Richard asked, rising.

'Be glad of it. Thanks.'

* * *

When Richard arrived home towards nine he received something of a surprise as old Baxter met him in the hall.

'A Mr. and Miss Prescott are here, sir — '

'They are! When did they arrive?'

'About an hour ago, Mr. Richard, sir. I said I had no idea when you would be home, but they insisted on waiting. They are in the library.'

'Thanks, Baxter. Bring in some sherry, will you?'

'Yes, Mr. Richard, sir.'

Richard hurried across the hall and pushed the library door open quickly. Joyce Prescott was seated before the fire, deep in an armchair, and her father in another armchair with a book in his hands.

'Ricky!' The girl got to her feet immediately, the light paling her face and setting the copper glinting in her hair. 'Ricky, I just *had* to come . . . to say I'm sorry . . . for this morning.'

Richard hesitated and then smiled

faintly. He turned and shook Dr. Prescott's hand as he rose from the chair and gave a slow, knowing smile.

'Remember, Richard, I said it couldn't be as bad as all that,' he murmured.

'I'd forgotten all about it, sir,' Richard said, shrugging.

'I don't think so, Ricky; you're simply trying to be nice about it.' Joyce gripped his arm tightly. 'You were hurt — and rightly! Dad here made me see that. I've been thinking about it ever since you rushed off in a huff this morning and I made up my mind to square things before the day ended. So I . . . That is, *we* . . . came over.'

Richard stood looking at her for a moment, then he turned as Baxter came in with the sherry.

'Just put it down, Baxter,' Richard said. 'I'll attend to it.'

'Sherry?' Richard questioned, and the girl and her father both nodded.

Richard gave Joyce a glass. 'Then the unknown woman doesn't matter any more?' he asked, then turned to hand Dr. Prescott's glass to him.

'I wouldn't quite say that . . . ' Joyce turned back to the armchair and perched on its arm, one graceful leg swinging. 'I'd still like to know who she is, but it occurred to me afterwards that you'll tell me in your own time — or so dad says. And he knows!'

'I am merely a student of human nature,' Dr. Prescott said benevolently, setting down his glass. 'And I don't like to see two young people heading for the rocks. You *will* tell Joyce, one day?'

Richard met the dark eyes behind the glasses and nodded slowly.

'Yes, of course I will . . . ' And for a moment Richard found himself dwelling on the twist of circumstances that had placed him beside Chief Inspector Garth all day. It had been Joyce herself who had done it. But for her making him dash off like that . . .

'You don't seem very pleased even now,' Joyce said irritably, pursing her lips. 'What's *wrong*, Ricky? Something bothering you?'

'Why, no!' He drained his glass and set it down. 'I've been thinking, though. I'd rather you didn't call me 'Ricky' any more.'

'And why not?' she demanded in surprise. 'Haven't I always called you that? Didn't you *ask* me to?'

'Yes, but . . . Well, *she* called me that, too. I don't want any reminders, that's all.'

Joyce drank her sherry and reflected. 'She's gone away, then?'

'Gone away?'

'You said 'called' me that. Isn't she here any more — or what?'

Richard tightened his lips, aware that he had made the same slip as he had made before the chauffeur. His damnable misuse of grammar: his seeming inability to realise that Valerie was alive until proven dead . . .

'To me,' he said with effort, 'she's in the past tense. Finished! Done with! Like the nickname she used for me and which I don't ever want to hear again.'

Joyce smiled coolly. 'All right then, I'll remember and call you 'Dick'.' She put her glass down and then added: 'But old habits die hard, you know. If I forget now and again you'll have to forgive me.'

'Just don't forget,' he suggested, with unintentional hardness.

Joyce got up and moved over to him, still smiling. Richard relaxed a little and his big mouth smiled back at her as he put an arm about her shoulders.

'That's better,' murmured Dr. Prescott. 'Much better.'

'Sorry, Joyce,' Richard said. 'I've been through some pretty tough moments behind the scenes — getting rid of entanglements, I mean. But let's see what we can do to sort it out . . . This, for instance . . .'

He took the ring case out of his pocket and snapped back the lid. This time the girl looked at the circlet of gold and single clawed diamond thereon in fascinated joy.

'It's wonderful!' she whispered. 'At last we're engaged for all the world to see!'

'For all the world to see,' Richard agreed, smiling as he slipped the ring on her finger.

She drew him across to the divan, forced him to sit down beside her.

'Don't mind me,' Prescott said, grinning.

'Let's — let's forget all about this woman, Dick,' Joyce said earnestly. 'Let's talk of other things. Where have you been all day?'

'Oh, I've wandered around. London chiefly.'

'Tomorrow we can go there together,' she said, sitting back and closing her eyes happily. 'Do all the things we should have done today.'

'Not tomorrow, Joyce — wouldn't be worth it. It's Sunday.'

She opened her eyes and looked surprised. 'So it is! I *must* be in love. No, not tomorrow,' she agreed somewhat ruefully. 'Dad and I will be going to church. Has to be done as a regular thing when he gives away so much money to it. Why don't you come to church, too?'

'Mmmm — no,' Richard answered, smiling. 'I'm no church man, dearest. I'll be better employed getting on with that garage.'

'Oh, that again! Anyway, we can go out together all day Monday?'

'I — I'm afraid not,' he said. 'Some business has come up. I may have to keep going up and down to London quite a lot in the next few days — '

'There you go again!' Joyce gazed at him in dismay. 'You said you'd finished all your business — that you were absolutely free all the way to our wedding!'

'I know — and I was, before we had our little argument this morning. I ran into some unexpected business in the city today and it's essential that I give it my attention.'

'Then it's more important than I am?' The suspicion of the morning was back in her voice.

'As if it could be! Joyce, dear, I never expected you'd be so unreasonable . . . '

'Ricky . . . I mean Dick, I'm *not* unreasonable. It's simply that as your wife-to-be I think we're entitled to be with each other a little, especially after you promising. If you love me the way you say you do you will cancel all this business and spend the next few weeks with me. Not necessarily all the time, of course, because I have to help Dad catch up on a lot of secretarial work, but at least don't make engagements which will keep us apart . . . '

Richard was silent. Everything depended on how long Chief Inspector Garth would take to arrive at a complete blank in the Valerie Hadfield case and admit himself beaten. After that . . .

'Well, I'll fix it so that we can be together after Monday,' Richard said finally, patting the girl's head. 'On Monday, though, I'll have to go through with my appointment, but I'll see to it that we're together from then on. And on Monday night we'll go that new musical comedy at the Regal and then on to the Blue Shadow for supper. How's that?'

'That's more like my own Ricky,' the girl said, getting to her feet; 'and I don't apologise for the usual nickname,' she added, wagging a finger at him as he frowned a protest. 'I'll simply never get out of calling you that. All right then, we're all fixed for Monday night. Where and when do we meet?'

'I expect to be in the city until towards tea-time . . . Might as well have tea at the

Blue Shadow if it comes to that. Yes, meet me there at about quarter-to-five. I'll book seats at the Regal first thing on Monday morning.'

Richard got to his feet and picked up her coat and held it for her. With a graceful movement of her hand she drew the coppery hair over the collar.

'I'm so glad we're not quarrelling,' she said simply. 'But don't think it isn't a hard sacrifice for me to quell my curiosity over this other woman . . . But I love you, Ricky, love you so much.'

She embraced him tightly for a moment and he patted her shoulder.

'Love makes one do odd things sometimes,' he said.

He went with her from the room to the hall door, opened it for her. Dr. Prescott came trailing behind them.

'Glad you two have seen sense at last,' he commented. 'Still going to try and finish that garage for when Joyce arrives to take over?'

'Going to do my best,' Richard acknowledged.

Prescott sighed, then he headed down

the steps to the front path as Joyce turned back to Richard and raised her lips to his.

★ ★ ★

At ten-thirty on Monday morning, after booking the Regal Theatre tickets, Richard called to see Chief Inspector Garth. When admitted by Sergeant Whittaker he found Garth at his desk, reading through mail and reports.

'Hello, Dick,' he greeted, looking up. 'You *do* mean to try and catch me out if you can, don't you?'

Richard smiled amiably, and it cost him considerable effort. He had had two bad nights for one thing and he felt nervy for another. All through the previous day as he had worked on the garage he had been haunted by uneasy premonitions. Though nothing was visibly wrong he had a conviction of movement going on below surface, of events conspiring against him, relentlessly, out of reach.

'Just thought I'd drop in and see if you're carrying the Valerie Hadfield business on,' he explained. 'I can hardly find any mention of it in the papers.'

'Oh, I'm carrying it on all right,' Garth assured him. 'As for the papers, I've clamped down somewhat on news. Doesn't pay to let a criminal know all you're doing.'

'Forgive me, Garth, but what *are* you doing?' Richard asked dryly, holding out his cigarette case and finding it waved away as a cheroot came into view. 'Just sitting here at your desk?'

Garth swung in his chair to face him, cheroot clamped between his teeth. 'I don't have to tear about like a track runner to get my facts, Dick . . . They come to me, or will do before long. I'm waiting for whatever reports the Twickenham Superintendent has to send — regarding house, furniture, car licensee — and coming nearer home I am waiting for the Home Office report on the tyre-lever which laid Peter Cranston low.'

'Tyre-lever?' Richard repeated. 'You mean that a tyre-lever was used as the weapon to kill him?'

'No doubt of it. Divisional Inspector Whiteside was on the job all day yesterday, checking and rechecking since the doctor's report of a blunt instrument. He found a tyre-lever with what might be traces of blood and human tissue upon it . . . Anyway, we dispatched it to pathology straight away and Dr. Winters is sweating over it at this very moment.'

Richard settled in the hide armchair by the doorway. The reaction would show Peter Cranston's blood — no doubt of that. Mentally Richard could see the antisera being added to the blood, could see the faint haze appearing in the test tube . . . Routine stuff that would not prove anything as far as his own participation in the business was concerned.

'Doesn't look like being a very exciting day, then?' he asked, sighing.

'Plenty may happen yet,' Garth told him. 'And if it does we . . . Oh, good!' he broke off, as the gnomelike, bald-headed Dr. Winters came in with his report.

'Group O,' Winters said, putting the report on the desk. 'Same group as the deceased's own blood. That doesn't prove that it is *his* blood, I know, but taking all things into consideration — wound, type of weapon, and so on — you can be pretty sure that the tyre-lever stunned Cranston and the carbon monoxide did the rest.'

'Mmmm,' Garth acknowledged. 'And the blood on the car was a different group altogether? AB? Bang goes my vague hope — very vague one, true — that maybe Cranston was mixed up in it somehow. Wish I could find a sample of Valerie Hadfield's blood somewhere. It would help a lot.'

Winters went out with an impersonal smile and Garth studied the report for a moment or two. Presently he set it on one side.

'Slow progress this,' he muttered, thumping his broad chest impatiently. 'Hell's bells, if only we could find the *body* we'd be getting somewhere . . . '

'Don't you mean — bodies?' Richard suggested.

'No. I cling to the singular. I believe Williams murdered Valerie Hadfield and then her chauffeur. Why he murdered Valerie I haven't the vaguest idea, but I am pretty sure the chauffeur was wiped out because he knew too much. The maid Ellen has testified that the chauffeur was more in his mistress's confidence than anybody else. That is understandable since he drove her everywhere and must have seen any companion she had . . . Possibly even he knew the identity of Valerie Hadfield's killer.'

'Logical enough,' Richard agreed. 'And you mean to say there were no finger-prints anywhere on the weapon?'

'Only blurs — and some fingerprints belonging to Cranston himself . . . And talking of fingerprints, one or two sets have been found in Valerie Hadfield's flat, that check with those in the back of her Daimler. *Somebody* whom she knew intimately obviously visited her flat, drove with her, and . . . ' Garth gave a shrug. 'Don't know who, but we'll find out.'

This news was not unexpected. The number of times Richard had been in Valerie's flat he could hardly expect that he had not left traces . . . Have to tackle that difficulty when he came to it . . .

'I suppose the maid Ellen hasn't had

anything to do with all this?' he asked.

'No. She has perfect alibis for everything, and her fingerprints don't lead anywhere conclusive. It's that *man* we want, Dick, and we've got to find him — '

Garth turned as the telephone shrilled. Sergeant Whittaker picked it up and listened.

'Superintendent Chalfont, sir — for you,' he said.

'Yes?' Garth put his cheroot in the ashtray and listened. Then he glanced up at Whittaker. 'Take this down — Furniture bought from Draycott's in Brandish Street, Twickenham. Yes, yes — and house bought through Amos Hardisty, Elm Crescent, Twickenham Green . . . Yes, I got it. Car licence owned by Rixton Williams and no private address . . . Blast! Eh? Yes, of course. Cover note was issued, was it? Car bought from Morgan & Lamvil, second hand dealers, Tithe Street, West Central? Yes, I'll take over from here. Many thanks.'

Garth put the instrument down and put the cheroot back between his teeth.

'Seems we should begin at Morgan and

Lamvil,' he said finally. 'Not far from here and we can go on to Twickenham later. Let's be going.'

Richard wondered for a brief moment if he should abandon accompanying the Inspector in his quest for a solution. He was risking a good deal, he realised, if some stray, unthought-of thing about him happened to betray him as the original Rixton Williams; but on the other hand the whole business had a morbid, deadly fascination for him. It was like being the spectator of an engrossing play. He just couldn't tear himself away from the scene.

In the back of the car, Whittaker driving as usual, Garth sat crumpled up and scowling.

'More I think of this,' Richard said, breaking the silence, 'the more I think you're up against a tough proposition, Garth. This Williams chap seems to have a peculiar genius all his own when it comes to vanishing completely. You've got to admit he is clever.'

'If I'm no nearer in another month I'll admit it then,' Garth growled, slanting his pale eyes. 'So far the thing's only two days old and I haven't even started to pull it to bits yet. Williams will eventually have to break cover. If he doesn't, then the only answer is that he is at large and that he created the character of Rixton Williams on purpose, dropping him like a thread-bare overcoat once his usefulness was finished.'

'Which still makes me wonder — *why*?' Richard muttered.

'Only answer to that — without proof — is that Valerie Hadfield *did* have one man in her life of whom she never spoke, and this one man had his reasons for wanting to be rid of her. No doubt that the chauffeur knew too, and that's why he's stretched out waiting for the inquest.'

'Doesn't anybody know the chauffeur's movements before he was murdered?' Richard questioned. 'Surely *somebody* must have seen him?'

'Whiteside's checking on that — getting the times from the theatre — the whole dope concerning him. There'll be some juice to squeeze out of it finally, don't you worry . . . Somebody unexpected happens to get up and go to a window to look for a late husband, and sees the murderer leaving the garage. Somebody stops to tie up his shoelace and sees the car entering the garage . . . Little things that tie up.'

'*If* they occur,' Richard said. 'You've no evidence of it as yet.'

'And from the look on your face you don't want me to have,' Garth said, grinning. 'You're itching to discover that this is a perfect crime which has got me licked, aren't you? Well . . . we'll see.'

Garth relaxed again, said no more until Whittaker had driven them to Morgan & Lamvil's. When they entered the big second-hand store Richard noted that it was the same spotless young salesman who had sold him the old saloon.

'Chief Inspector Garth?' The salesman looked at the warrant card Garth held out and then nodded. 'I've been expecting you, sir. Superintendent Chalfont of the Twickenham police rang us up. Got to know of us through the licensing authorities when we transferred the log book. You'd prefer to see the manager, I suppose? Unfortunately he's out just now.'

'It's not essential,' Garth told him. 'All I want to know is who it was that sold Rixton Williams a car?'

'I did, sir — and I know what's happened since. I saw a small bit about it in the newspaper. I hope I'm not likely to get involved in something unpleasant . . . '

'No reason why you should. How much did the car cost, and in what manner was it paid?'

'Sixty-seven pounds, sir, inclusive of licence,' the salesman said. 'Naturally we transferred the licence to the new owner along with the log book. The money was paid in one pound notes.'

'Mmmm,' Garth mused, and Richard, looking on casually, knew the Chief Inspector was disappointed. Five pound or ten pound notes could have been traced . . . but then Richard knew that too.

'What did he look like?' Sergeant Whittaker inquired, as his Chief stood thinking.

'About five feet nine, round shouldered, left foot limp, cap, raincoat, and from his voice I'd say he was a Northerner. Said he wasn't looking for anything fancy. I gave him cover note insurance until he could get his address fixed. I arranged it so that he could temporarily use our address — '

'Which is illegal,' Garth commented.

'I know, sir.' The salesman shrugged. 'The law blinks at that sort of thing as a rule . . . I mean, live and let live. Nine times out of ten it is convenient to us and the customer. This time, though — '

'He did not drop any hints about a lady?' Garth asked.

'No, sir. Never mentioned one.'

'You can't recall anything peculiar about him, can you? Any outstanding physical oddity?'

Pause, then: 'No, I can't recall anything, I'm afraid — except the limp.'

'All right, thanks. We're wasting time here. Let's get along to Twickenham.'

Richard grinned faintly when he sat next to Garth and their car was moving through the congested streets.

'All right, say it,' Garth invited. 'I'm battering my bonny napper against a brick wall!'

'Well, aren't you?'

'Mebbe — dammit! In a while — and probably before the month's out, too — I'll start admitting that it *is* clever! Even now I'll admit that Rixton Williams has made a grand job of covering up his tracks. If I can get nothing out of Twickenham I'll have the Lancashire constabulary see what they can find out about our friend.'

Thereafter Garth became moodily silent, gazing out on to the gradually quietening suburban road. Richard no longer sensed those relentless undercurrents. If anything, he was agreeably surprised at the masterly perfection of the scheme he had woven. The human bloodhound already admitted that he was at a standstill.

Finally Whittaker pulled up outside the Twickenham police headquarters. They went into Superintendent Chalfont's private office.

''Morning, gentlemen,' he greeted,

nodding. 'Been looking around?'

'No, because if I get no more damned sense out of it than I have out of the car dealers I'm wasting my time,' Garth retorted, sitting down. 'Maybe I can get most of it out of you . . . What about the estate agent's? How much did you find out?'

Chalfont nodded to a half completed report in the typewriter where a sergeant sat waiting before it.

'I was just getting it ready to send to you, sir. Anyway, I can give you the details. Rixton Williams called in Hardisty's in his saloon a week last Thursday, October tenth. It was about three-thirty in the afternoon. He paid a cover charge for the key, went to look at the house which he eventually bought and then — '

'To blazes with that!' Garth interrupted crossly. 'What did he *pay* in? Cash? For the house, I mean . . . '

'No — cheque. The sum of sixteen hundred pounds, drawn on the Sub-District Middlesex Bank. He did not buy the house on the same day as he viewed it. He paid five pounds in one pound notes to hold the place and said he'd bring a cheque next day. That he did, arriving about the same time. In fact, judging from the times he could hardly have put his money in the bank — two thousand in one pound notes — before he paid out sixteen hundred of it for the house. After that — same afternoon, Friday — he paid two hundred and ninety-eight pounds to Draycott's, the furnishers, by cheque, which is still there . . .'

'Two thousand in ones,' Garth murmured at length. 'The benighted dimwit!'

Richard tensed in his chair. All of a sudden the pulses in his throat felt as though they would stifle him.

12

'Yes, a benighted dimwit!' Garth repeated, looking up from his desk. 'That's a tall order for any bank to carry out — supplying two thousand in one pound notes. I can send out a call to every bank in the country and have them try and trace which customer has drawn out two thousand in ones fairly recently. There'll be a record of it; I'll gamble on that.'

'But why should the two thousand have come from a *bank*?' asked Sergeant Whittaker, clinging to logic.

'Why not? I can't see any man in his right senses walking about with two thousand in ones when there are banks who'll take care of it for him . . . '

Richard jumped in and seized his chance desperately, though his voice was languid enough.

'I agree a person of average sagacity *wouldn't* walk about with two thousand in ones, Garth — but I'd place Williams as the kind of man who has saved all his life and maybe put the notes in an old biscuit tin. Lots of people don't trust banks. Then he drifted down this end of the world and, for reasons best known to himself, decided to blue most of it. House — furniture — car. It's natural enough when you come to think of it.'

'Natural enough for a genuine lower middle-class man setting out on a new line of life,' Garth agreed; 'but I doubt that Rixton Williams is — or was — a *genuine* lower middle-class man. I have the impression that he created the character purely to kill Valerie Hadfield and the chauffeur, and then disappear. The limp in particular is very amateur; easiest gag in the world. These things being taken into account we are not looking for Rixton Williams but for the person who behaved *as* him. And that person, I insist, would in all probability have a bank account.'

'Why?' Richard persisted.

'Because Valerie Hadfield was not the kind of girl to be mixed up with a man who *hadn't!*' Garth sat back, beaming.

'Think back on what Timothy Potter said — 'I cannot understand a woman of Miss Hadfield's obvious style eloping with him. It seemed to me — unnatural.' Quite right! Why *should* she fall for such a specimen to the extent of eloping with him? Not she! The probability is that she only stayed beside him because she knew his real identity but *not* his villainous purpose, and we know from reports that socially she was hardly the kind of woman to tolerate anybody who could not advance her . . . '

Garth paused and selected a cheroot. 'No, she would never fall for a man who had no bank account! Therefore I insist that this unknown, hoping to make himself safe, refrained from having the money withdrawn in fivers and tenners which could be traced, and instead used one pound notes — but they in their own innocent way can be even more obvious. I'll have the banks check up on it the moment I get back to my office . . . And don't forget the letter we found, which had never come through the Twickenham mail. I'll gamble that Rixton Williams had

had that letter by him for long enough and simply took advantage of the absence of date.'

Richard sat stunned, bewildered by the fact that the bank evasion he had adopted had turned right round on him.

Garth turned to Chalfont. 'Now, Super, I want you to get the exact times — or as near as you can — when Williams came and went from his home, the bank, the agent's, everywhere. Get as near a full résumé of his actions as possible. From the times we may get a lead on where he actually came from. Since he arrived at three-thirty one afternoon and about the same time the following afternoon it seems to suggest a given period to cover a certain distance on each occasion.'

'London maybe,' Sergeant Whittaker said. 'It would take about that long by car, leaving after lunch.'

'Perhaps,' Garth agreed. 'Anyway, Super, check up on it.'

'I will, sir, and I'll let you know as soon as possible. Anything else?'

'For you, no. You made arrangements

to have the car brought to your headquarters here? Well, that's all for now. I've a few things to do on my own. Coming, Dick?'

Set-faced, Richard got to his feet slowly, keeping a hold over himself. On the way back to London he sat motionless as an image, lost in thought. Garth looked at him curiously.

'Something wrong?'

'Eh? No, I was just thinking. This case is pretty intricate, isn't it? But I've got an idea about it . . . I'll think it out and let you know my opinions. Meanwhile, however, I don't think I'll tag round with you any more today. I've things to do at home. Maybe I'll turn up again tomorrow.'

'Okay.' Garth gave a grin. 'But I notice you're clearing off just as you see that I've made a crack in the armour!'

Richard smiled, said nothing. At the corner of Whitehall he got out of the car and returned to his Jaguar parked on a public ground. Sliding into the driving seat he sat meditating. He had slipped — horribly, and if he didn't think of a logical explanation for the withdrawing of two thousand in ones from his bank — which the manager would be sure to remember — he might find a rope not very far from his neck.

But whilst one shred of reasonable doubt remained the law could not operate. That doubt might be made to function and throw Chief Inspector Garth off the track. An idea began to form in his mind.

After lunching at a restaurant, Richard drove on home. He told Baxter he was not requiring anything and would be leaving again almost immediately. He went to his study, took a stamp album out of the safe — an exquisite affair of leather with gold clasp and edges — wrapped it in brown paper and then hurried out again to his car.

Half an hour later he had the album on the desk of M. Cardieux, one of London's most eminent philatelists.

A desk light glowing down in a cone upon the stamps, M. Cardieux himself sat with his polished thinning grey hair swept back from his forehead, lens screwed in his eye, breathing harshly through thin-edged nostrils.

'*Magnifique*!' he commented at last, sitting back with a sigh and taking the lens from his eye. 'And Monsieur wishes to dispose? But why? The longer you keep a collection like this the more value it will accrue.'

'I just don't want it,' Richard answered, coming forward to the desk. 'I came across it among my late father's effects and I realised it was of some value. So I came to you . . . What is it worth?'

The dealer considered, then: 'To me, Monsieur, three thousand pounds. No more.'

'That suits me and I'm not going to bargain — but I will ask a favour of you. Let me have two thousand of it in pound notes and the remaining thousand in fives or tens.'

'Monsieur does not trust me?' asked the philatelist dryly.

'Nothing of the kind, M. Cardieux. It is simply that I have a special reason for wishing to have the money in that form.'

The philatelist got to his feet and

nodded. 'Very well, Mr. — er — ?'

'Graham,' Richard said briefly. 'Thomas Graham.'

'Very well, Mr. Graham. I will have a receipt made out for the stamps, which will contain an undertaking for the money to be paid in the form you ask — tomorrow morning. Naturally it is too late now for the bank to oblige us.'

Richard compressed his lips as he glanced at his watch. 'Yes, I suppose it is. A pity . . . Very well, I'll call first thing after the banks have opened.'

M. Cardieux excused himself gracefully, then returned presently with the receipt and undertaking in his hand, duly signed. Richard studied them, then put them in his wallet.

'Tomorrow morning then, M. Cardieux. And thank you. Good day.'

Richard left the establishment unobtrusively, walked along the block and down a side street to his car. By detouring routes he made his way back home again.

The car he left in the driveway, then hurrying up to his bedroom he got into the old suit and overalls he used while performing dirty jobs and returned downstairs to the outdoors. The mild, intermittently sunny afternoon was just right for further garage work, and the Baxters who had heard him come in saw him next through the back windows as he set the concrete mixer going and, half an hour later, began to add the necessary two inches of height to the garage floor with the wet, cloying substance, beating it down with the flat of the shovel.

Altogether he worked for about an hour, and in that time completed the flooring — the previous day he had worked mainly on the walls — then he returned inside to wash, shave, and change for his appointment with Joyce at quarter-to-five . . . It was just on the quarter-hour when he drew up his Jaguar outside the Blue Shadow in London to find the girl, in neat blue costume and hat, approaching from the opposite end of the short street.

'Timed to perfection,' she laughed, as he got out of the car.

He smiled, took her arm, and they went inside together. The inevitable Alberti was hovering beside the dried palms.

'Ah, Meester Harvey, gooda afternoon . . . An' Mees Prescott! Thees way . . . Same place? But of course!'

After Richard had given their order and Alberti departed, Joyce asked a question.

'How about your engagements? Did you cancel them?'

'Er — yes, except for a small one tomorrow morning. That I have to keep otherwise I'm free. And I've been thinking — before long I'd better be seeing the verger about the banns. No use dragging the engagement on, is there? Unless we use a special licence.'

Joyce shook her auburn head. 'Not for me, Ricky . . . I — I mean Dick. I want a full dress wedding. It's an important event to a woman, remember.'

'Either way suits me,' Richard smiled; then he became silent as Alberti reappeared with his big, loaded tray.

'A thought occurs to me,' Joyce said as she poured out the tea. 'You gave me an engagement ring on Saturday night' — the girl studied it on her finger — 'and it seems to me that if this other woman is still wearing hers too, and is asked about it, she might say that *you* gave it her. If that happened some folks round our neighbourhood might get to hear of it and they'd rise up and say they had just cause and impediment.'

Richard laughed softly. 'You don't have to worry, dearest. The woman in question will not give us away. That's as sure as tomorrow's sunrise.'

'Oh is it?' Joyce raised her level dark eyes to him for a moment. 'I don't think I could ever be *that* sure of a woman's silence — knowing women where a man is concerned, I mean.'

'I can,' he answered. 'You have my word that she will never speak, and she returned my ring. I wouldn't insult you by giving it to you, of course. Yours is a different one.'

'And what became of hers?'

'I — er — I got rid of it. Seemed the safest, though it was costly.'

Joyce said nothing, but he noticed a frown on her forehead as she began to eat.

'Look, Dick,' she said at last, 'I have

tried everything to convince myself it doesn't signify. I've asked dad what *he* thinks and he simply says I have my own decisions to make; and I've resolved to trust you to the end because I love you. *But* . . . I can't understand why I feel as though I ought to hold back. I wonder if it is because we'll not be happy together after all? That the thought of this past shadow will always be cropping up?'

'Why should it?' he asked harshly. 'People divorce each other and marry other people, and they live happily. I was only engaged to her, and a pretty offhand sort of business at that. It's childish to feel slighted because another woman happened to see me before you did!'

He expected sudden anger, but instead she nodded composedly.

'That must be what it is,' she decided. 'Childish! All right, the matter drops from here on.'

Richard wondered if it would. It seemed as though she sensed there was something criminal, something diabolical, somewhere and could not quite put her finger on it. He must never breathe so much as a hint of the name of Valerie Hadfield, never reveal how utterly he had destroyed her and everything belonging to her which could conceivably point back at him. He must keep quiet about her for the rest of his life.

Suddenly he felt appalled. Such an exacting punishment had never occurred to him. The eternal necessity of never using a word out of place in order that the vultures of the law could pounce on it and tear it to shreds . . .

The remainder of the time during and after tea he kept the conversation on commonplace topics. When darkness had settled outside they departed to the good wishes of the ebullient Alberti and went out to the Jaguar. Half an hour later the car was parked and they were seated in the Dress Circle of the Regal Theatre — Joyce well groomed and smiling, Richard trying to look genial.

What if he talked in his sleep? Or talked in the delirium of illness? Two thousand in one pound notes! The fact that Valerie's letter had been written a year ago and had never been delivered through the mails! Joyce's innate feeling that all was not well . . .

Though Joyce smiled as she listened to the songs, laughing openly now and again, he remained stone-faced, his eyes fixed on the stage. For some reason he kept thinking he was looking at Valerie when he saw the bright limes trained on the white-gowned soprano with the voice of a bird. Valerie who had died, whom he had murdered, whose body was . . .

To him, the two and a half hours had never seemed longer. As the girl and he went up the gangway steps with the press of warm, talkative people he glanced down at her.

'Drinks before supper? In the bar?' he asked.

'Why not?'

When they reached the top of the steps he escorted her into the long Spanish galleon type of bar with brass-banded tubs for tables.

'Well, I thought it was a lovely show,' Joyce said, sitting back in her chair and waiting. 'Did *you* enjoy it?'

'Yes, I — '

'Well, well, Dick — hel*lo! M*y turn to meet you for a change, eh?'

Richard glanced up, pulses racing. Chief Inspector Garth's voice!

'Hello, Garth,' With a smile that looked ghastly in the amber lighting Richard got to his feet. 'Been to the show?'

'Yes. Even the police like to relax sometimes.'

'Er — May I introduce Miss Prescott? My fiancée. Dear, this is Chief Inspector Garth of Scotland Yard, a good friend of mine.'

'Oh, really?' Joyce smiled up at him as he bowed genially. 'But I always thought Chief Inspectors were stern-looking men with bowler hats which they never take off.'

'You mustn't believe all you see in films, Miss Prescott,' Garth laughed. 'You behold a very ordinary human being who spends his time becoming increasingly astonished at the subterfuges of his fellowmen, and whose lack of vigorous exercise makes him a martyr to dyspepsia. Unromantic, eh?' He turned and glanced towards a distant table-tub, motioned. A dark, still-pretty woman nearing middle age got up and came through the smoke haze.

'Your wife?' Richard inquired tautly.

'Yes indeed . . . Ah, here you are, my dear. Meet Miss Prescott, and here is Mr. Harvey, the chemist who gives us a hand now and again. You've heard me speak of him.'

'I have indeed,' Mrs. Garth said, smiling and shaking hands. 'My hubby is very fond of you and your chemicals, Mr. Harvey.'

Richard smiled, said nothing. He felt like a man waiting for the shot of a gun in his heart. At any moment Garth might let something slip about Valerie, and not being exactly a fool Joyce would immediately start to put things together . . .

'Well, I — ' Richard broke off and gestured. 'Will you come over and have a drink, Garth?'

'No, seems to me it's time I ordered something for you. We might as well make a party of it. Hey, there!' He motioned to a waiter dressed as a pirate. 'Bring those drinks over here, please.'

The man nodded his scarlet-bandeaued head and came across with two glasses of stout. Garth sat down heavily and beamed, his wife sitting behind him. As Richard crept down into his chair the port he had ordered was brought and set down too.

'I'll pay,' Garth insisted firmly.

For one piercing second Richard thought of bolting . . . Then he forced himself to relax. Valerie Hadfield's body could never be found. And without the *corpus delicti* the law was impotent . . .

' . . . and her top notes were really exquisite,' Joyce was saying, as he drifted back to realities. 'Don't you think so, Dick?'

'I — er — yes indeed,' he acknowledged, picking up his port.

'Your fiancé seems rather preoccupied at present, Miss Prescott,' Garth commented, grinning. 'He should be like me — shut up shop completely when he goes out for a change. Only place I ever talk shop is at the club, and then it's only to save myself from being bored to distraction by stories of what happened to the old codgers who were in at the relief of Mafeking.'

There was silence for a moment as Garth drank from his glass. His wife said nothing. She appeared to be a happy, understanding woman who preferred to let her husband do the talking.

'You're working on the Valerie Hadfield case, aren't you, Inspector?' Joyce asked presently — and Richard set down his glass so clumsily on the tub top he spilt some of the wine.

'Nerves?' Garth asked dryly; then he looked at Joyce and nodded. 'Yes, I am — and I suppose you noticed it from the brief announcements in the newspapers. Well, I don't expect your doctor to tell me the exact state of your health . . . Now, what about some more drinks?'

Richard found himself breathing hard, partly in relief. Garth had deliberately cut the subject dead. But as long as he remained in the party he was a potential menace, especially with Joyce so obviously curious.

'No more drink for me, thanks,' Richard said, as the pale eyes glanced inquiry at him. 'In fact I think we'd better be on our way to supper, hadn't we, Joyce?'

She looked at her half-empty glass. 'I'll just finish this first.'

She drained it, set it down, then got to her feet. Garth rose too and shook her hand. He was smiling generously.

'Coming down in the morning, Dick?' he asked.

Richard hesitated as he saw Joyce's dark eyes glance at him curiously.

'I — er — probably,' he muttered. 'See how things go, anyway. Good night, Mrs. Garth. 'Night, Garth.'

He turned aside and caught Joyce's arm tightly, moved her so firmly she fell over her chair and then stumbled.

'For heaven's sake, Ricky, what's the hurry?' she demanded. 'I've given my leg an awful crack — '

'Don't *call* me that!' he breathed harshly. 'You hear? *Don't!*'

By this time they were some distance from Garth, but there was no way of telling whether he had heard the nickname of 'Ricky'. Glancing anxiously back across the smoke filled room, Joyce limping painfully beside him, Richard saw that square, broad figure still standing by the table-tub, cheroot jutting from the corner of the mouth, the impassive rigidity of the death-mask on his face.

13

To Richard's surprise Joyce did not flare at him for his almost brutal demand for her to cease calling him 'Ricky'. Instead she set her firm little jaw and walked with him in silence to the lift — and so down to the theatre foyer. She still said nothing as they crossed the road to the car park. Richard did not attempt to break the quiet as he drove through the busy streets to the neighbourhood of the Blue Shadow, but when at last they were both seated at supper with the tireless Alberti retreating from them Richard looked at the girl curiously.

'Sorry I spoke so snappishly, Joyce,' he apologised. 'It was just that that name gets on my nerves.'

'Name?' Joyce repeated absently, looking at him, and he felt a shock at the whiteness of her face. 'Oh, that . . . I'd forgotten about it. It's something else. What did Inspector Garth mean by asking you if you were coming down in the morning?'

'Why the devil do you have to question every one of my actions?' he demanded fiercely. 'Hang it all, Joyce, I'm not accountable to you for everything I do!'

'Maybe not, but why should you want to go and see Inspector Garth?'

'Why not? You heard him say I do pathological work for the Yard sometimes. That fact you know yourself . . . ' Richard seized his chance. 'And that's what I'm doing now, but of course the fact can't be advertised in case it helps the criminals.'

'What criminals? Those connected with Valerie Hadfield and Rixton Williams?'

Richard looked at her fixedly and answered, 'Yes!'

'Then I don't understand it!' she said, sighing. 'What need is there of your services at the Yard at this juncture? I've read the few details about the case, same as everybody else, but . . . Well, both this actress and her apparent lover have vanished into thin air. As far as I can see there's no *need* for a pathological investigation.'

Richard took out a cigarette and lighted it. His nerves steadied a little as he inhaled. Absently he watched Alberti called away urgently by an under-waiter and wondered disinterestedly who could want Alberti at this hour. Never gave the man any rest — like himself . . .

'You forget the chauffeur, Joyce,' he found himself saying. 'Pathology is playing quite an important part concerning his death. There'll be an inquest on him and the Yard is ranging the facts. I'm in on that. That's the important business I've been on, only I'm not supposed to tell anybody.'

'Garth didn't seem to mind me knowing,' Joyce pointed out, looking at the supper as though she wondered what it was.

Richard turned and faced her directly.

'Look here, Joyce, what are you *getting* at? What's on your mind? If you are nursing some absurd, dark suspicion then for God's sake drag it out into the open — but don't keep on with these confounded pin-pricks.'

Her face was still white.

'I can't help remembering,' she said slowly, 'that inhuman look on your face when I called you 'Ricky' in front of Inspector Garth — granting that he heard it. It was a terrible look . . . It frightened me!'

'You're imagining things, Joyce!'

'I'm also remembering something else,' she went on steadily. 'You said you were going out of town and couldn't see me for a week, and yet dad noticed that you'd found time to build a little bit of your garage. That means you told me a deliberate lie . . . And what is more,' Joyce continued, with strained emphasis, 'the week you were missing — or said you would be missing — was the same week during which Rixton Williams appeared and disappeared, according to the newspapers, anyway. The final disappearance occurred last Friday, and on the Saturday morning you came to me and said all your business was finished. You couldn't have been working for the Yard then because the disappearance of Valerie Hadfield and Rixton Williams hadn't happened before last Friday.'

Richard looked at the coffee going cold, then across the café to where the diners were flocking in from the night shows — and, unusually, Alberti was still leaving things to the care of the under-waiters.

'From all of which tangled jumble of nonsense and coincidence you infer what?' Richard asked finally, a razor-sharp edge in his voice.

'I don't know.' Joyce got to her feet abruptly, deathly, her dark eyes half frightened and half bitter. 'But the feeling is so strong on me that there is something *wrong* that I'm not going any further with our engagement . . . ' She tugged at the ring on her finger and dropped it on the spotless cloth. 'Good night,' she added.

Richard couldn't believe it for a moment. He stared at the ring, then at her slender figure in the blue costume as she went gracefully across the café. Irritably he put the ring in his pocket and motioned a waiter.

'But you haven't eaten anything, sir!' the man protested, as he was asked for the check.

'Never mind that!' Richard retorted. 'Give me the check . . . And where's Alberti, by the way?'

'Talking business with a gentlemen, sir . . . ' The waiter put the check down and bowed his way from the table. Scowling, Richard paid at the cash desk, and then stalked outside. No sign of Joyce. Presumably she had gone to the Underground station.

He got into the Jaguar, drove away from the kerb, leaving behind him Inspector Garth and Alberti in the manager's office.

Garth was pacing slowly up and down, cheroot between his teeth.

'And that's all you can tell me, eh? The manager wouldn't know any more if he were here?'

'Nothing more at all, sir,' Alberti slapped his hands on his fat thighs emphatically. 'I tella all that I know. Meester Harvey he comes in here many times — so, an' often with thees Miss Prescott . . .'

'For how long has he been doing this?' Garth snapped, jaw muscles bulging.

'Er, for perhaps eight months, mebbe a beet more. But no less. I tella the truth!'

'Has she ever called him by the name of 'Ricky' within your hearing?'

''Reeky? Ah, no — not as I know.'

Finally Garth shrugged. 'All right, thanks,' he said briefly. 'And don't forget to keep this conversation to yourself. Good night.'

'Gooda the night, sir . . . '

Garth left the way he had come, by the side door where the diners could not see him. In the alleyway outside he climbed into a taxi where his wife was waiting.

'Why did we have to chase Mr. Harvey and Miss Prescott in that fashion, Mort?' she asked curiously. 'What in the world suddenly bit you?'

'Perhaps a mad dog,' he answered broodingly. 'I'll know for sure as time goes on.'

* * *

As he drove home, Richard was thinking furiously. He had mapped out everything to the last tiny detail, yet at every step he made now some new unexpected thing seemed to crop up. It was frightening, and a killing strain on the nerves.

Had Chief Inspector Garth heard the name 'Ricky,' and was he even now working things out in his analytical fashion; and would Joyce think further, abandon all pretence of love, and go and tell Garth everything she suspected? Well, what if she did? They *still* could not produce Valerie Hadfield's body!

But it was galling, stunning even, to have fought so hard for the girl he loved, to have twice come so near to possessing her, and then to find her turned away by some new suspicion. The idea of wiping her out — as he had the chauffeur — before she could say anything was the thought furthest from his mind. He felt that this showed how much he loved her. What failed to penetrate the blur of his egomania was the fact that he didn't want to kill Joyce for three reasons: he wanted her for himself; he knew another murder after the chauffeur incident might easily prove his undoing; and he was afraid of Dr. Howard Prescott. A good deal of calm, calculating reasoning went on behind that ready smile. The murder of his daughter would arouse every outraged instinct and might turn the pleasant philanthropist into a ruthless avenger.

When he got into the house, leaving the Jaguar in the drive because he did not want the bother of garaging it in his present turbulent state of mind, Richard found that the Baxters had as usual gone to bed.

He made up for his missing supper with sandwiches he prepared for himself in the kitchen; then instead of going to bed he went into the laboratory, switched on all the lights and studied the place circumspectly from end to end. It took him an hour, but at the end of it he was completely satisfied that not a single clue remained if Garth should ever get this far.

If Garth should ever get this far . . . There was a vast difference between him perhaps having heard the name 'Ricky' to getting a warrant issued for murder. No *corpus delicti* either — and a cast-iron alibi.

Somewhat easier in his mind Richard

left the laboratory and went up to his bedroom. Thoughts, grim and macabre, kept him wakeful.

* * *

By dawn, after a hellish night, Richard had come to a decision. He would continue to stay beside Chief Inspector Garth and give him no reason to think he was afraid. If the worst happened he still had his alibi and the knowledge of the missing *corpus delicti*. Even if Joyce decided to talk it could only end the same way . . . Suspicion would be piled on suspicion, certainly, but without proof it couldn't mean anything.

Immediately after breakfast, and a glance through the morning paper, which failed to tell anything, Richard set off for the city in the Jaguar, made his first call the establishment of M. Cardieux. The money was ready and waiting in a large heavily sealed envelope. Richard took it, thanked the philatelist gravely, and put the envelope away carefully in the cubby-hole of his car.

Returning home again, he went through to the study with the package. He transferred two thousand in ones into his safe, and the remaining amount he locked away in a drawer in his desk. Then, somewhat relieved, he went out to the car again and so back to the city. It was close on eleven o'clock as he mounted the stairs to Chief Inspector Garth's office.

Sergeant Whittaker admitted him and he entered slowly, expecting to find a pair of merciless eyes upon him, but instead Garth greeted him with a cordial wave of the hand and stabbed a finger towards the armchair by the doorway.

'Still waiting for my downfall, Dick?' Garth asked dryly, leafing through the papers on his desk.

'Why not?' Richard asked. 'Every time I come to see how you're getting on I find you squatting here reading reports and letters . . . How are things going?'

'Oh — not at all badly.' Garth sat back, selected a cheroot, then thumped his chest meditatively. 'I've got the full reports from Divisional Inspector Whiteside and Superintendent Chalfont.

Whiteside's report tells how the chauffeur left the theatre at such and such a time, how a neighbour at the end of the avenue in which he lived and garaged the car saw him turn into the avenue and head towards the garage about eleven-thirty . . . Said neighbour was just drawing the curtains in the bedroom preparatory to switching on the light . . . One of those little things that I said might happen.'

'Interesting,' Richard acknowledged.

'Peter Cranston had somebody with him in the Daimler,' Garth added. 'Naturally it was too dark to see whether it was man or woman, but it doesn't require genius to know that whoever it was who murdered Cranston was *that person*.' Garth deliberated for a moment. 'Unfortunately there are no details about this person, no clues as to why he or she did it, or *what* he or she did. The person was extra careful evidently since all the fingerprint impressions we can find on the front of the car, where this unknown person was seated, were Cranston's own.'

'And those in the back of the car, not yet identified?' Richard asked.

'Probably from a friend of Valerie Hadfield's. A man friend, since prints are distinctive of sex. It would be too big an assumption, without a good deal of corroborative evidence, to say that they belong to the person who murdered her. We prefer facts here — not guesswork.'

Richard said nothing, mentally cursing the neighbour who had been drawing bedroom window curtains. Garth turned aside and picked up another report.

'This is from Chalfont — a very commendable report on the comings and goings of the mysterious Rixton Williams. He first appeared in Twickenham on the afternoon of Thursday, October tenth, and came and went pretty methodically, sleeping some nights and not others . . . I'll not weary you with all the details and times,' Garth added, grinning, 'but you can take it for granted that we know almost to the minute the times he came and went. Most of the information has come from Timothy Potter, who has been invaluable to us.'

Richard wished he could ask for the details without sounding too suspicious

— but that simply could not be.

'Well,' he admitted, 'you've been busier than I thought. What happens now?'

Garth shifted uncomfortably. 'At this moment, I'm going to have a brandy-and-soda and try and shift this infernal breakfast lodging in my chest. Hand it over, Whittaker. Join me, Dick?'

'A bit early for me — but I don't want to be unsociable,' Richard said.

Whittaker poured out the drinks and then went back to his own small table in the corner, began to work at a noiseless typewriter transcribing from shorthand notes.

'I like your fiancée, Dick,' Garth commented presently, setting down his empty glass and stifling a belch. 'Nice girl . . . Known her long?'

'Long enough to be very fond of her,' Richard answered, and he drained his own glass and put it on the desk. Then he waited, on the defensive, but Garth did not pursue the subject.

'You were asking what I'm going to do next? Well, frankly, I don't know! I have to attend the inquest on that chauffeur at eleven-forty-five. Shouldn't take long, but it means I'm not going far from here . . . So I'm afraid there isn't much that will interest you.'

Richard nodded and got to his feet. 'All right — then I'll get some business of my own finished up. This afternoon, maybe?'

Garth's pale eyes looked at him through the haze of the cheroot.

'Surely! I'll probably have had the bank reports in by then. That should start the wheels moving again.'

At the door Richard hesitated and looked back, a taut smile on his big mouth. 'No power on earth will make you admit that this is a perfect crime, will it?' he asked dryly.

Garth looked up. 'What makes you think it is?'

'Everything! Total disappearance of Valerie Hadfield, and even more total disappearance of her killer — if she *was* killed — and likewise total disappearance of Peter Cranston's killer. No clue — not as much as a fingerprint. If that isn't a perfect crime, just what *do* you want?'

Garth smiled suddenly. 'This isn't such

a perfect crime as it may look superficially, Dick. Later I'll probably tell you why.'

Their eyes met for a moment, full on, but Richard read no hint of hostility or suspicion in those colourless depths. With a faint smile he turned and left. Whittaker stopped typing, got to his feet and came over to the desk. Garth sat looking at the drained glass of brandy-and-soda Richard had used.

'Okay, sir?' Whittaker asked.

'Get it tested,' Garth said briefly, and the sergeant straddled his fingers inside the glass and carried it from the room. In a few minutes he was back.

'They'll report as soon as possible,' he announced; and then he looked at his superior pensively. 'Do you really think that Mr. Harvey *is* mixed up in this lot, sir?'

'In this business, Whittaker, I'm not entitled to think — only to prove certain conclusions on known facts. Richard Harvey has known this girl Joyce Prescott for approximately eight months — if Alberti at the Blue Shadow is to be relied upon — and the general impression is that he loves her deeply. All right . . . so fish around and see what you get out of that fact.'

'A motive?' Whittaker suggested.

'Exactly!' Garth confirmed, slapping his palm on the desk. 'The one damned thing that has stopped us so far in this business has been the *reason* for killing Valerie Hadfield — or otherwise causing her to disappear. We still don't know if she *is* dead. But now we see a motive — purely theoretical, on which we cannot pin an atom of guilt as yet. But consider: suppose Richard Harvey *is* the man who has been in Valerie's life, and that he fell in love with somebody else whom he liked much more? What course then but to *kill* Valerie Hadfield?'

'There might have been other ways of shaking free of her, sir.'

'Not Valerie Hadfield!' Garth declared. 'You study the reports, take a consensus on them all, the folk who knew her, and you'll soon see that she was not the forgiving type. I imagine that once her hooks landed in a man they'd stay there

— until death us do part.'

'It's — it's unbelievable!' Whittaker said finally. 'A man like Mr. Harvey doing such a thing . . . Wealthy, clever, genial . . . '

'In our business, Whitty, we've known murderesses with a face like the Madonna and child-stranglers as holy-looking as an archbishop. Remember we've more or less satisfied ourselves on the point that Valerie Hadfield would only take on a man of position and money, *not* the kind of man Rixton Williams seems to have been. Richard Harvey, I'm sorry to say, fits the bill for money and position. We have also to remember his scorn for Scotland Yard and his skilled handling of chemistry. That makes him damned dangerous, even clever enough to perform the perfect crime he's always talking about . . . '

Garth scowled from beneath lowered brows.

'About a fortnight ago we were on the topic of perfect crimes at the Stag Club, with relative anecdotes concerning Crippen and a few others. Dick bet me that a perfect crime could exist even in these scientific days, and I'm — almost — sure . . . '

'But there's not a single clue anywhere to show that Mr. Harvey had any connection with Valerie, sir,' Whittaker pointed out. 'Her flat has been turned inside out, her car examined, her acquaintances cross-examined, and nobody has ever mentioned Mr. Harvey.'

'Only one man would perhaps know of it,' Garth answered, alert again. 'The chauffeur! In the back of Valerie's car are unexplained fingerprints. They belong to somebody not yet identified — and those same prints are in the flat. In view of having found a motive, however hazy it may be, I'm going to check Dick's fingerprints on those of the glass that contained b. and s. And since the prints *are* in the car the chauffeur must obviously have known the identity of the person — therefore he had to be removed.'

'But no fingerprints to prove the chauffeur's killer,' Whittaker said, clamping down on the essentials of logic.

'No. The absence of which points again

to a mind remarkably agile in foreseeing police procedure . . . '

'You have a possible motive, sir,' Whittaker said, 'and other points, to a degree, fit in — wealth, position, *etceteras*. But isn't there something stronger?'

'Yes, the nickname of 'Ricky',' Garth answered him. 'It is the same nickname which Valerie had for Rixton Williams, and it was on that note left in the Twickenham house. I've been through all the letters — the one from Twickenham in particular — and one fact emerges. Namely, that Richard Harvey — granting that it *is* he — took advantage of the fact that Valerie always wrote to him with only the day instead of the date at the top of her letters. We know that that particular letter from Twickenham is a year old at least, so the assumption is that Harvey — possessing the letter — made an appointment as Rixton Williams, knowing he was on safe ground because he *already had the answer* in Valerie's own handwriting. Understand? He made it look as if he had written Valerie and that she answered him accepting his proposition. He insisted that she come to his home, which fitted in perfectly with her pre-written answer. It made it seem she really was in love with Rixton Williams and went to see him of her own free will.'

'Crikey!' Whittaker said blankly. 'Yes!'

'The name of 'Rixton Williams' is the next significant thing — a Christian name of such a phonetic sound that it could abbreviate to 'Ricky' without seeming too outlandish; though, as I said earlier, 'Rixy' would have been more appropriate. Thereby it matches the name 'Ricky' on the pre-written note from Valerie . . . *But*, Whitty, the whole scheme is dependent on the name 'Ricky' never being used again — or at least within hearing of anybody knowing Valerie, and particularly within hearing of the Police. Last night Dick's fiancée used that name for *him*. I just caught it, and I never saw such a look of diabolical ferocity on a man's face as there was at that moment. He grabbed the girl's arm, pulled her away so violently she banged her leg on her chair . . . Well, from now on I don't feel at all comfortable concerning Miss Joyce Prescott's future.'

'Since the ink on that letter is over a year old,' Whittaker said slowly, 'it means Mr. Harvey must have known Valerie that long ago.'

'Exactly — unless the evidence is somehow amazingly twisted.'

'Do you think Valerie Hadfield knew who Rixton Williams was?'

'I think that she must have done, finally — judging from her manner as described by Timothy Potter, but it is possible that she never expected anything dastardly was in store for her.' Garth got to his feet, crushed out his cheroot in the ashtray.

'The hunt for absolute proof comes next — but I'm willing to gamble that Richard Harvey and Rixton Williams are one and the same person . . . To leg him down will be difficult. But I'll get him — sure as he's born!'

His fist thumped firmly on his desk; then Garth smiled wryly. 'Now I must be on my way to that damned inquest.'

14

Not knowing whether to feel disturbed or satisfied by Chief Inspector Garth's manner, Richard lunched in the city and returned to Scotland Yard towards half-past two to find Garth writing busily at his desk. He glanced up as Richard entered, no sign of hostility about him.

'Well, how did the inquest go?' Richard settled in the armchair by the doorway.

Garth shrugged. 'It merely determined that Peter Cranston met his death at the hands of a person or persons unknown. The rest is up to me.'

'You're pretty sure then that it was murder?'

'I have yet to see the man who can commit suicide by hitting himself in the back of the neck with a tyre-lever and then put the tyre-lever back,' Garth answered grimly.

Was there a sharp cutting edge in the voice? Richard sensed that Garth was holding something back, waiting to explode it at a chosen moment. But Garth prolonged the suspense by continuing with his writing, and Sergeant Whittaker typed away on his noiseless machine in the corner. Then at last Garth put his pen down, sat back, and selected a cheroot from his case.

'Dick,' he said quietly without looking at him, 'why did you draw two thousand pounds in one pound notes from your bank on October eleventh, a week last Friday?'

'I thought you'd get round to it finally,' Richard said, sighing. 'I've been scared stiff of you jumping to the wrong conclusion ever since I heard you mentioning that cash in Twickenham. Naturally, I didn't have anything to do with the Valerie Hadfield business.'

'I never said that you did. I merely asked you why you drew two thousand in ones from your bank. I got back here after the inquest to find the first local bank reports coming through and one from your bank was among them. I went over and had a chat with the manager.'

'By what damned right?' Richard demanded angrily. 'Look here, Garth, I know my rights as a citizen and you had no reason for making scandal about me — !'

'I made no scandal,' Garth said levelly, quite unmoved. 'I merely checked up. Bank managers are accustomed to that when something is — er — not quite as it should be. I merely ask: *why* did you draw out two thousand in ones on the very day that Rixton Williams deposited a similar amount in a bank in Twickenham?'

Richard gave a crooked smile. 'Just to show you how crazy you are, Garth, you can come and look at that two thousand in notes in my home this minute! In my safe! It can't be there and disseminated about Twickenham as well, can it?'

'Granting it is the same two thousand, no,' Garth admitted.

'Damn you, Garth! What do you have to twist things for? Come and look for yourself!'

Garth smiled round his cheroot. 'Maybe I will, just to take the damned impulsiveness out of you. Hang it all,

Dick, I'm your friend and you know I have a job to do. I'm not throwing any accusations at you. I'm merely asking a question. Why did you withdraw two thousand pounds?'

'I did it to give to Howard Prescott's orphanage — he's founded one, as you may know. I felt that I should, seeing I'm going to marry his daughter. I've more money than I'll ever need, and so . . . Well, just as a gift.'

'Mmmm . . . But why in one pound notes? Why not a cheque?'

'I was going to send it anonymously, and a cheque would have given me away, just as five or ten pound notes would have done had Prescott chosen to investigate. I didn't want my act of — well, generosity, to be found out.'

'Uh-huh.' Garth drew hard on his cheroot. 'Then you were *going* to send it? Why didn't you? What held things up?'

'You are holding things up.' Richard told him calmly. 'I was going to do it yesterday, then you blasted off about the two thousand in ones and I thought perhaps I'd better hold my horses.'

Garth thumped his chest. 'I can't see what difference that would have made. Two thousand couldn't be in the orphanage *and* in Twickenham, any more than two thousand could be in your *home* and in Twickenham . . . ' He got to his feet. 'Anyway, I think I'll come over to your place in the purely routine way and take a look at those two thousand notes. Just in the line of duty, you understand.'

Richard forced a grin and rose. 'As you like. I've nothing to hide.'

'Y'know, you're not entirely alone in being a drawer of two thousand in ones,' Garth added, grinning as he got into his overcoat. 'I have reports of three other people at different banks who also drew money in that form on the self-same day — all of them local enough to be a possible Rixton Williams. We'll check back on them all, but since you're the nearest I'll start with you . . . ' Garth turned and glanced at Whittaker as he still plugged the typewriter.

'Back later, Whitty. Try and get that report finished in detail for when I return:

the Assistant Commissioner will want to see it.'

Richard followed Garth from the office and glanced questioningly as they emerged on the pavement opposite to his Jaguar.

'Might as well ride in your tub for a change,' Garth said. 'I get a bit sick of that official car of mine.'

'Not often a suspect drives the Chief Inspector to the spot in question, is it, Garth?' Richard asked after a while, nosing through the traffic. 'Co-operation to the *nth* degree, eh?'

'You're not a suspect, Dick; you simply happen to have come straight in line with circumstantial evidence. I've got to check on it or else have the Assistant Commissioner jump down my throat. He's already been asking me how much longer this Valerie Hadfield business is going to take.'

Around three o'clock, they gained Richard's home. The sprawling old-fashioned residence was no new place to Garth: he had been here before when pathological business for the Yard had demanded it — but his eyes did stray to the half-completed garage and remain there for a moment. Then he got out of the car in the driveway and waited for Richard to join him.

Together they entered the house and Richard led the way across the wide hall to his study, motioning Baxter away as he came shambling out of the back regions.

'Take a seat, Garth,' Richard invited briefly, nodding to a chair. 'I'll soon dispel your suspicions for you.'

Garth remained standing, his hat on the desk, his pale eyes watching Richard as he went to the safe and opened it. Taking out the two thousand one pound notes he had collected from M. Cardieux that morning he tossed them contemptuously on the desk.

'Do you want to count them?' he asked briefly.

'Counting or examining 'em won't do me any good, Dick, and you know it. Pound notes can't be traced — not in the usual way; unless they're marked or something beforehand. I only wanted to satisfy myself as to the truth of your statement so I can tell it to the Assistant

Commissioner. I don't like having to butt in on you like this, you know, and I appreciate the way you've helped me. You must realise I find my job distasteful sometimes.'

Richard picked the bundle of notes up again, put them back into the safe and closed the door. Then he went over to the cocktail cabinet. 'Brandy-and-soda?' he asked.

Garth grinned. 'Thanks for remembering the indigestion. Yes, I'd be glad of it.'

He turned aside to survey the room in its ordered cosiness. In an apparently idle glance, he noted everything he needed, and arrived at no conclusions worth retaining. Then Richard had come to him with the glass of brandy-and-soda held forth. They both drank with the easy calmness of old friends and at length Richard took the empty glasses and put them back on the cabinet.

'Well, Garth, what now? Satisfied I'm no suspect?'

'Good Lord, man, of course!' Garth clapped him on the shoulder and smiled. 'You, of all people! As if you could be, knowing the array of power there is behind Scotland Yard . . . No, I'm quite satisfied, but now I am here I'd like to look at your laboratory — unless you're on with something secret?'

Richard hesitated. To refuse would seem suspicious: to accept might be to gratify some unexplained curiosity that Garth was hiding behind his disarming smile.

'You can look around with pleasure — though I can't think why you should want to. First you say you no longer suspect me, and then you ask to see my laboratory?'

'Purely as a friend, Dick.' Garth picked up his hat as he followed Richard into the hall. 'That lab of yours has always had a curious fascination for me.'

Richard led the way into the annex and Garth strolled in, walking slowly down the space beside the centre benches and the right hand wall. Once again his pale eyes were darting everywhere. He turned as Richard caught up with him and stood looking round with hands pushed in his overcoat pockets.

'Lovely stuff you've got, Dick!' Garth wagged his head admiringly. 'X-ray equipment, liquid air compressor . . . Everything of the best, eh? Mmm — and ground glass windows too. Don't mean anybody peeping in, do you?'

'You know as well as I do, Garth, that I have to do important research jobs sometimes, and secrecy is vital.'

'Yes, I suppose it is.'

Garth's gaze wandered to the rack where tools were fitted and then back again to a contemplation of the bench beside him. The movement of his eyes had been so swift that Richard had hardly noticed it: certainly he did not know that Garth had, in that one snapshotting glance, calculated the number and type of tools in the rack.

'Incidentally . . . ' Garth turned from meditation. 'Did I see a garage outside? I didn't think you had one.'

'Why such interest?' Richard asked. 'You did see one, as a matter of fact — part of one, anyway. But — '

'I'm only wondering if you are building it yourself — though I suppose you must be otherwise the contractors would be working on it at this time of day.' Garth smiled. 'You didn't forget to tell all of us how you were building this annex, remember . . . Though why a man of your capabilities should stick bricks and mortar together for a hobby I don't know. Still, since I do crossword puzzles for a spare time occupation I guess both of us are crazy!'

Richard motioned to the side door of the laboratory and opened it. Garth followed him outside and they stood looking at the half-completed structure, the walls part of the way up and the floor bedded down solid. Garth's eyes wandered to a plane, saw, and general building tackle and materials.

'I'm building it for Joyce,' Richard explained, his iciness slowly thawing as he saw Garth was quite inoffensive. 'She likes the Jaguar and there's no sense in having it pushed away in a public garage when it can be on the premises. Didn't matter for me alone but different when you have a wife.'

He waved a hand to the structure and

for a moment Garth's eyes sifted to an oval patch of plaster just above the inside of Richard's wrist.

'Did you do that building this?' he questioned.

'Eh? Do what?' Richard turned to him quickly; then he understood. 'Oh, my wrist? No, I did it in the lab — deep flesh cut on a piece of metal. Nothing serious.'

Garth said nothing. His gaze strayed to the bags of powder, to the concrete mixer, the stacked timber, the pyramid of bricks. Richard watched him intently, trying to make up his mind whether Garth was just casually curious or whether he was trying to prove some point of his own.

'Oh, Mr. Richard, sir . . . ' Old Baxter appeared in the doorway of the laboratory. 'There's somebody on the telephone — wishes to speak to you.'

Richard muttered an excuse to Garth, then hurried back through the laboratory. Garth watched him go, smiled to himself and stepped back amidst the benches and test tubes. Quickly he searched under the benches until he came to that commonplace adjunct of any laboratory — the swab-bin. He looked inside it, shifted the waste rags about hurriedly, then whipped out a bloodstained piece of cotton wool and thrust it in his pocket. Silently he drifted outside again just as Richard came hurrying back to join him.

'It's for you Garth — Sergeant Whittaker. He didn't want to ask for you without asking me first if you were here. He says he has something important.'

Garth went back through the laboratory and Richard stood studying his retreating figure. Once again the brief relapse into ease of mind was undergoing convulsions. Quickly he looked about the laboratory. Nothing was changed; and as he knew already from careful checking and rechecking there was not a single thing out of place or any clue as to his activities . . . At least, not as far as he could remember.

When Garth came back there was a curious half-drawn look on his face, as though he had received a shock and had not fully recovered.

'I'll have to get back right away,' he said. 'Something important has turned up

. . . See you again one of these days if you care to drop in at my office. Thanks for showing me round.'

'Shall I drive you back into town?' Richard offered, walking with him to the drive outside.

'No, no, I'll take the tube. I've one or two calls to make anyway.'

'Just what *has* happened, Garth? I'm as interested in this case as you, remember.'

Garth shrugged. 'To be truthful I don't know the exact details myself: Whittaker wouldn't give them over the 'phone. Just like him — always secretive . . . Well, see you again, Dick.'

He went off down the drive, leaving Richard gazing after him in puzzlement. What else *could* there be that had turned up? Perhaps Joyce? Richard's grey eyes hardened; then he shrugged. What if it were? His alibi was perfect . . .

He turned back towards the garage, and decided it might be as well to put in a few hours work on it until dusk. Joyce was no longer the incentive behind him wanting to finish it, but he had simply *got* to complete it, as fast as possible, and preferably before Chief Inspector Garth came up again on a 'routine' round . . .

Meanwhile. Garth was striding through the mellow afternoon. His death-mask was completely in place.

'The Goddamned swine!' he murmured once, the muscles of his jaw suddenly taut; then he swung off the road in which Richard's home stood and turned into a side street. The rest he accomplished mainly by instinct and asking his way. He had noticed the home of the Prescotts when they had driven up from London: Richard had pointed it out to him.

At the house a grey-haired woman of middle age and ample bust opened the door.

'Might I see Miss Prescott?' Garth asked briefly.

'The name, sir?' the housekeeper asked.

'I'm Chief Inspector Garth of Scotland Yard . . . '

There was a movement in the hall behind. Joyce herself came into view as the housekeeper retired back to her duties.

'Why, Inspector Garth! Of all people!'

'I'd just like a word with you, Miss Prescott. If you don't mind — '

'Why no, of course not. Please come in.'

He took off his hat, and followed her across the hall into the study. Her father glanced up in surprise from his desk.

'This is Chief Inspector Garth of Scotland Yard, dad,' the girl said rather timidly. 'You remember me telling you I met him last night when I was with — Dick? My father, Inspector — Dr. Prescott. You see, we — we have no secrets from each other, so whatever you have to say to me can be said before him too.'

'How are you, Doctor?' Garth shook hands as Howard Prescott came round the desk. 'And I may as well tell both of you I don't exactly like my job at the moment. I wanted to check up on something from you, Miss Prescott . . . Last night, as you left Dick — I'm calling him that because he is as much my friend as he is your fiancé — did I hear you call him . . . 'Ricky'?'

'Yes.' Joyce spoke very quietly as she motioned Garth to an easy chair. Then she added, 'And he's not my fiancé any more, Inspector. It's all over.'

Garth looked sympathetic. 'Oh, I'm sorry about that. Just why?'

As Joyce remained silent, her father said: 'You see, Inspector, Joyce here is a girl of most vacillating moods. She has always been that way. All eagerness in one direction, then the next moment she flies off at a tangent and tears everything she has done up by the roots. That's how it is now. Fortunately she tells me everything, so I can usually straighten her out. Last night she came home with the conviction that Dick is mixed up in the disappearance of this woman Valerie Hadfield, and because of that she's given the poor chap his ring back and has sworn never to see him again.'

'What started this idea, Miss Prescott? Was it the name of 'Ricky'?'

She turned suddenly from the window where the weak sunshine made her hair like a copper halo.

'Yes — it was that really.' She sounded

half afraid. 'Somehow I — I sort of tied up the name of Ricky with Rixton Williams and then . . . Oh, I don't know!' She made a helpless gesture. 'Perhaps I am being unforgivably mean towards Dick, but for the moment I had the awful feeling that *he* caused Valerie Hadfield to disappear.'

'As to that,' Garth said, 'you have only the guide of your own judgement. I'd rather like to know how long you've been engaged to him.'

'Eight months.'

'Forgive me if I sound indelicate,' Garth said, 'but isn't that rather a long engagement?'

'There was a reason.' Joyce answered. 'Dick was struggling to break an engagement to some other woman during that time . . . You see, during that period we weren't officially engaged. The moment he did at last break free of this unknown woman he gave me a ring and sealed the bargain.'

'When?' Garth asked quietly.

'Well, when he came to give it to me last Saturday morning we had a bit of a tiff and finally it got to Saturday night before we patched things up . . . ' The girls' round chin quivered a little but her dark eyes were defiant. 'Last night I gave it him back! And until he tells me who the woman is that has been standing between us I won't ever speak to him again.'

'So *that's* the bone of contention, is it?' Garth asked, a deadly glint in his pale eyes. 'He has never told you the name of this former fiancée?'

'Never — and things have so sort of linked up with Valerie Hadfield that I . . . ' Joyce stopped and shook her head wearily, pressed her finger and thumb to her eyes.

'Just why do you want to know so much about Richard, Inspector?' Howard Prescott asked. 'What's *wrong*?'

'Wrong?' Garth was at his blandest as he turned his palms upward. 'Nothing at all, Doctor, and even if there were I wouldn't dare say so.'

'Then if there's nothing wrong why did you come here in an official capacity?'

Garth looked at the shrewd dark eyes behind the horn-rimmed glasses and saw a man far removed from a gentle philanthropist and professor of philosophy.

'I came,' Garth said deliberately, 'to find out whether Miss Prescott said 'Ricky' or 'Rixy' last night. Between those two names is a world of difference. Had it been the latter it would have been the same name as Valerie Hadfield had for her lover Rixton Williams, and things might have looked rather peculiar for Dick. As it is . . . . Well, you've cleared the air nicely, Miss Prescott.'

'Have I?' she gave a listless smile. 'You can put it that way if you want, Inspector — maybe you *have* to in your job — but I'm as sure as I'm born that Dick's other woman was Valerie Hadfield, and that only he knows what has become of her!'

'Careful, dear!' her father warned her.

'I can't help seeing it!' she insisted. 'And you think so too, Inspector, otherwise you wouldn't be here. And I'll tell you something else, too,' she went on, colouring emotionally. 'Dick said he couldn't see me for a week just before he gave me the ring. That week was the same one in which Valerie Hadfield and Rixton Williams had their whirlwind courtship. I noticed that when I read the brief accounts in the papers. But Dick *could* have seen me had he wanted because he was at home at intervals during that week building his garage.'

'Really?' Garth remained impassive but he cocked a questioning eye on Howard Prescott. The Doctor nodded rather reluctantly.

'I'm afraid it's true, Inspector, but it's understandable. He wanted to get the garage finished in time for Joyce to be able to use it — '

'Which is something I just don't understand!' the girl interrupted. 'I have never expressed any particular desire for a garage on the premises. In fact, I can't recall saying that I ever wanted a garage — or a car — at all. It's Dick's idea, and it seems to have become a positive obsession. Anyway, I know what *I* think, and believe me, Inspector Garth, it doesn't make me feel at all happy.'

Garth got to his feet. 'Well, I have to be on my way,' he said, holding out his hand.

'I'm so glad to have met you again, Miss Prescott. As I said earlier, you must use your own judgement in this — er — affair of the heart. Thank you for all you have told me . . . And good day to you, Doctor. Glad to have made your acquaintance.'

As he left, Garth knew he had been particularly evasive to two decent, down-to-earth souls who deserved infinitely better treatment, but as a servant of the law he had certain ethics to preserve.

Thoughtfully he made his way to the Underground station, and returned to his office. As Garth came in Sergeant Whittaker got to his feet.

'It's the biggest thing so far, sir!' he declared urgently. 'Look for yourself! We couldn't have had better proof if we'd wanted . . . It was delivered to Valerie Hadfield's flat by Kerrigan's the jewellers, and of course P.C. Gordon sent it on here. Apparently the lid had been smashed and Valerie had sent it to be repaired. Seems they'd have sent it here sooner only they weren't quite sure of procedure . . . '

Without a word Garth raised a silver

cigarette box from the desk. Slowly he opened the lid and read the inscription inside — *To Val, from Ricky, with all my love*.

'We've got him, sir!' Whittaker declared. 'We've got him because this box was in existence long before Rixton Williams even came into being . . . '

15

Garth returned the box to the desk, hung up his hat and coat. Slowly he settled down in his swivel chair, his expression one of hurt wonderment.

'It's damnable!' he said bitterly. 'Dick Harvey is one of the few men I have always admired — for his ability, social standing, his charm of manner . . . And now we have all the evidence lined up we know that he was the man in Valerie Hadfield's life. It means I've got to hound him to the ends of the earth if need be until I either batter the truth out of him or prove every one of his actions to the hilt. To have to do that to one of one's best friends is tough, Whitty.'

'Yes, sir,' Whittaker agreed quietly; then added naively, 'But we're police officers.'

'All right! So we know he's the man in whom Valerie Hadfield was interested. How far does it get us? Does it prove he killed her? No! Does it prove he killed

Peter Cranston? No! Where *is* Valerie Hadfield? It isn't murder until we find out . . . The evidence so far? We know from the fingerprints on the empty glass of brandy-and-soda this morning that the prints on it tally exactly with those in the back of the Daimler and in Valerie's flat. We knew *then* that he was the man in her life, but somehow I've kept hoping he'd explain it away. I've kept the truth from him for that very reason — to lure him out, but he's refused to be baited. We know, too, about the name 'Ricky', and we know other things. He wangled that two thousand pounds somehow knowing we couldn't check up, and to allay his suspicions I told him that others had drawn out two thousand in ones . . . Also I spent half an hour with his former fiancée, Joyce Prescott, this afternoon and that girl has guessed the whole truth if only she knew it. She even admitted that Dick had — or has — another woman in his life and that he only freed himself from her the *day after* Valerie Hadfield and the bogus Rixton Williams vanished. Yes, it all adds up . . . '

Garth went to his overcoat pocket, and took out a ball of blood-stained cotton wool from it.

'This is from Dick Harvey's swab-bin,' he said. 'I noticed a cut on his wrist and he told me he'd done it in the laboratory. In any event, whether he did it there or elsewhere, the probability struck me that he'd wash the wound in the lab where he keeps all the disinfectant. So, thanks to your fortunate ring on the 'phone I was able to take a quick look round for traces, and found this. If you hadn't rung I'd have had to wait and then break in the place later. Anyway, let's see what we get. Follow me . . .'

Before long they were entering the Home Office pathological department and heading towards Dr. Winters as he pored over some abstruse chemical problem at the far end of the enormous room.

'Oh, hello, Inspector . . .' Colourless as ever Winters looked up, then took the stained fluff Garth handed to him.

'Can you test it?' Garth asked. 'I've reason to think it may match that blood-group we found on the car belonging to Rixton Williams.'

'Easy enough,' Winters said, and began to busy himself with the preparation of a saline solution into which he finally placed the small wad of cotton wool containing the blood-stain. Then he watched the effect in the ampule as hazy, dirty sediment appeared. Carefully he set the ampule in a rack and waited for the liquid to settle itself.

'Will it take long?' Garth asked.

'I'm afraid it will need at least a fourteen-hour steeping,' Winters said. 'It's not a recent stain and I've got to have it absolutely clear before using the antiserum controls on the stain extract . . . Better leave it with me, Inspector, and I'll let you have my report as soon as I can.'

'Okay.' Garth had to accept it.

'What now, sir?' Whittaker asked as they returned to the office. 'Confront Mr. Harvey with all you know about him so far?'

'Partly yes — partly no. I shall certainly let him know that we have proof of his connection with Valerie Hadfield, but what we have to do is to get evidence of what happened to her — and that is going to take some doing because . . . '

Garth broke off and his eyes widened momentarily.

'My God, of course! Another motive, apart from the obvious one of wanting to be rid of a woman who wouldn't let him go. A *perfect crime*! Now I know why he was so sure that one could exist! He must have planned it from that very time, and damn me, I'm not so sure that he hasn't succeeded! Unless he betrays himself somewhere we can never pin anything on him . . . '

Garth reached his desk. 'My only hope lies in subtlety. Let him think that I still don't suspect him, until that moment comes when he slips — as they all do finally — and the whole rotten pack of lies comes down in an avalanche!'

* * *

Richard did not stop working on his garage until half-past ten that evening, except for a brief interval for dinner towards eight o'clock. Once the daylight had gone he carried an extension flex and lamp out from the laboratory and continued by its brilliance. He made no attempt to explain his actions to the puzzled Baxters. He no longer considered it necessary to maintain his pose of geniality. What the devil did it matter, anyway? He had lost Joyce, presumably for good; he knew full well that Chief Inspector Garth had strong suspicions, despite his assertions to the contrary . . . With these major distractions the puzzlement of two old fools like the Baxters simply didn't signify.

So by half-past ten that night he had completed the brick walls and laid the timber beams across them which were to form the basis for the ceiling and angled roof. Then he went in the house, washed, and retired to bed and relaxed between the sheets.

He was commencing to feel the strain of insomnia. His nerves were no longer as steady as they had been. He kept going back and forth over his actions of the past two or three weeks, tearing each act to pieces to see if it would stand up to the acid test.

He was awake until well after two in the morning, then at last a half-hearted nightmarish slumber did come to him. It was worse than being awake. Valerie Hadfield, thin and elongated beyond all natural dimensions, was helping Chief Inspector Garth to build a garage, and every time he laid one brick he dashed off somewhere to answer a telephone, and returned with a brandy-and-soda. Inchoate, tangled mix-up which ended with Garth falling into a bag of cement powder and emerging as dishevelled as a tramp and white as a wedding cake doll.

Richard awoke, laughing painfully, and found that it was half-past three. He did not sleep again. He did not even want to. Dream of the dead and be troubled with the living . . . His father had always believed that, and now he believed it too — bitterly, intensively. In fact it was more than a belief: it was a deadly fear that clung to him through the abysmal dark hours that creep into the grey of dawn.

Towards six o'clock he got up stiffly, dressed in his old clothes, and went outside to continue with the garage, working until breakfast-time on jobs that made little noise so the Baxters would have no idea what he was doing. After breakfast he went out and hammered the roof-stanchions into position, added the laths that would take the ceiling plaster . . . Then as he poised high on the crossbeam of the roof he became aware of a figure looking up at him quizzically.

It was Chief Inspector Garth.

'Hello, Dick!' he greeted.

'Soon back, aren't you?' Richard wriggled his way along the crossbeam and came down the ladder to the ground. Garth's face was quite expressionless, dough-white from his eternal dyspepsia, a cheroot half-burned down between his teeth.

'Yes, I'm afraid I am. I'd like to ask you something, Dick . . . Why didn't you tell me of your intimate association with Valerie Hadfield?'

Richard examined his dirty hands,

searching his mind frantically to anticipate what might be coming. 'What in the world are you talking about?' he asked calmly.

'I'm talking about a cigarette box inscribed on the lid — 'To Val, from Ricky, with all my love'!'

That infernal silver cigarette box! The one thing he hadn't been able to fit into his plan because he couldn't find it . . . Now, of all times, it had reappeared!

'I see you're familiar with it,' Garth commented, digging his hands deep in his overcoat pockets. 'The jeweller's returned it after repairing a broken lid.'

'I'm not necessarily familiar with it!' Richard retorted. 'I'm just plain surprised that you should dig up such a thing and throw it at me in this fashion! What's 'Ricky' got to do with me?'

'Look here, old man, I'm not a damned fool,' Garth said quietly. 'I know your nickname is 'Ricky' because Miss Prescott called you that.'

Richard smiled coldly. 'So she's been blabbing to you, has she?'

'The matter doesn't concern her, Dick;

it concerns *you*! You knew — and may still know — Valerie Hadfield. I've no proof that she is dead, but you are the one man in her life. Right?'

'Except for Rixton Williams . . . yes,' Richard said deliberately. The gloves were off now, and he knew it.

'You admit that you know Valerie Hadfield then?'

'I knew her very well, Garth, up to the time of her disappearance that is . . . ' Richard was talking easily now, his mind far ahead of his words, preparing a path through the jungle lying ahead.

'You didn't help a fellow much, did you?'

'Why should I? You were so infernally self-assured I didn't intend to give you an atom of help until you got things so tied up that I *had* to. And besides, I didn't admit my association with her because I realised what a frightful spot it could put me in.'

'And you risked losing Joyce — in fact *did* lose her — for the same reason?' Garth questioned.

'Yes — and you must have done plenty

of talking to her to know that I *have* lost her. I knew she suspected lots of things but I couldn't admit anything to her any more than to you because I realised she might talk to you, or vice versa, when Valerie vanished — her disappearance coinciding most inconveniently with my own excursions on business out of town — I knew I'd better keep quiet, even at the risk of losing Joyce and exciting your suspicions. As for this mysterious Rixton Williams, I don't know a thing about him. His name happens to be applicable to my own nickname, and the only solution I can think of is that Val has — or had — a second man in her life and maybe put him up to all this to get me in bad odour when she realised that I wanted to get her out of my system.'

'So that's your theory?' Garth gave a fleeting smile. 'You think she got somebody to make it look as if *you* had done it? You suggest that at this moment she still lives and is laughing at you from somewhere?'

'Knowing Val, yes,' Richard agreed, conscious of agreeable surprise that everything was working out so well.

'Well, it's certainly a theory,' Garth admitted, throwing down his cheroot stump and grinding it under his foot. 'But how do you explain the death of the chauffeur?'

'Simple. The same unknown did it — maybe not so much at Val's behest as for reasons of his own. Anyway, you can't prove that *I* did it!'

Richard wished that he had not added the last words. He had the uneasy feeling that they untied everything he had said — but if Garth thought the same thing he made no sign of it.

'Well, Dick, I'm glad you've been so frank about your friendship with Valerie Hadfield. It helps me a lot . . . But whether you are the victim of circumstantial evidence or not, you must realise that I have to check on everything?'

'Naturally,' Richard agreed, with a trace of his normal, easy-going smile. 'What do you want to know?'

'Where you were last Friday evening between six o'clock and midnight. It was during that time — approximately between eight and nine — when Timothy Potter drank his champagne with Valerie and Williams in Twickenham, and also when Valerie, dead drunk, was being hauled down the front path.'

'Yes, I recall that,' Richard nodded, completely at his ease. 'Well, I was working here — all evening.'

'Can you prove it?'

'Very easily. Ask my servants.'

A vague doubt crossed Garth's face as he led the way back through the laboratory and into the hall. Richard called the Baxters out of their quarters.

'Okay, Garth, you do the talking,' Richard invited dryly. 'That's the normal procedure, isn't it? So I can't drop any hints?'

'Can either of you tell me what Mr. Harvey was doing last Friday night?' Garth asked. 'Whether he was at home or not?'

'Oh, yes, sir — he was at home.' Mrs. Baxter made the reply and looked questioningly at Richard.

'The gentleman is a Chief Inspector from Scotland Yard, Mrs. Baxter,' Richard explained blandly. 'Tell him all he wants to know; he's entitled to it.'

'I can verify what my wife says, Inspector,' old Baxter put in. 'He was away most of Friday and came in about five o'clock — '

'And had a few sandwiches in place of the usual dinner,' Mrs. Baxter added. 'I remember that I asked him why and he said it was because he had plenty of laboratory work to do and didn't want to try and think on a full stomach. He said he'd perhaps be working from quarter-to-six that night until quarter-to-six next morning. And — and he insisted that he wasn't to be disturbed.'

'Then?' Garth asked, his jaw set.

'Er — he said something about us going to bed earlier if we wanted, but as I told him fixed habits don't alter that much and I said we'd go at our usual time. Then he said something about us being able to see him working in the laboratory if we wanted, because of the lighted windows . . . '

'Uh-huh,' Garth acknowledged, staring into space.

'I — I saw Mr. Harvey at work about eight o'clock, sir,' old Baxter ventured, and Richard found himself quivering with excited relief.

'You did?' Garth's voice was steady. 'Personally?'

'No — I didn't dare disturb him. I never do. I went out to get the coal and wood for the next morning's fires and I saw that the laboratory lights were on.'

Garth said nothing.

'At about a quarter-past ten,' Mrs. Baxter resumed, thinking, 'Mr. Richard came into the house from the laboratory and asked for a sandwich. He said he was hungry and that — er — oh, his back was stiff from so much stooping. I don't know any more than that, sir. We went to bed, my husband and I.'

'Well, thanks very much,' Garth said, smiling. 'I shan't need to trouble you again. You can return to your quarters.'

'Well, master mind?' Richard asked.

'Only one conclusion I can come to,' Garth answered, shrugging. 'My infernal dyspepsia must be clouding my judgement! Obviously you can't have had anything to do with Valerie's disappearance or with Peter Cranston's murder. Two unimpeachable witnesses making a voluntary statement, and I can tell when anybody is lying or not . . . ' His eyes rested on Richard's for a moment, steadily; then he added, 'Those two believe what they saw.'

Richard nodded. 'I'm really glad to get that worry off my mind, Garth. Now you know everything I think I'll see what I can do to patch things up with Joyce . . . I gather that you have seen her. What did she say about me?'

Garth raised his hands in protest. 'A referee usually gets his head punched and I'm not going to risk it. You'd better do your own dirty work . . . Now, how about a brandy-and-soda for an old friend — and one who's made about the biggest *faux pas* of his investigative life?'

'Surely!' Genial once more, Richard led the way from the hall and into the lounge, motioned to a chair while he mixed a drink and handed it across.

'Well, what happens now?' Richard asked, looking at his drink.

'Oh, have to switch things round a bit and find out who Rixton Williams really is — and, above all, we've got to make some sort of show at finding Valerie. That's the big snag — her missing body.'

Garth got to his feet, put down his glass, then held out his hand. 'No hard feelings, Dick?'

'Lord, no! I'll be only too glad to help you if I can — but please tell me one thing, and admit it like a man. Isn't this a perfect crime? Such as you said could never exist?'

'Yes, it is. It's clever — diabolically clever — with every clue so neatly eradicated that we stop almost before we start . . . But perfect crime or otherwise, Dick, the hunt isn't over yet. I still maintain that the Yard can beat any criminal alive . . . or dead.'

They went out together into the hall.

'Drop around to my office when you're in town and I'll tell you how far I've got. Failing that I may drop in here now and again.'

'Do that,' Richard agreed, shaking hands — and he watched Garth go off down the driveway. He closed the door and strolled back into the lounge, grinning. Until this moment he had never known what freedom really meant. All along the line he had won. Chief Inspector Garth was beaten . . . Utterly.

* * *

Garth, however, was not quite such a fool as Richard imagined.

'There is no doubt any more,' Garth said, when he got back to his office in Whitehall towards midday, 'that Dick Harvey is our man; and there is also no doubt that he has devised a perfect crime which only an unguarded move can betray.'

'Yes, sir,' Sergeant Whittaker agreed. 'Everything checks up — even to Doc Winters' precipitin test on that blood-stained cotton wool. The blood is in the same group as that found on the car — Group AB, the rare blood-group as he calls it. It doesn't prove that it is Mr. Harvey's blood, but it looks as if the thing is too obvious to admit of doubt.'

'Of course it is Harvey's blood!' Garth snapped. 'He engineered the whole damned thing from start to finish and the only thing stopping us arresting him is proof. Look how the facts are now ranged against him: One — away from home at the approximate time Williams came into being in Twickenham; two — withdrew two thousand from his bank and two thousand appeared in Twickenham; three — his nickname is the same as Williams'; four — he admits he was intimate with Valerie and found her a nuisance to him; five — his fingerprints on the back of the Daimler and in the flat; six — the inscribed cigarette box; seven — his blood-stain-group tallying with that on the abandoned car; eight — his desire to be rid of Valerie and marry Joyce Prescott; and nine — the year-old ink on the letter from Valerie found in Twickenham. I didn't refer to it when talking to him, and I imagine that he has too many other things on his mind at the moment to recall its significance . . . All that is on the debit side, Whitty. On the credit side we have . . . '

Garth mused and ticked the items off on his fingers.

'One — his alibi that he was working in his laboratory when Valerie and Rixton were in Twickenham and when Peter Cranston was murdered; two — the two thousand pounds which he showed me to explain away his actions and which he must have wangled somehow; three — his clever removal of all clues which might have proved he murdered Peter Cranston . . . '

'What do you make of his alibi, sir? Has he bribed those two servants of his to get him out of a jam?'

'No, they're not the bribing sort. They saw the lighted laboratory windows but *not* Dick Harvey. They *assumed* he was in there, which was exactly the reaction he had expected. He wasn't there, but I've got to *prove* it.'

'Then things being as they are, sir, what's your proposition?'

'I shall have to remain friendly with him. He's quite convinced now that I don't suspect him any more. I've even let him think that we may need his *help*.

Anyway, I'll stay beside him until I get the clue we need . . . ' Garth was silent for a moment, inspecting his empty cheroot case woefully. 'Y'know,' he said, 'there's one thing I can't understand.'

'Sir?'

'Why the hell he's working so hard on that *garage*! At first he said he was doing it for Joyce Prescott. But he has lost the girl completely because of her well-formed suspicions and yet he *still* goes on building the damned thing! I've looked at it, searched it, but there's nothing unusual about it as far as I can see. What's his game?'

Whittaker shrugged. 'I should imagine it's an outlet for nervous tension, sir. Harvey feels with so much bottled up in his consciousness that he must *do* something. Just as some men fly to drink, as others seek out a — er — woman. Escape mechanism, sort of.'

'Suffering snakes, man, you should have been a professor of psychology! You're just wasted here!'

'Thank you, sir.'

'I just wonder though what *did* become

of Valerie Hadfield?' Garth scowled. 'I still don't know whether she is dead or not, but something inside me keeps insisting that she is — but even if dead her body should remain. That was one of the main points Dick and I argued over at the club. I pointed out the terrific difficulties presented to murderers in trying to be rid of the victim.'

'Perhaps it's hidden somewhere near where we found the car, sir?'

'No, no — don't forget the absence of footprints, and besides Chalfont's men have toothcombed that area. No reports of any suspicious parcels anywhere or anything like that. I can conceive of Dick in his disguise as Rixton Williams doing a perfect vanishing act by simply becoming himself and destroying the clothes of his alias, but the disappearance of the girl is a real stinger. Doesn't seem to be any clue in Dick's laboratory either. I could of course take out a warrant and have the grounds of his home dug up, but that would make my friendship with him extinct. Besides, I can't imagine him being such a fool as to use such a clumsy method of disposal. No, I think there's an answer in that laboratory somewhere . . .'

Garth closed his eyes, visualising its layout.

'Door to the house — there! Door to the drive — there! Benches down the middle and along the sides. Three Dewar flasks near the outer door on the floor. An X-ray machine facing a liquid-air compressor apparatus across the laboratory. Shelves full of chemical bottles; racks full of test tubes, and a separate rack containing joinery and metalwork tools . . .'

Garth stopped, and his eyes opened suddenly, pale, blank — even horrified.

'Great God!' he whispered. 'Surely it *couldn't* be . . .'

16

Richard worked on with the garage throughout the day, believing he had circumvented the last problem. The alibi had apparently done the trick by reason of its very ordinariness. No case could ever be brought satisfactorily against him. He even felt proud of his brilliance in having perpetrated a perfect crime.

Perhaps now, able to make a clean breast of the thing as he had to Garth, he could get Joyce back for himself? Worth a try . . .

He chose the evening for the attempt, after he had slated the garage roof and nailed the ceiling laths in position to take the plaster on the morrow. Towards seven he arrived at the Prescott home. He was quite unaware as the housekeeper opened the door to him that out in the quiet suburban road Chief Inspector Garth stood watching, well hidden by the shadow of the trees lining the road.

'Miss Prescott in?' Richard asked briefly.

The woman gazed at him in the fan of light cutting the dark. 'I'm sorry, Mr. Harvey, but my instructions are to say that she is not at home — ever. So — '

The woman's adamancy faded as there was a sound behind her and Dr. Howard Prescott came out of the drawing room, his glasses gleaming in the hall light.

'All right,' he said quietly. 'I'll attend to it.'

Richard stepped into the hall without being invited and closed the front door.

'Just because Joyce and I have broken things off because of a misunderstanding it doesn't make me a social outcast, does it?'

'She's in the drawing room,' Howard Prescott said, nodding towards it. 'Go in and see her if you want. I'm going to my study.'

There was studied indifference to the words. It set Richard's darkly suspicious mind wondering just how much Garth had told . . .

Joyce looked up quickly as he entered the drawing room. She was seated on a swollen leather buffet beside the fire, her legs tucked under her and a book in her lap. She did not get up, but her eyes followed him.

'Hello — Joyce,' he said awkwardly and came to a stop with his hand on the back of the hide armchair.

'What do you want?' the girl asked, not a trace of affection in her dark eyes. Nor was there fear either. They stared out of a pale face, silently accusing.

'I've something I must say to you, Joyce.' He came to the front of the chair and sat in it.

'You have me weighed up all wrong, you know. About the woman in my life, I mean. It was Valerie Hadfield. I told Inspector Garth as much this morning.'

'It's no surprise,' Joyce said finally, looking into the fire. 'You must have known that I'd guessed it but you hadn't the decency to admit it outright. You had to wait until a Scotland Yard official hammered it out of you.'

'He *didn't* hammer it!' Richard retorted. 'I admitted it in the course of conversation because I saw no point in concealing it any more. Garth was actually beginning to think that I had done away with Valerie so it was time to clear myself . . . and I did, to his entire satisfaction.'

'Well, since you've done that what more is there to be said?'

Cold viciousness crept into Richard's grey eyes. One thing he could not stand was being treated with contempt by a woman. Perhaps it was even one of the prime reasons why he had killed Valerie.

'I don't understand you Joyce,' he said, controlling his voice. 'I came here to make a confession, expecting you to behave with ordinary decency and forget the troubles we have had . . . you haven't even the manners to look at me when you speak!'

The girl still stared into the fire, hiding the fact that she was nervous. Her hands were shaking — so much so she clasped them together about her knees.

'I don't want to look at you,' she said. 'I don't ever want to see you again.'

'Why? Just because I kept quiet about Valerie to save myself getting into a mess?'

For the first time Joyce turned and looked into his angry eyes.

'No! Because I believe you know what happened to Valerie Hadfield! I believe . . . that you *murdered* her! *And* her chauffeur!'

Richard overcame an overwhelming desire to strike her with all his force across the face.

'What a damned vivid imagination you've got!' he breathed. 'And how little faith in me!'

'Little faith is right,' she agreed, getting to her feet abruptly. 'Now I'd be glad if you'd get out! It's time you understood that we have not got a single thing in common any more!'

Richard jumped up, caught the girl's shoulders fiercely.

'That swine Garth's been feeding you some sort of story!' he shouted, shaking her. 'Go on, you little fool, admit it! He's been telling you that I killed Val and her chauffeur, hasn't he?'

Joyce tore free of his prisoning grip and stood beside the table, her breath coming quickly. Her eyes were blazing.

'He *didn't* say anything of the sort — how *could* he in his position? I've simply arrived at my own conclusions. You know perfectly well what you've done, so how can you expect me to have anything in common with *you*? You . . . a murderer!'

'Take care what you're saying!' Richard whispered, clenching his fists.

'Why?' the girl asked defiantly. 'If you're not guilty why should you care what I say?'

'If Garth didn't tell you anything then you must have told *him* something!' Richard snapped. 'You sold me to him, invented all sorts of wild stories, and that was why he came chasing after me. I see it all now. Idiot that I was ever to trust you.'

There was hostile silence as they measured each other. Richard failed to see a spark of pity in the girl's face.

'You — *bitch!*' he shouted harshly; then turned and strode from the room. The slam he gave in closing the front door reverberated through the house and brought Dr. Prescott out of his study — to suddenly find himself with a weeping girl clasping her arms about his neck.

'Dad — why did it have to be — Dick?' Her voice was choked, hardly audible. '*Why?* I *really* love him! Why did I have to fall in love with a man who's a killer? What have I done to get a deal like this . . . ?'

'You told him your real feelings?'

'Yes. I — '

'Good!' Prescott patted her quivering shoulders gently. 'It's hard now, dear, but it's the best way. Neither you nor anybody else is safe in the company of Richard. He's going downhill fast. I can see it in his eyes . . . '

When he left the Prescott house Richard did not return home. Home was the last thing he wanted. It would never have Joyce for its mistress: he would never have her for his wife — only her cold contempt until the end of his days . . .

Hair ruffled by the wind, he marched through the mild autumn night, struggling to comprehend how his scheme had come so completely unstuck — during which time Inspector Garth was in the laboratory-annex, a silent, shadowy figure, having let himself in at the laboratory's driveway door with a master-key. Now he prowled about the long place, a tiny rod of light projecting from the masked lens of the torch he carried.

He soon found that which he sought — the hacksaw hanging in the tool-rack at the far end of the laboratory. He inspected the blade, its small razor-edged teeth, and then unscrewed the blade quickly and slipped it in a long cellophane envelope. From his inside pocket be brought out another blade to replace the one he had taken. Being standard size the difference was unlikely to be noticed.

Job done, Garth departed as silently as he had arrived, anxious to be away before there was any chance of Richard returning . . .

He need not have worried. Richard was some distance from his home, standing by the slack wire rail overlooking open fields. He was remembering how he had thought of himself as something godlike in the devising of his scheme.

Now depression gripped him; as the mild wind blew in his face. Once Valerie had been alive, Joyce had been desperately in love with him, and he had been planning a masterpiece of strategy to defeat Scotland Yard . . . Now Valerie was dead, Joyce was utterly against him, everything he had striven for had been wiped out. He wondered about leaving the country and making a fresh start somewhere else, then rejected the idea. It would draw suspicion. No, he'd stay and finish the job, prove that he could beat Scotland Yard.

Some day perhaps Joyce would reconsider when she saw that he was not arrested. He still loved her, otherwise the fury that had lashed him at her words would still be with him and waiting, prompting him to destroy her. She was the only girl he ever wanted to possess . . .

Turning up his coat collar about his ears he wandered off into the night.

* * *

Towards half-past eight Chief Inspector Garth entered his office to find the indefatigable Whittaker busy at his type-writer setting out the details of the Valerie Hadfield case in readiness for the day when the evidence would have to be presented. Normally Whittaker would have been at home by now, but at times like these — with the Assistant Commis-sioner on the prod — he became secretary to his chief.

'Any luck, sir?' he asked Garth as he came in.

'Well, I managed to play my hunch, anyway. I got the hacksaw blade and replaced it with another one.'

Whittaker got up and looked at the blade in the cellophane envelope as his superior put it on the desk.

'I think,' Garth said, 'we can safely assume by this time that had Valerie Hadfield's body been anywhere to *be* found it would have been. The police of the entire country have been looking for it, using the most modern equipment — without result. The only other alternative is . . . dismemberment.'

'Uh-huh,' Whittaker admitted. 'Nothing new about that, sir. Crippen and others . . . They all tried it.'

'Exactly — and it seemed to me that we might have the same thing here. Dick Harvey's laboratory is not that of a surgeon, of course, and the only instrument I noticed that could have done a dismemberment job was a hacksaw. Certainly I don't think he'd use an ordinary wood-saw such as he is using for the building of that garage. In fact, I think those particular tools have been loaned by the builders. I admit that there might be other instruments hidden away — but my interest centred on the hacksaw, chiefly because it is a common fault of a self-assured killer to be so convinced of his own immunity that he leaves the fatal weapon in full view. I decided it could do no harm to look . . . And here's the blade.'

'But surely, sir, if Mr. Harvey did chop up Valerie Hadfield he'd have taken care to clean up everything afterwards? Remove bloodstains and so on?'

'I grant you that he has got rid of

bloodstains, but I am inclined to doubt over-scrupulousness with the hacksaw. It has a myriad of tiny teeth for material to lodge between. Ordinary cleaning would leave slight deposit between the teeth. Acid alone could make it absolutely clean, but that on the other hand would leave visible markings on the steel blade that would draw attention to it. So, I think Dick Harvey cleaned the blade as well as possible, and left it at that.'

'But — but why *should* he leave it at that, sir?'

'Because, my both-feet-on-the-ground friend, he had such a foolproof scheme for disposing of Valerie he might easily have been over-confident on the smaller, less important details.

Whittaker frowned. 'Then just what do you think he *did* do with that woman?'

'It's a pretty ghastly idea I have in mind, Whitty,' he muttered. 'Too ghastly to mention yet in case I'm wrong . . . ' He brisked suddenly and whipped up the long envelope. 'Anyway, let's see what pathology has to say.'

They left the office together and to

Garth's satisfaction Dr. Winters was present finishing an overtime analysis when they arrived in his department. He took the hacksaw blade Garth handed to him and studied it through the transparency of the envelope.

'Find out if this blade is clean, will you, Doc?' Garth asked. 'Or whether anything is on it which might help us.'

'With pleasure.' Winters stripped the cellophane away. 'But I can't give you an immediate answer. If there's anything to be found on the blade it means a good deal of steeping, and then there's foam reaction and filtration to be done. I might have something for you by this time tomorrow. All depends.'

'That'll do,' Garth said quietly. 'And use every trick you know with these bottles and beakers of yours to make that blade sit up and beg. My whole reputation may depend on it!'

* * *

Richard had spent another sleepless night. Any hope of sleep had vanished after

Joyce had delivered her farewell speech.

When he got up he felt too leaden to shave and so came downstairs unshaven in his old working suit. Mrs. Baxter found him short tempered, vindictive about the quality of his breakfast — and finally he stalked outside with nothing more inside him than some tea and a good deal of cigarette smoke.

He worked until noon applying plaster to the garage ceiling, came in and had a good lunch and a shave — after which he felt a trifle better — and then during the afternoon he finished the plastering and began the task of making the garage doors. Towards nightfall he gave up, moved all the timber to one side and left the driveway free. Nothing to prevent him bringing the Jaguar home now and telling the contractors to take away the remains of their stuff. The doors would be finished and on by the next night. Be something to do to walk over and fetch the Jaguar . . .

He was just leaving the driveway towards seven o'clock when he collided with somebody coming along the street. Under the street lamp he saw the black

Homberg hat and horn-rimmed glasses of Dr. Prescott.

'Hello, Richard,' Howard Prescott acknowledged quietly.

'Sorry I bumped into you . . . Er . . . How's Joyce?'

'Quite well, thank you.' Howard Prescott prepared to move on but Richard caught his arm fiercely.

'Doctor Prescott, can't you convince Joyce that she's all wrong about me — convince her that I love her. God knows, I do!'

'Joyce is an adult with a mind of her own. It's not my job to influence her — and besides I couldn't and remain truthful.'

'If you think that about me why don't you turn me over to the police?'

'I am not a police officer, Richard. I shall not state my private opinion to anybody else. That is the work of the law.'

'Look here, Doctor. Just supposing I *had* done the thing you and Joyce believe — which I haven't — speaking as a philosopher, what do you think I should do?'

Richard found Prescott's hand gripping his arm.

'Admit the fact! Go to Scotland Yard and give yourself up! I know what you've done, even if the police haven't arrested you, even if you haven't admitted the fact. Your eyes are haunted by something that is in your mind . . . I've seen men like that before, men with some great anguish in their souls. There's no way to cure it except by expiating your sin. All of us have something to expiate, be it big or small.'

'Including you?'

'Naturally. As your friend I'm telling you the way out. The horror of the thing you've done will never leave you, Richard, until you drag it into the open . . . Good night.'

Richard stared after him, then turned and continued up the street towards the public garage. Confess! What sort of a damned fool did Howard Prescott take him for? But at the back of his mind the suggestion had taken root. If there was no other surcease from this deepening anguish of mind and body he might be forced into it — or die. Finish it quickly.

'Fool!' Richard whispered angrily. 'Garth believes you're *innocent!* He said so! When the Yard gives up the chase go abroad and find another girl . . . '

Meanwhile, Garth had come to the end of his day's vigil of fretting. Doctor Winters was in the office with his report in his hand.

'Well, doctor,' Garth asked. 'Is the blade clean — or not?'

'Not! The precipitin reaction shows traces of tissue which have yielded human protein, as opposed to animal tissue.' Winters let the report fall from his fingers on to the desk. 'There's not enough residue to say anything much or to identify sex or age, but you can rest assured that that hacksaw has been deep inside a human being's flesh . . . somewhere.'

Garth felt for his cheroots. He wasn't conscious of Winter's departure or of Whittaker's tense, questioning face.

'Human protein,' he said. 'Now I'm as good as *sure* where the body of Valerie Hadfield went!'

17

Next morning Garth arrived at his office to find Whittaker studying a report from Divisional Inspector Whiteside.

'You're looking darned pleased with yourself,' Garth commented.

'Read this, sir!'

'This, sir. Maybe the last link in the evidence.'

Garth picked up the report and read it aloud slowly:

' 'Divisional Inspector's Report: Acting on the instructions of Chief Inspector Garth have contacted all outfitters and emporia in a general area between Belsize Park and the city. A firm by the name of Flensburg in Medville Street, Camden Town, has reported that one of their salesmen sold a ready-made suit, raincoat, *et cetera*, to a person who gave his name — for invoice purposes — as Kenneth Garson. The salesman remembers him because there was an error in the change. The clothes are identical with those worn by Rixton Williams (according to spectators) and Kenneth Garson's description would fit perfectly with that of Richard Harvey. The clothes were bought on Thursday, October tenth. Would suggest interview with Flensburg's salesman to clear up details.' '

'Looks like *it*, sir, doesn't it?' Whittaker asked.

'Definitely!' Garth answered grimly. 'I'll go over right away and see this chap. The chances are that he is the only person who has ever seen Rixton Williams before he *became* that person. You'd better stay here in case anything else comes in. I'll be back here as soon as I can.'

Garth hurried out to his official car. Half an hour later he returned to find Richard in the office, seated in the armchair by the door, smoking and talking to Whittaker.

Richard waved a hand to him. 'Taking a change from sitting in the chair, eh?'

'Good for the indigestion,' Garth replied, hanging up his hat and coat.

'How are things with you?'

'I'm afraid I'm in the dog house.'

'Oh?' Garth sat at his desk and began to write something swiftly.

'Joyce Prescott won't have a thing to do with me. She thinks that because I've admitted knowing Valerie Hadfield I must necessarily have murdered her, or made her magically vanish. Damned tough on me, I can tell you.'

Garth finished writing and handed the slip to Whittaker. The sergeant read: *Flensburg's salesman has identified Harvey as Rixton Williams. Add this to report in preparation*.

Whittaker went over to the noiseless typewriter and settled down to work, half an ear cocked for what his chief was going to say next.

'So you've lost your lady love, eh?' Garth sat back and grinned. 'What makes you so cocksure that you don't deserve it?'

'You well know I *don't* deserve it!' Richard retorted. 'And the sooner you find out who Rixton Williams is the better I'll like it! Then I can come out into the open and reclaim Joyce and my self respect. It's not exactly pleasant when the woman you love thinks you're a killer.'

'Dick, I'm afraid your lady love is going to have to think nasty things about you for a long time to come,' Garth admitted. 'Between us three here, this case has me licked! I just don't *know* who killed Peter Cranston or who caused Valerie to disappear!'

Richard felt a wild drumming in his ears.

'I'll probably get my ears boxed by the Assistant Commissioner. Every lead we've had so far travels a certain distance and then stops dead. Every time I find myself hamstrung for lack of proof.' Garth slammed his fist on the desk. 'There isn't a scrap of proof! This Mr. X, Mr. Williams, whatever in hell you like to call him, has played a brilliant hand and got me tied in knots. In other words, Dick — you win our bet! You said a perfect crime could exist, and I said it couldn't. I thank my lucky stars we didn't actually play for real stakes.'

Richard laughed silently to himself at

the memory of the advice of Dr. Prescott. *Confess*, he had said!

Richard smiled and got to his feet, crushing out his cigarette in the ashtray. 'Well, so you're beaten. What's next?'

'Relegate the case to the files of the unsolved,' Garth said moodily. 'I've never had one like this since I became Chief Inspector — but to every man his Waterloo . . . And since you are the victor,' he added briefly, 'you might at least be magnanimous. Haven't you any suggestions to cheer me on my way?'

'I'll buy you a lunch,' Richard said. 'Just to show you that there's no hard feelings. Then, as part of my terms as victor, I think I should drive you to Miss Prescott's this afternoon and make you admit that you can't solve this business. That should put her in the right mood for accepting me again.'

Garth shook his head. 'Sorry Dick, that's out. My admission of defeat is for you and the Assistant Commissioner. No outsiders. But I'll come and have lunch with you with pleasure.'

As he followed Richard out of the

office, only Sergeant Whittaker saw the profound wink aimed back at him.

⋆ ⋆ ⋆

Garth stayed beside Richard for the rest of the day. They had lunch together and for the afternoon turned in to see a film — entirely at Garth's request to 'take his mind off things.' It went towards five when they emerged again into the waning daylight and walked slowly towards the car park.

'Well, I feel a heap better for your company, Dick,' Garth confessed, smiling. 'I've even lost my indigestion for a while. Only thing spoiling my peace of mind now is going back to the office to see if anything fresh has turned up.'

Richard could not quite fathom the Chief Inspector's mood. It seemed odd that he could take nearly a whole day off and do nothing except what he wanted — unless his high position entitled him to do so. Anyway, the case was closed and that was all that mattered, and because of it ego still ruled Richard.

He felt somehow tempted to rub it in even more — display everything openly, flaunt it in Garth's face, knowing all the time he couldn't derive a single clue from it all. Be a good idea to force Garth to inspect his garage now it was finished. Let him look at the very thing he was seeking and come away unaware of it. Then indeed it would be a perfect crime.

As they reached the car, Richard said, 'Why go back to that dump of yours in Whitehall? Why not come home with me? I'm alone and I could do with a bit of cheering up.'

Garth grinned as he considered the truth propounded by many a psychologist — that the criminal mind, when it believes itself safe, seeks only one thing: the glorification of its actions. A crime, as such, loses all its magnificence if there be none but the criminal to appreciate it. Richard, running true to type, was about to reveal the final shadings in his masterpiece that so far had been forced into the background from sheer necessity.

'Okay, might as well make a day of it,' Garth agreed. 'Besides I like your brandy.

Does my stomach good.'

At length, as their car approached Richard's house, Garth saw the newly completed garage, minus doors, looming up along the drive of the house in the glare of the headlights.

'So you actually built it!' he exclaimed.

'And had Rothwell's take the surplus away. Only the doors to finish.' Richard grinned cynically as he switched off the ignition. 'Didn't think I would do it, did you?'

Garth grinned. 'I admit I thought you'd make a mess of it!'

'I'll show you it properly after dinner and make you admit once again that you're wrong. I'll leave the car here and then we can use the headlights later. I've taken the extension flex back into the laboratory . . . Come along.'

Garth followed Richard to the front door of the house. Old Baxter came out of the back regions to take their coats.

'The Inspector will be staying for dinner, Baxter,' Richard told him. 'Tell your wife, will you please?'

'Yes, Mr. Richard, sir.'

Richard took Garth's arm. 'Come along upstairs and freshen up . . . '

Garth went with him up the broad staircase and ten minutes later they were both seated in the library awaiting dinner, discussing everything except the one thing they were both thinking about . . . the garage. Even at dinner they both avoided the subject, but at last Richard drifted round to it when they got to the coffee.

'Funny, I suppose, that I should take such pride in a garage,' he mused, studying the pale eyes across the table. 'Only I don't look at it that way. I simply regard it as a work of art brought to a successful conclusion.'

'Is that why you went on building it even though you knew Joyce had turned against you?' Garth inquired.

'Of course. I began to build it originally for Joyce, but I didn't see any reason for pulling it down once I'd started on it.' Richard got to his feet. 'Anyway, come and have a look and admit that I'm not such an amateur after all.'

Together they strolled round into the

driveway and Richard switched on the Jaguar's headlights. The doorless garage became brilliantly clear and he led the way towards it and into it. Garth followed, hands in trousers pockets, came to a halt in the centre of the concrete floor and looked about him.

'Well?' Richard asked dryly. 'Did I make a good job of it, or not?'

Garth had been waiting for a moment like this ever since he had guessed how Valerie Hadfield has disappeared. He studied the brick walls, the concrete floor, the window frame without glass as yet, then he looked above him at the plaster ceiling.

'Ceiling, eh?' he asked in surprise. 'Unusual!'

'In a way, perhaps, but it saves dropping chunks of mortar on the car in wet and rough weather. Some better class garages have them . . . Anyway this one has.'

Garth surveyed the ceiling again, brilliantly clear in the light of the headlamps, and then looked back towards the walls . . . But he jerked his gaze once more to the plaster. For a moment he had seen something that had not registered immediately — but it did now . . .

Something gleaming faintly golden, curling out of the plaster, a tiny little loop. A coldness went through him, and passed.

'You've made a good job of it, Dick, and I congratulate you. Maybe you'll come over and build a house for me sometime?'

Richard only smiled — the cold, deathly smile of a criminal who has achieved his fondest hope and escaped unharmed. He had made Chief Inspector Garth look on the last resting place of Valerie Hadfield — and his lynx-eyes, the eyes of the man without a failure in his record, had not for a moment been aware of it.

Richard was still smiling as he led the way back into the house. So was Chief Inspector Garth — for quite a different reason.

18

Determined not to reveal his hand, Garth was in no hurry to leave Richard's company. He spent the evening with him talking, playing a couple of short games of chess — in which Richard forced a stalemate both times — then, towards nine o'clock, Garth insisted that he must be on his way if his wife was ever to forgive him.

'You'll keep me in touch with any developments in the Hadfield case?' Richard asked, seeing Garth to the front door.

'Surely — though I don't expect anything. Still, I hope something does turn up because I appreciate how you must feel about Joyce Prescott . . . Well, thanks for everything.'

'I can't run you home?'

'No, thanks all the same. The exercise to the Tube will do me good.'

Richard frowned as he closed the door.

Still he did not feel sure. *Was* there something at the back of Garth's mind, or was he really beaten? If he was not, what point was there in maintaining friendship? Richard gave it up and returned to the lounge for a spell of serious thinking before retiring.

And while he tried to map out his future, Chief Inspector Garth remained in the road running past the house, on the opposite side facing the driveway gates. Well away from the nearest street lamp he stood in shadow, watching — and waiting.

Towards half-past-ten he saw Richard come out and drive the Jaguar into the doorless garage. The lights went out and the throb of the engine ceased. Richard reappeared and went back into the house. Not ten minutes later lights came up in one of the upstairs rooms. It might be either the Baxters or Richard. Not being sure, Garth fumed and waited, cursing the impossibility of a cheroot for fear of its glow being seen.

It was eleven-thirty before he felt safe to venture. He drifted across the quiet, empty road, entered the driveway and crept close in by the screening trees. As he moved he pulled a pair of folding scissors from his pocket and snapped them open. Without a sound he gained the garage on the side further from the house, crept within, and then very gently eased himself on to the Jaguar's bonnet so that he could reach the ceiling.

He kneeled, listening. There were no sounds. Carefully he pulled forth his fountain pen torch and switched on the tiny needle of beam, flicking it round until it reflected back from that tiny golden loop. He held it gently, snipped it with the scissors. With finger and thumb crushed together he extinguished the torch with his free hand, slid down to the floor and left the way he had come.

At the first street lamp he paused and heaved a sigh of relief as he saw the single hair still in his grip. He transferred it to a cellophane envelope, thrust it in his wallet, then went on briskly into the night . . .

* * *

First thing the following morning Garth appeared in the pathological department, accompanied by Sergeant Whittaker. The pale-faced Winters came over as he was signalled.

'You've got some hair somewhere, Doc, taken from that house in Twickenham in the Valerie Hadfield case,' Garth said. 'I want you to check it with this one.'

Winters took the cellophane envelope and peered at the single strand.

'Getting down to single hairs now, Garth? Where's this from?'

'I'll tell you when you've identified it — if you can. My guess is that it matches Valerie Hadfield. Will it take you long to find out?'

'Not very,' Winters answered. 'I can tell you straight off that it is a woman's hair. Male hair is shorter, thicker, and more wiry. And it isn't an animal's. So female is the answer, and from the head too . . . Now, let's see.'

Winters went over to the bench, studied the packed shelves above it and then took down ether and rectified spirits. Carefully he poured equal parts of both into a tube and placed the hair within it, shaking it gently.

'Cleansing agent,' he explained, as Garth and Whittaker looked on. 'Seems to be a lot of rubbish sticking to it. What is it?'

'Plaster,' Garth said mechanically.

'Plaster? But what's human hair doing in plaster?'

'This,' Garth said, his pale eyes fixed on the tube, 'is not ordinary plaster.'

Winters shook the tube again — and again, during a period of ten minutes; then he removed the hair with forceps and put it into a clear fluid of oil of turpentine and finally dried it between blotters. This done he went to the filing cabinets and returned presently with a few hairs mounted on microscopic slides with Canada balsam.

'Are you in a hurry for this examination?' he asked, and Garth gave a grim nod.

'All right; I'll have to leave this specimen unmounted and make only a rough comparison. It'll probably do for you and I'll give you the proper thing later on. Takes forty-eight hours at least to mount a hair, you see. Anyway, let's see what we have.'

He made up a rough slide with Canada Balsam for the single hair Garth had brought and, side by side, examined it with the mounted hairs in the comparison-microscope. For several minutes he studied the two specimens, then at last looked up.

'Identical!' he said. 'The fact that this latest single specimen hasn't set in the balsam properly blurs the details a little, but there's no doubt but what this hair came from the same head as these other mounted ones. Colour, cuticle, cortex and medulla are all the same. It has been cut off, by the way, not torn out.'

'Thanks, Doc,' Garth said, his face grim. 'Make a proper job of the mounting for when I need it, will you? Come on, Whittaker, we've things to do.'

The sergeant followed from the laboratory and back to the office. 'What,' he asked slowly, 'does all this mean, sir?'

'It means that Valerie Hadfield's hair was used to mix in the plaster of the ceiling of Richard Harvey's garage,' Garth told him. 'That poor woman's hair wasn't burned, perhaps because the odour of burning might have been detected. Nor was it scattered to the four winds, nor was it destroyed by acids. Why this latter method wasn't used I can't imagine, unless it was because of Dick's fear that some hairs might escape somewhere and be detected — or else, most probable reason of all, it was because he was fanatically determined to use every part of that woman's body to good advantage!'

Whittaker said nothing. His mind was crawling with horrible possibilities.

'My God, sir,' he said suddenly, 'if Valerie's hair is mixed up in the garage ceiling plaster her body might be somewhere in that garage! After all, we did find human tissue on that hacksaw blade. Do you suppose that he cut her up and buried her remains under the concrete floor of the garage?'

'I believe,' Garth replied deliberately, 'that Valerie Hadfield is not buried under the garage, but that she *is* the garage!'

'But that's impossible, sir! You just

couldn't mix up parts of a body in building materials and get away with it. If that's what you are suggesting?'

Garth reached his desk and sat down in the chair.

'Don't forget that we are dealing with a scientist, and a clever chemist. Such a man would not use the methods of Crippen and others, cutting a corpse up and then trying to dispose of the pieces. He would, I imagine, strive for the *total elimination* of the corpse, if only to create the perfect crime. So, if the hair of the missing woman is mixed up in the garage plaster — thereby proving at last the situation of her body — and we can be pretty sure it didn't get there by accident and that there may be her whole head of hair mixed up in that plaster, neatly cut into short lengths — the *rest* of her body might quite easily be mixed up with the concrete that forms the floor, or in the mortar between the bricks!'

'But a corpse just couldn't be cut up that finely, sir.'

'That,' Garth smiled grimly, 'is where

the chemist walks into the picture! The answer, I think, is — liquid air! Quite a modern product of science and used a good deal in industry. The air is drawn into a compressor, pistons compress the air and drive it into a coil round which cold water circulates. Heat is constantly drawn out of the compressed air until a certain percentage of it is made liquid, at the frigidly low temperature of minus one hundred and ninety degrees Centigrade. This resultant liquid air is a pale blue mobile fluid and is stored in what are called Dewar flasks, stoppered with cotton. Actually they are on the principle of a thermos-flask.'

Whittaker nodded, thinking it out, though still obviously puzzled.

'There is a liquid air compressor in Dick Harvey's laboratory,' Garth resumed slowly. 'Also there are three Dewar flasks against the wall. Flesh, in contact with liquid air — if the process be prolonged — changes to the consistency of grey powder. It shrivels, blights, rots away under the unimaginable cold. Dip a living flower in liquid air and when you take it out you can snap it to bits like a piece of matchstick or . . . you can pulverise it! — with a pestle, hammer, or whatever you like.'

'Pulverise it?' Whittaker repeated, starting.

'So you begin to see? Maybe for convenience Richard had to dismember the corpse into sections, for a full sized adult body is a difficult thing to handle under liquid air processes. If we assume that diabolical process *was* carried out, there is no scientific reason why every scrap of Valerie Hadfield could not have been reduced to powder — flesh, bones, all the lot, turned into brittle residue which in turn was pulverised and then added to the sand and cement powder being used for the garage. Perfect dismemberment and elimination and not a trace remaining.'

'But the blood?' Whittaker questioned. 'If he started dismemberment before the liquid air experiment some blood *must* have flowed!'

'Only very slightly, if at all, depending on how soon after death he cut up the body. Hypostasis — post-mortem coagulation — is complete in six hours as a rule and if there is any flow of blood at all it is only minute. What there was he could easily move from the floor, or wherever he performed his grisly task, with a cleansing fluid. As for the blood left in the body, he certainly knew what he was about!'

Garth gave a grim chuckle.

'There's a hellish touch of genius about this, Whittaker!' he declared. 'The only thing that might have given normal dismemberment away would have been blood-staining — signs of it in the concrete, in the mortar, but under liquid air treatment the blood would be frozen to minus one hundred and ninety degrees Centigrade, and blood at that temperature won't give the slightest reaction in a laboratory! Damned clever! That's what happens when an expert chemist takes to murder.'

Whittaker rubbed his jaw. 'It's only a theory though, sir . . . That single hair may not *really* mean such a diabolical, fiendishly clever plan was carried out.'

'You haven't been tagging around with

Dick Harvey as I have Whitty. You haven't seen the pride with which he showed me that garage of his — and looking back on it I can see that it was desperate desire to prove his own criminal brilliance that made him show me the place. Normally, no man would waste his time showing a friend his garage. That craving of the ego for recognition of his handiwork — and the brilliant headlights revealing that single hair — will prove his undoing! Right from the start his interest in that garage has been unnatural. Amidst it all is Valerie Hadfield, and we've got to find some traces.'

'Even if we do they'll be unidentifiable,' Whittaker sighed. 'You know as well as I do, sir, that unless we can *prove* the traces belong to Valerie, we're sunk. Even if Harvey should openly confess to his crime and we can't identify the traces of Valerie, he's still a free man.'

'I know — but he murdered Peter Cranston, and we *have* his body. Make Richard confess to the murder of Valerie and I'll stake everything I've got that he'll admit he murdered Cranston too. Then

— and only then — can we charge him with murder.'

'How do you propose going about finding some traces of Valerie, sir?'

Garth got to his feet and strolled to the window.

'Yes, *how*?' he muttered. 'I could take out a search warrant and have the garage pulled down and analysed, but that would shatter the friendship between us, which I must preserve if I'm ever to tempt a confession out of him.'

'Would that matter so much now we know everything, sir?'

'I think it does, yes. Besides, I have a personal stake in this. Dick Harvey thinks he has proved to me that a perfect crime can exist. I want to prove to him that law and order can in the end beat the best modern criminal brain, if only as a lesson to other misguided mutts who try the same thing.'

Whittaker waited expectantly and Garth returned to the desk.

'I've just remembered something! He told me last evening that he had sent all surplus material back to the building contractors — Rothwell's — having finished with it. It means that there may be some sand, cement powder, and so forth still *in* the sacks he sent back, and the residue in the concrete mixer might be worth analysing too. The next point of call is Rothwell's, where Richard won't have the least idea what I'm up to.'

* * *

In forty minutes they had reached Rothwell's disordered timber and brick-yard, and found the builder himself in his little shack. He looked up expectantly at his two visitors and set aside a sheet of specifications.

'This won't take long, Mr. Rothwell,' Garth said, and the builder's eyes widened at the sight of the warrant card.

'Say, look 'ere! What did I do?'

'Nothing,' Garth assured him with a grim smile. 'All I want to know is, are you the man who sold a load of bricks, cement powder, sand, timber, and so forth to Richard Harvey recently?'

'That's right,' Rothwell nodded. 'For

his garage . . . 'E makes an 'obby of buildin'.'

'I believe you loaned him a concrete mixer, too?'

'Aye — an' tools. But 'e's had us collect what's left o' the stuff.'

'Was there any material left in the sand bags or cement bags?'

'Might be,' Rothwell admitted, rubbing his chin. 'Nothin' t' shout about though . . . Why?'

'That part needn't concern you, Mr. Rothwell. Let us say it is a check-up on building materials, shall we? I'd like to see those bags, and the concrete-mixer.'

'Okay,' Rothwell agreed, shambling out into the chaotic yard; 'but I can't think why. There y'are, gents — take your pick. Just as the stuff were dumped down. I 'aven't even moved it yet.'

Garth and Whittaker moved over to where the nearby empty bags were standing and looked into them. In each was about two inches of powder remaining.

'I can take these by getting the necessary authority,' Garth said, turning and looking at Rothwell and then nodding to the bags, 'but that would waste valuable time. Do you mind if I borrow them for analysis?'

''Elp yourself — though I'll be 'anged if I can see what you're up to.'

Garth jerked his head and Whittaker picked up the two bags and walked off with them to the waiting car in the roadway. Garth moved across to the concrete-mixer and peered inside it. Then he put his hand in the mixing crucible. The material within was hard as iron. Taking out his penknife he snapped open the blade and dug out enough of the hard substance in powdery, chipped formation to fill a small cellophane envelope that Whittaker produced from his wallet.

'Look 'ere, gents, are you sure I ain't in a mess?' Rothwell insisted.

'You have nothing to fear, Mr. Rothwell,' Garth said quietly. 'That is, as long as you say nothing about what has happened. It is to be kept a complete secret. You understand?'

'Uh-huh, I understand,' Rothwell agreed.

Garth nodded a farewell, and then followed Whittaker out of the yard to the car. They drove back in the direction of the city.

'Think we'll have any luck with this stuff, sir?'

'I don't know. It's the last chance we've got of proving my theory outside of dismantling the garage and analysing it bit by bit. Of course we'll do that in any case when we've arrested Dick, in order to complete our evidence, but let's hope we find something here to go on . . . Doc Winters is in for a busy day!'

Winters did not seem in the least disturbed when Garth and Whittaker appeared in the laboratory for the second time that morning with one sandbag, one grey paper bag, and the cellophane envelope full of residue from the concrete-mixer. He merely raised an eyebrow and listened attentively while Garth explained the position.

'Liquid air, eh?' Winters shook his head doubtfully. 'You're setting me a mighty tough problem. Liquid air, depending of course on the period of immersion, should have destroyed both bone and flesh and powdered the blood as well, and the pulverising process would complete it. Our only chance is that perhaps the time was not long enough and that parts of the bone, the most resistant of all human material, will have survived. Anyway, I'll go to work and probably have a report by tomorrow.'

'Not before?' Garth asked disappointedly.

'Can't be done, sorry. There's the steeping and filtering to be gone through, and then I've got to sort out the genuine powder from bone traces — if any. Not a thing before tomorrow!'

'Okay,' Garth sighed. 'And it seems to me, Whitty, that we've about earned some lunch. Come on.'

* * *

So neatly had Garth concealed his hand so far, Richard felt almost happy as during the day he worked on the completion of the doors for his garage. Now it was purely a matter of finishing off the job for appearances' sake — and besides it gave him a chance to think.

As he worked he began to realise the empty futility of everything he was doing — and had done. His whole sinister plot, magnificently successful though it had apparently been, had failed in its objective in that he had not got Joyce.

Now, after a night during which he had actually managed to sleep for three consecutive hours, he realised what he had got to do. He must exert his authority and force Joyce back to his side. Only by accomplishing it could he consummate his masterpiece.

By five o'clock, as the light was commencing to wane and the doors were finished and on their hinges, he had his plan worked out.

Without bothering with evening dinner in the usual way, making do with a few sandwiches, he went upstairs to shave, changed into a lounge suit, then left the house in his very latest style of overcoat, his dark hair shining smoothly groomed

As usual it was the impassive-faced housekeeper who opened the door to him at the Prescott home.

'I know,' Richard commented, raising a hand. 'Miss Prescott won't see me!'

'Those are my instructions, Mr. Harvey — and from the master, too.'

'I refuse to go without seeing either Miss Prescott or her father,' Richard said briefly.

The woman turned away from the doorway, and Richard deliberately walked into the hall and stood waiting, grimly expectant. After a moment or two the housekeeper reappeared from the study, glanced towards him, then went on to her own quarters. The door opened again and Dr. Prescott himself came out, adjusting his horn-rimmed glasses.

'What do you want?' Howard Prescott asked, stopping a couple of feet away.

'To see Joyce, of course. What else? And you're the only one who can fix it for me.'

'We've been over all this before. I made it perfectly clear to you when we last met how you stand with Joyce — and me. Will you please go?'

Richard measured him. 'You told me you were not responsible for Joyce's actions. That being so, suppose you let *her* speak? I want to see her. If she refuses, I'll go, but at least give her and me a chance.'

Howard Prescott hesitated, then glanced towards the door of the drawing room under which a light showed.

'Joyce!' he called. 'Come here a moment, will you please?'

The door opened and the girl appeared, simply dressed, vague surprise on her face. Catching sight of Richard she backed into the room again.

'Just a minute!' Richard snapped, striding across the hall. 'I'm putting and end to this tomfoolery once and for all!'

He strode after her into the drawing room. Prescott followed him and stood watching expectantly. Joyce was near to the fire, her back to it, studying Richard with nervous dark eyes.

'How much longer is your crazy delusion about me going to stand between us, Joyce?' he demanded, standing by the divan and resting his palms flat on the back of it. 'Can't you and your father here get it through your heads how unjust you're being?'

'Do we *have* to go through all this again?' Joyce asked, her voice quivering. 'I haven't forgotten what you called me when you left here last time.'

'I'm sorry,' Richard said quietly. 'I was furious — just as you'd be if accused of something you haven't done. Things have happened since I was here last. Chief Inspector Garth has given up the case of Valerie Hadfield completely because he can't find the person who killed her, or else made her disappear. My alibi is absolutely watertight. If it satisfies Scotland Yard surely it ought to satisfy you?'

The girl's eyes remained fixed on him for a while and he saw them undergo a slight change. She looked away from him suddenly to her father. Dr. Prescott had his lips compressed and a tiny frown of doubt puckering his forehead.

'I can quite understand how both of you arrived at your conclusions, and I don't blame you for it. Circumstantial evidence has ruined many a life before now. I've admitted that I know Valerie Hadfield — or that I *did* know her, if she is now dead — but there the story ends as far as I'm concerned. Garth is satisfied about everything else, even to my visits away from home unfortunately coinciding with Valerie's mysterious love affair with Rixton Williams. As for the name of 'Ricky' that is purely coincidence again — but naturally I wanted to keep things dark when I saw how all these coincidences were going to add up and make things look bad for me . . . '

Joyce stirred restlessly.

'You know how impulsive I am. If I've been wrong about you I'll never be able to make it up to you . . . '

'But of course you will,' Richard said, smiling and coming round the divan to her. 'I was determined I'd make one last effort to save our lives from being shattered. If any trace of doubt remains let me tell you that I was out all day yesterday with Inspector Garth — socially, not officially, that is. In the evening he came up to dinner at my place. Do you think a Scotland Yard official would do *that* to a suspected man?'

There was silence, almost of shame.

'If you doubt it — though I'd rather hoped you'd take my word for it — ring him up,' Richard added. 'It was when I realised that the case was closed and marked uncompleted, and that I had therefore become free of suspicion, that I resolved to come here. Please, Joyce, for the love of Heaven, don't *still* nurse your delusion about me.'

'I don't want to, Ricky,' she muttered, and he noticed there were real tears in her dark eyes. 'In spite of everything, I still love you. If all that you've said is true — '

'It *is* true! Don't I keep telling you? The whole thing's done with! My name never got into the paper to start a scandal, and it certainly won't now. We're right back where we were on the Saturday morning when I told you I'd freed myself.'

Richard waited — then suddenly Joyce's arms were about him tightly. He stooped and kissed her forehead gently, stroked back the gleaming hair with a faintly trembling hand.

'That's better,' he whispered, and raised his eyes to meet those of Howard

Prescott across the room.

'Why don't you say something, Dad?' the girl asked, as her father remained silent. 'Don't you see how wrong we've been . . . ?'

Dr. Prescott shrugged. 'I can only offer my apologies, Richard. As for Joyce, she really *is* desperately in love with you: I've known that from the start. I — er — perhaps you'd prefer to be alone? This is no moment for a third party.'

As he left the room, unsmiling, Richard looked after him with a puzzled frown.

'I'm so glad . . . Dick,' Joyce whispered, looking up at him. 'Here take off your coat. Sit down. We've such a lot of time to make up.'

Richard let her help him off with his overcoat, and at the same moment Dr. Prescott was sitting down at his desk in the study and picking up the telephone.

'Whitehall, one two one two,' he requested; then when he was connected, 'C.I.D., please — Chief Inspector Garth, if he's still there. If not let me know where I can contact him.'

After an interval Garth's voice came

over the wire. 'Hello? Garth speaking. Who's that?'

'This is Dr. Prescott, Inspector — It's about Richard Harvey. He's here now, having patched things up with my daughter. He insists that he is a free man and that you've given up the Valerie Hadfield case. He also says that you had dinner with him last night, glorying in the fact that you and he are on the best of terms. Is that — the truth? *Have* you given up the case?'

There was silence from the other end of the wire.

'You see my position, Inspector?' Prescott insisted. 'Joyce is my daughter. I am responsible for her. Because she loves young Harvey so deeply she is willing to listen to the first plausible excuse that gives him back to her. But I'm trying to look further, as a father should . . . If Richard be still suspect there may be danger. You understand?'

'Yes, Doctor, I see the awkwardness of your position,' Garth admitted. 'But I *did* have dinner with Dick last night. As for your daughter being in love with him there is no actual harm or danger in that. Two people in love don't hurt each other as a general rule.'

'What exactly do you mean by that, Inspector? It sounds as though you're saying Richard won't hurt Joyce because he's in love with her. If that be so it means — '

'I realise your position, Dr. Prescott, but I must ask you to realise mine! I am unable for obvious reasons to talk upon everything I do. All I can say is that your daughter won't by all ordinary standards, come to any harm through being in love with Richard Harvey all over again. In fact, maybe it is better that way. Jealousy and hatred have vicious reactions sometimes.'

'Answer me one question: have you given up the Valerie Hadfield case or not?' Prescott asked deliberately.

'Unofficially, yes. But a case is never really given up. It is simply a matter of putting it in abeyance until some new development occurs.'

'Well, I suppose I'll have to let things stay as they are, then,' Prescott sighed. 'I don't want to influence Joyce in any way — unless it be for her own good. Going to be difficult to reconcile myself to the situation as far as Richard is concerned. I told him the other night that his only chance to save himself was by confession — '

'You what?' Garth interrupted sharply. 'Why? Did he admit something?'

'On the contrary, he denied everything. But he asked me, if he *had* committed the crime of murder — which he swore he hadn't — what he should do about it, and I told him his only chance lay in confession. He looked so ill, so haunted, his guilt so self-evident — to me, anyway.'

'Hmmm . . . Sound advice,' Garth said slowly. 'And instead he reclaimed your daughter?'

'Obviously. Meeting you the day after and hearing that you had given the case up seems to have given him fresh hope.'

'I am afraid,' Garth said carefully, 'that there is nothing you can do in this situation. Don't take back what you told him if it hurts your ethics. Let the thing slide. Simply treat him as you treated him before the trouble arose, and leave it at that. You may hear from me again before very long. Goodbye.'

''Bye,' Prescott sighed, and put the instrument down.

At this moment Garth was in Whitehall, ready to depart for home, his hand gripping the telephone he had only just replaced. Sergeant Whittaker was by the door, also ready for off

'That was Prescott. He just told me, *inter alia*, that he met Richard the other night and told him to confess . . . And that gives me an idea! Get the file out and get the name of Valerie Hadfield's manager, will you?'

Wondering, Whittaker came back to the steel cabinets and began a search. Presently he handed over the memo containing the information.

'Good!' Garth got to his feet. 'I'm going to take a long chance on stirring up a guilty conscience into following Dr. Prescott's advice. Nothing but a confession will do the trick now. Come with me and we'll see this manager of Valerie's. If we can get what we want out of him we're liable to be busy during the night.'

'Oh?' Whittaker said resignedly. 'Where, sir?'

'In Richard Harvey's laboratory — and God help us if he sees or hears us.'

'Do you think it was good advice to let Miss Prescott fall in love with Mr. Harvey again?'

'It was the *only* advice I could give. I can't betray my hand at the moment and I firmly believe that Joyce Prescott is safe enough as long as she and Richard Harvey remain in love. He really *does* have an affection for her . . . ' Garth reflected then nodded firmly. 'She'll be all right. Come on.'

19

Eleven o'clock was just striking from the drawing room clock when Richard insisted on leaving. He was smiling; the lines of anxiety had gone from his mouth and eyes. The evening had gone perfectly. Dr. Prescott had not interfered, and the only interruption had been when the housekeeper had brought in light refreshment.

'All forgiven?' Richard rose, stretching his arms.

Joyce held up her hand upon which the engagement ring gleamed, and stood up beside him.

'Proof!' she smiled.

'You mean so much to me, dearest,' he murmured, stooping to kiss her hair.

'A fresh start,' she said. 'Tomorrow we begin all over again. And soon . . . We'll be married.'

'Time's getting on, Joyce, and I want to catch up on some more sleep. I've been having unholy nights since you turned me down.'

She smiled ruefully at the thought and helped him into his overcoat. They went out of the room and across the hall just as Dr. Prescott emerged from his study — or else he had been listening for the pair coming.

'Good night, Richard,' he said quietly, and turned away to the staircase.

'I have an idea he still doesn't believe me,' Richard sighed. 'Well, have to leave it to you to soften him up.'

'I will,' the girl promised, smiling.

Richard kissed her again and then went off down the front path. 'Tomorrow morning,' he called back. 'I'll be here for ten o-clock. See that you're ready!'

Humming to himself Richard turned out into the road. He had achieved his final victory — beaten Scotland Yard and brought Joyce back to his side. Nothing whatever to worry about any more, except perhaps Dr. Prescott who seemed vaguely uncertain. But he didn't matter.

Completely enveloped in his own thoughts, Richard failed to see that he was being watched as he walked home. He had not used the Jaguar for so short a journey.

On the opposite side of the road two pairs of eyes were fixed on him.

'Looks cheerful, sir,' murmured Sergeant Whittaker. 'Tied up with his girl again, I suppose.'

'He shouldn't be long going up to bed,' Garth said. 'That's his room over the front there . . . Wish I'd known he had been out. We might have fixed things before he got back. My feet are about frozen.'

'Let's hope he doesn't decide to spend the night doing laboratory work,' Whittaker said.

'A man in love for the second time doesn't spend his night doing that,' Garth answered.

Garth's guess was right. As he entered the house Richard's only desire was to get to bed and dream of Joyce, crush into the background those vile visions that had haunted him since he had rid the world of Valerie Hadfield and her chauffeur.

He went upstairs to bed, and it was not

long before he dozed off. Then he stirred in his sleep at the consciousness of a distant, far-off ringing. Opening his eyes he gazed into the darkness of the room. The noise was louder now — piercing —

Trrrrring . . . Trrrrring . . .

He turned over and switched on the bedside lamp, felt out lazily for the extension telephone. As he raised it he peered with one eye at the clock. It said quarter-past one.

'Yes . . . ?' he mumbled.

'Is that you, Ricky?'

He gripped the telephone rigidly, suddenly fully awake. Or *was* he awake? Perhaps he was dreaming. It was a woman's voice, intensely distinct in the quiet of the night . . .

'Ye-es,' he whispered, staring fascinatedly in front of him. 'Who's speaking?'

'Good Lord, Ricky, don't you recognise the voice of Valerie?'

All of a sudden Richard's pulses were leaping and bounding. '*Who* did you say?' he yelled.

'Hello? I can't hear you . . . The line's awful. This is Valerie, Ricky — Valerie

Hadfield. You ought to remember me! Even if we have been apart for a few weeks. I stepped out of town without telling anybody . . . Answer, can't you?'

'You *can't* be Valerie!' Richard shouted, drenched in perspiration.

'I can't hear what you say, not properly,' the girl said. 'I'll try from another kiosk somewhere later on. Probably when I get into town. Can you hear me?'

Richard fancied he heard an impatient sigh, then the line went dead. The telephone dropped from his hand back on to the cradle with a hollow rattle.

Suddenly, devastatingly, the horrors were queuing up to enter his mind, the ghouls of dreadful uncertainty, the thundering conviction that he was going insane. Valerie! But he had choked her to death in that house in Twickenham. With his own two hands. He had brought her here in his Jaguar to this very residence. Then he had . . . God! Had it not *been* Valerie after all, but somebody else? So like her that he had been completely fooled?

Shaking, he clambered out of bed, pushed his feet in slippers. In the dim glow of the bed lamp he lighted a cigarette and sat trying to reconcile the impossible. *Had* he made a mistake? After all this was Valerie alive? But surely she must have seen the papers? Or had she? She had said she had stepped out of town without telling anybody. Maybe to some remote part of the country where papers were behind time . . .

'You damned idiot!' Richard breathed. 'She's dead! It's a trick! It was Valerie you killed . . .'

He got up and began pacing up and down the shadowy room restlessly, smoking cigarette after cigarette. Then, viciously —

Trrrrring . . . Trrrrring . . . Trrr —

'Hello!' he barked, as he whipped the instrument up.

'Can you hear me, Ricky? Is the line any better? This is Val, speaking, from a different call-box.'

Richard shuddered. It was definitely Valerie's voice — !

'In God's name, Val, from where are

you speaking?' Richard demanded hoarsely. 'Tell me, before I go crazy!'

'Hello?' her voice questioned plaintively. 'Can you *hear* me? I can't get a word out of this line. It's blurred and muffled. Ricky, *can you hear me?*'

'Of course I can hear you!' he yelled. 'Tell me where you are! Tell me — '

'No use,' she said, sighing. 'I'll have to come over myself first thing in the morning. Maybe you can hear what I say: I hope so. 'Bye for now, Ricky.'

'Valerie!' Richard screamed.

The line blanked. Richard's hand was shaking so violently he could hardly return the 'phone to its cradle. He tried to think, to decide if this incredible thing really were possible . . . But such chaos surged in his brain that he had hardly any conception of what he was doing. Abruptly he snatched up the telephone.

'Operator! Operator!' He joggled the rest viciously.

'Number, please?'

'Look here, I'm Circle four-oh-nine-eight. Somebody has called me up twice tonight — a woman. Can you trace where the call came from?'

There was a pause, then, 'Sorry, sir, your number is on the dialling system. It's impossible to trace dial calls.'

'Oh — damn!' Richard slammed the 'phone back and tightened his lips. If it had all been a trick . . . But the purpose behind such a trick? And if Garth had spoken the truth, the case of Valerie Hadfield was closed, anyway . . .

Stupidly Richard sat down on the edge of the bed. He never closed his eyes again that night. He spent the time smoking, pondering, brooding, darting frightened glances about the room now and again. For the life of him he could not see how he could have made a mistake in killing Valerie. No other woman could have been so identical or in possession of so many private facts. And certainly, as far as he was aware, she had not got a twin sister . . .

Slowly the memory of her words came back to him — 'I'll have to come over myself first thing in the morning.'

Richard staggered to the window, drew back the heavy draperies. Grey daylight was just coming into the autumn dawn. To a certain extent it banished the terror of the night. Purely for the sake of something to do he began to dress, shaved, then went downstairs as the hall clock struck seven. He went outside and to the garage, stared at it fixedly, then came back into the house and spent the time until breakfast wandering up and down his study, thinking, wishing his head did not ache so intolerably.

When he went in to breakfast Mrs. Baxter looked at him curiously. 'You don't look too well, Mr. Richard, and — '

'Nothing's the matter! Get out and leave me alone!'

Mrs. Baxter tightened her lips, hesitated, then left without further words. Richard stared at the food before him, then pushing the plate on one side irritably he sipped the coffee instead and forced himself to concentrate on the morning paper. Not that there was anything significant in it. No mention at all of the Valerie Hadfield case — even less reference to the return of Valerie.

He threw the paper on one side

impatiently, finished the coffee and lighted a cigarette. The clock on the mantelpiece reminded him that it was nine-thirty and across the turmoil of his mind floated the remembrance that he had promised to call for Joyce at ten o'clock.

He got up, bracing himself. Then he stiffened suddenly at the sound of the doorbell. Forcing calmness upon himself he went to the door of the dining room and opened it to see the familiar figure of Chief Inspector Garth being admitted by Baxter.

'Hello there, Dick!' Garth waved a hand cordially. 'I'm an early bird, eh?'

Richard fought to control himself, trying to imagine what Garth wanted at this unearthly hour. 'Come in and have a cup of coffee.'

'Thanks, I could do with it . . . ' Garth thumped his chest, held his hat in his hand, and followed Richard into the room. Silently Richard poured out coffee.

'Something happened?' he asked casually as Garth sipped the coffee slowly.

'Yes,' he said, his pale eyes ranging

Richard's sunken face. 'And you don't look too well, either. Been working too hard — ?'

'To hell with how I look!' Richard blazed. 'What do *you* want?'

Garth smiled faintly and set the cup down. 'This is hardly the place to tell you. Let's go into your laboratory. Quieter there, and we can't be overheard.'

'Does it matter if anything is?' Richard asked deliberately. 'And I have an appointment at ten o'clock — '

'With Miss Prescott?'

'Yes, if you must know. I've squared things up with her.'

'Before you go,' Garth said, 'you'd better hear what I've got to say. Come along to the lab.'

Richard hesitated, then he led the way out of the room, Garth following him. When they reached the laboratory Richard shut the door turned.

'Well? And make it short. I'm in a hurry.'

'No you're not, Dick.' Garth's face was expressionless as he put down his hat on the bench. 'You can't continue your association with Joyce Prescott because Valerie Hadfield is alive.'

The last trace of colour went out of Richard's face.

'Then — it's true?' he whispered.

'True?' Garth looked surprised. 'What is? Why look so staggered, man? It was never proved that she died, remember: simply that she was *presumed* murdered. Now it seems she merely stepped out of town, and the revue. Sudden impulse, and for reasons of her own. Never can tell what a woman'll do next!'

Richard said nothing. He turned away slowly, pressing a hand to his eyes. He stopped finally beside the bench and looked up again to find Garth's pale eyes fixed on him unwaveringly.

'She rang me up twice — during the night . . . ' Richard gestured helplessly. 'I heard every word she said, but she seemed as if she couldn't hear me. I tried to convince myself that I dreamed it, but . . . Now you know about it, too.'

'But why should you wish to convince yourself that you dreamed it?' Garth asked. 'You couldn't know any more than

I whether she was dead or alive . . . could you?'

To Richard the laboratory seemed intensely quiet. A sense of intense pressure was upon him — strangling pressure, and it seemed to be emanating from Garth.

'When — did Val contact you?' Richard inquired haltingly.

'First thing this morning. She walked into my office as large as life, demanding to know what all the fuss was about. Wanted to know where the silly story about her being murdered had come from. Seems she's been out of touch with things and had only just heard . . . ' Garth took out and lit a cheroot. 'Matter of fact she's in my car at the front. That's why I'm here. I thought you'd like to see her, just to reassure yourself after all the fuss there was. She said she'd decided to come and see you this morning.'

'And — what about her chauffeur?' Richard muttered.

'I dunno — that's still a problem. I'll sort it out.'

'And — and she's here . . . ? Outside?'

'I'll have her come in,' Garth said. 'Just a moment.'

Richard watched him stupidly as he went to the driveway door and opened it, then signalled down the drive to somebody in the roadway. Motionless, Richard waited, conscious of perspiration trickling down his forehead. The laboratory seemed blurred and far away. Garth was standing at the outer doorway, cheroot smouldering fragrantly, his merciless eyes staring across the gap.

There were sounds — light, obviously feminine footsteps, coming along the driveway. They came nearer. The sunlight caught a slender silhouette as the girl hesitated in the doorway just out of Richard's line of vision. Richard watched the shadow as an animal watches a striking snake . . .

Then the girl came in — slim, in a neat costume, blonde hair to her shoulders.

'*No!*' Richard shrieked, everything within him exploding. 'No, you can't be Valerie! You're dead — dead! I killed you! Destroyed you! Bit by bit . . . *You can't be Valerie!*'

The girl came nearer and Richard's pounding heart nearly choked him as he realised now it was *not* Valerie. There were subtle differences, but the general figure, the make-up on her face, and his own crashing mind had caused his momentary leap at the obvious. The girl waited, then turned as Garth took her arm and led her outside. He came in again, closed and locked the door.

'You mean that you dismembered Valerie's body, immersed the pieces in liquid air, pulverised them, and then added them to the ingredients for the garage outside. Don't you?'

Garth's ice-cold voice came from far away.

'I never said that!' Sweat was pouring down Richard's face. 'Leave me alone, Garth — for Christ's sake! Leave me — '

'You've already admitted that you murdered Valerie!'

'I — I didn't! You tricked me into saying so!'

'Don't lie,' Garth breathed, walking forward slowly. 'I know the whole foul story, Dick! I've untied your perfect crime knot by knot. I know you were Rixton Williams. I know you disposed of Valerie . . . The hacksaw blade had human protein on it.'

Richard stared across at the tool-rack dully and shook his head.

'Your garage ceiling had a single hair protruding out of it. Valerie Hadfield's hair! Since then I've had the remains of the cement and concrete analysed — the stuff you returned to Rothwell. Doc Winters found tiny shards of bone in the cement powder — scraps which had escaped ultimate freezing and pulverisation. Maybe you hurried the job and ruined your plan for that reason. You've been clever — damned clever — even to knowing the blood at that temperature could never be detected . . . But you have not been quite clever enough.'

With an effort Richard straightened and drew the back of his sleeve over his dripping forehead.

'All right, I did do just that,' he whispered, smiling crookedly. 'And I killed the chauffeur too — and fixed an alibi. You have no *corpus delicti* for

Valerie and in the case of the chauffeur there are no witnesses here to listen to what I am saying to you. What was the idea of all that piffle in recreating Valerie?'

'To get this confession out of you, Dick — and it worked. You broke under the unbearable tension, just as I'd hoped.'

'*And no witnesses!*' Richard repeated, laughing softly. 'You are a bigger fool than I thought, Garth. I admit everything and you neglect the precaution of a witness. While that bogus Valerie was in here I merely said I'd murdered Valerie — but without her identifiable corpse that confession means nothing, not even though that woman heard me say it. She was *not* here when I admitted I murdered Peter Cranston. Only you! Galling, isn't it?'

'That girl is Valerie Hadfield's understudy,' Garth said. 'Last night I heard from Dr. Prescott that he had suggested to you that confession was your only way out. That gave me the idea that under stress you *might* blurt out the truth. I had a talk with Valerie's manager, and several of her speaking parts, on recordings, were dug out and transported to my office. There we had an expert policewoman mimic study them and use her powers on you during the night, imitating Valerie's voice. The telephone disguised whatever imperfections there were and your mind was too harassed to be analytical. I softened you up, Dick, and topped it off with the understudy this morning. Her make-up is identical to the late Valerie's and physically she very much resembles her. That's my part of the story . . . '

'You dirty, scheming swine!' Richard breathed hoarsely. 'Pretending to be my friend, pretending you'd given up the case, and all the time you — '

'I had a job to do, Dick, and I've done it!'

'Like hell you have! I keep telling you — no witnesses to what I have said, and — '

'But I *have!*' Garth's voice was so quiet it stilled Richard's outburst. 'I have the aid of that very science at which you sneered so heartily. During the night sergeant Whittaker and I came in here and fixed a microphone under the bench there. Look for yourself . . . '

Richard stared unbelievingly for a moment, then ducked down and gazed at the small service microphone under the bench against the outside wall.

'Its wires pass under this outside door here' — Garth nodded to it — 'and then are buried in the soil among the trees at the side of the drive. Well concealed, so you'd never notice. This morning we had only to connect them to the radio transmitter in the car. I came out early just to make sure you'd have no chance of perhaps discovering the dodge. Every word you have said since you came in this lab — our words now, in fact — are being relayed into the office of Assistant Commissioner Farley at Scotland Yard by short-wave radio, and at the same time being recorded for reproduction in Court . . . '

Garth stopped, dropped his cheroot to the floor and trod on it. 'We've got you, Dick! And we *can* produce the body of Peter Cranston!'

For a full half minute Richard stood by the bench, his chest rising and falling.

'Clever, aren't you?' he blazed. 'Where's your warrant?'

'That'll be taken out — '

'Will it? Perhaps!' Richard straightened up again, his dark hair dishevelled. 'I've a last trick to play yet before anybody can get in here from your car outside — '

He whirled, dived his hand at a bottle from long accustomedness and snatched it from the shelf. In a split second he had the cork out. Garth watched narrowly.

'It's nitric acid,' Richard explained, grinning, raising it over his head. 'Eats steel, you know. I'm going to give you something to remember me by for the rest of your life, even if I *am* caught!'

Suddenly Garth flung himself forward as he saw Richard hurl the bottle straight at him. Flinging himself to one side he missed it by a fraction and it splintered on the wall, splashing its sizzling, fuming contents to the concrete floor. Hardly had it landed before Garth found himself fighting for his life. Richard's hands were clawing at his throat, dragging him forward towards that searing corrosive.

Garth staggered, drove his first up into

Richard's stomach. Richard doubled up, then straightened at a bone-cracking impact under his jaw. He tottered backwards, recovered his balance, and saw Garth diving for him.

With every ounce of his strength and despairing fury Richard drove with a piston-rod blow into Garth's face. It rocked him on his heels. He felt blood salty in his mouth. Again Richard's hands were tearing at his throat. With a supreme effort Garth forced himself round, tore away from the grip and swept up an uppercut that jerked Richard's head back. Helplessly he crashed into the central bench, his flailing hands clutching at jars and bottles. He glanced at one in his right hand, smashed the bottom off it, and retained the viciously sharp jagged-edged neck in his grip.

Murderously he flung himself forward, his terrible weapon swinging down towards Garth's unprotected face in a gouging movement. Garth held his ground until the last second, then jerked his head to one side and flung out his foot. Richard staggered and tripped, helped on his way by a blow to the base of the skull which knocked half the senses out of him. He crashed forwards and downwards against the wall — clean into the midst of the Dewar flasks with their stoppered necks!

'*Richard!*' Garth shrieked — and flung himself away from the smashing of glass and cascading of searingly cold liquid. He heard one unholy scream and saw the pale blue fluid flooding down Richard's head and shoulders . . .

Blindly Garth fought his way to the outer door and opened it. He stood breathing hard, motioning Sergeant Whittaker and the two constables coming hurriedly up the drive.

'My God!' Whittaker gasped, staring into the laboratory. 'He got it himself!'

Garth wiped a streak of blood from under his nose. Sudden unexpected light footsteps made him glance up. The slender figure of Joyce Prescott was coming up the drive. He went forward towards her, caught her arm and stopped her.

'What in the world's going on,

Inspector?' she asked blankly. 'You've hurt yourself, haven't you? Your nose is bleeding . . . Where's Ricky?' Her voice slowed. 'Has anything happened to him?'

Garth led her as far as the road before he spoke.

'Go home, Miss Prescott, and don't think any more about him,' he said, levelly. 'Just catch the News and read the evening papers, and then . . . Well, a girl as pretty as you is worth something much better.'

'What do you mean?' Her dark eyes searched him.

'I insist. Please go — for your own sake.'

Joyce hesitated, looked at the blonde in the police car, then with a puzzled frown she began to move up the road. Garth watched her go, turned as Whittaker came hurrying down the drive.

'Shall I 'phone for the ambulance, sir?'

'Naturally,' Garth said. 'Stay here until it comes. I'm going back to headquarters. Don't let the Baxters know too much.'

'Looks like the perfect crime came unstuck, sir, after all!'

'The poor, damned fool!' Garth gave a sigh. 'Summing it up I do believe he made more mistakes than the old masters themselves. Well, there it is . . . '

He took out a cheroot, lighted it. All of a sudden the autumn morning seemed intensely quiet. The fragrant blue smoke hung on the still air . . .

THE END

Other titles in the
Linford Mystery Library:

SHERLOCK HOLMES AND THE DISAPPEARING PRINCE

Edmund Hastie

The Crown Prince of Japan disappears without trace from his Oxbridge college rooms. Relatives of an heiress meet, one by one, with suspicious and grisly deaths. The thief of confidential battleship plans must be identified and located before the documents are leaked to the German military. And what nefarious activity links a cabman charging extortionate fares with a musically-minded butler? Narrated with wry affection by the long-suffering Dr Watson, each problem in this collection of four short stories showcases Holmes' well-honed skills of ingenious analysis and consequential deduction to perfection . . .

CLIMATE INCORPORATED

John Russell Fearn

When meteorologist Alvin Brook invents a means of controlling the weather, he imagines it will lead to his becoming a world benefactor, with riches for him and his family. Instead, Brook and his wife are murdered, and his invention is stolen and misused by industrialist Marcus Denham. Denham creates the mighty empire of Climate Incorporated, controlling the world's weather and holding nations to ransom . . . but he does not anticipate that outraged Nature — and Brook's son — will take their revenge.

DR. MORELLE AT MIDNIGHT

Ernest Dudley

Ian Laking is pathologically jealous of his beautiful wife, and obsessed with murder. His only hope lies in treatment by Dr. Morelle, the psychiatrist and criminologist. However Laking, suspecting his business associate Dyke Fenton of being his wife's lover, is plotting revenge . . . Dr. Morelle and his secretary, Miss Frayle, become caught up in the drama of jealousy and revenge. When the plan fatally recoils upon Laking himself, will Dr. Morelle be able to unmask the murderer?